PRIDE

Book One, In Wilde Country

By Sandra Marton

For Linda —
All Best Always —
Sandra Marton
xx

COPYRIGHT

CHAPTER ONE

LUCA BELLINI SHOT upright in bed, torn from sleep as abruptly as he had tumbled into it.

Cristo!

His head felt as if someone were inside it, pounding to get out. His mouth was coated with a substance that was best politely described as foul. His belly was cramped into an ever-tightening Gordian knot.

And where in hell was he? A bedroom, but what bedroom? Better yet, whose bedroom?

Luca scrubbed his hands over his face.

It surely was not his.

This was not the bedroom in his flat in Rome. It was not the one in his home in Tuscany or in his New York condo.

A light current of cool air fanned his naked torso. He looked up, saw the big fan slowly rotating in the center of the high, beamed ceiling…

And remembered.

He was in Texas, in an overblown mansion on an overblown chunk of real estate known as El Sueño.

It was the last place on the planet he wanted to be.

He fell back against the pillows, his face twisted in the kind of glower that would have sent those who worked for him running for cover.

El Sueño. His father's ranch in Wilde's Crossing. Texas.

"Fuck," he snarled, because only that most basic of American curses suited the anger simmering inside him.

And what time was it? Early morning, most probably, judging by the bright sunlight leaking into the room through the vertical blinds that hung at the windows and wide French doors.

Luca plucked his watch from the nightstand and peered at it. Six. Six in the miserable a.m. No wonder his head felt as if it was going to explode. He'd gotten to bed somewhere around three, his belly filled with the booze he and Matteo had driven sixty miles to find, some hideous stuff he'd never heard of, because no way in the world would he or his brother have touched a drop of whiskey from this house.

Alessandra and Bianca had called them *idioti* as much for wanting to drink themselves insensible as for refusing to drink anything that had been paid for with Wilde money, but what did women know of these things?

Luca had made the mistake of voicing that opinion. Alessandra had responded by jabbing her index finger into the center of his chest.

"We are not women," she had said hotly, "we are your sisters!"

Any other time, he would have laughed. But there was nothing to laugh about when it came to discussing the Wildes or anything to do with them. There hadn't been, for months.

"And we are sensible," Bianca had added, filling a pair of crystal goblets to the brim with a decent Argentinian Malbec she'd liberated from the wine rack in the library. "Booze is booze."

Actually, what she'd said was *boose is boose.*

Alessandra had swung toward her sister.

"We grew up speaking English," she'd snapped. "Can you not speak it properly now?"

"We grew up speaking *Siciliano* far more often than we spoke *Inglese*," Bianca had replied. "And unless you wish to wear this wine instead of drinking it, you will not correct my speech."

Alessandra had countered with a classic Sicilian gesture that proper young women were not supposed to make.

Bianca's response had been to offer the same gesture—and then the sisters had rolled their eyes and stepped into each other's arms for a hug.

The memory of that sharp exchange followed by an embrace was bittersweet.

Luca's sisters were like Mama. Direct. Passionate. Quick to anger, but quick to forgive.

He supposed those traits were common to all four of them: the girls, himself and Matteo. None of them took after their cold, removed, lying son of a bitch of a father, and *grazie a Dio* for that.

The Bellini offspring—not one of them considered themselves Wildes—had seen the truth about John Hamilton

Wilde long ago. Well, perhaps not the actual truth. Who in the name of all the saints would have managed that? But they'd certainly begun to question damn near everything he said and did.

But bigamy?

That had come as one hell of a shock.

It had taken them a long time to figure out that he had never been legally married to their mother, and the worst of it was that when they finally did, they had not been able to tell her for fear of what the news would have done to her.

And then, without warning, their mother was gone.

She had drowned in the very sea she'd loved. Then they'd been free to confront the man whose cursed blood flowed in their veins.

Luca rose from the bed, went into the connecting bathroom, relieved himself, dug his toothbrush from his overnight kit and scrubbed his teeth.

That was a little better.

Now to get dressed.

Someone tapped at the French doors that opened onto a wide wraparound porch. Luca frowned and stepped back into the bedroom.

"Who's there?"

The sound was repeated, more a hard rap of the knuckles than a tap this time, and the door handle rattled.

Whoever it was, was impatient.

Luca snatched his jeans from the chair where he'd dumped them, pulled them on, zipped up the fly, went to the doors and opened them. Matteo stood in the morning sun, feet apart, hands fisted on his hips.

He looked awful.

Hair uncombed. Jaw bristling with early morning stubble. Expression grim.

In other words, he looked pretty much the same way Luca looked this morning, but why wouldn't he?

Looking at Matteo was almost, but not quite, like looking in a mirror.

They were twins. Fraternal, not identical, born two minutes apart. They were the same height: six feet three in their bare feet. Both had the bodies of athletes: wide shoulders, narrow hips, long legs. Women said they were handsome. One in particular had even gushed that he, Luca, was a magnificent male specimen.

She hadn't lasted long after that.

Emotion had its place. In bed. Not out of it. Luca knew what he wanted from a woman, knew what he was prepared to deliver, and out of control emotion was not on the list.

It was too dangerous.

A man should always be in charge of his emotions.

If anything could be said to be his mantra, it was that.

Of course, there were physical differences between them. Luca's hair was the color of dark, rich coffee; his eyes were a deep sapphire blue. Matteo's hair was an inky black. His eyes were sea green.

Matteo had a dimple in his right cheek—his sisters teased him unmercifully about that dimple, sometimes faking exaggerated Victorian swoons complete with deep sighs and hands pressed to their hearts.

Luca also had a dimple. It was in the center of his square, very masculine chin, though when Bianca or Alessandra called it a dimple he would say, sternly, that it was a cleft.

And then one sister or the other would do that hand-to-the-heart routine and say *Oh my God, a cleft!*

"*Si.* A cleft," Luca would growl.

And then, inevitably, he'd give up being stern and he'd laugh.

He laughed with his sisters. With Matteo. But not very much with others.

Luca was a serious man. It was the thing about control again. It was important to both brothers.

Growing up as they had with a hot-blooded, hot-tempered mother—she was Sicilian, after all—and a father who was often withdrawn and generally unavailable had shaped Matteo into a man who knew emotions were best kept to himself.

Luca had taken things a step further.

Emotions were best avoided altogether.

He had adhered to that conviction his entire life.

But last night, when he and Matteo, Alessandra and Bianca had finally confronted the damnable Wilde clan, more than fireworks had exploded into the hot Fourth of July night.

Months worth of rage had overtaken him.

"Luca."

It had seemed impossible that they were finally confronting the Wildes. The other children of John Hamilton Wilde. The sons and daughters they had not known existed.

The sons and daughters born to legitimacy.

"Luca?"

No shameful secrets for them. No wondering why their

father had never really seemed a part of their lives.

"Luca! Dude, are you deaf?"

Luca, hands fisted at his sides, glared at his brother.

"Do not start with me, Matteo. I am not in a good frame of mind this morning."

"Do you think I am?"

Luca took a deep breath, let it out and unfisted his hands.

"No," he said quietly, "of course not." He stepped back so Matteo could enter the room. "Did you get any sleep?"

"A couple of hours. You?"

"About the same. "

"We should not have spent the night under this roof."

"No," Bianca Bellini said dryly, "certainly not."

The brothers turned toward the French doors where their sisters stood glowering at them.

"Ladies," Luca said calmly, "how nice of you to drop by."

Bianca tossed back her mane of long, straight blonde hair and marched into the room, followed by Alessandra. Alessandra's gold curls were drawn back in a low ponytail, but she managed to toss them just the same.

"Are you still complaining because we refused to drive back to Dallas in the middle of the night? It was bad enough that you two went in search of liquor on a strange road in a strange place in such furious anger. When you sit behind the wheel of a car in such a mood, terrible accidents happen."

"No accident happened. And we were not in any kind of mood," Matteo said with dignity.

"Of course not," Alessandra said. "All that fist-clenching and tooth-grinding was for dramatic effect."

Luca narrowed his eyes. "Is this why you're here? To criticize our behavior last night?" His jaw tightened. "Because I think we behaved with great restraint."

His sisters glanced at each other. Then they sighed. Bianca sank into a chintz-covered armchair near the windows; Alessandra dropped onto the edge of the bed.

"You did," she said. "We all did. We all deserve awards for outstanding behavior."

Luca paced across the room, grabbed his T-shirt and yanked it over his head.

"I hate this place," he growled. "The land. The house. The people in it, the endless Wildes, their wives and their husbands…"

"For what reason?" Bianca asked wearily. "They're no more responsible for this situation than we are."

"They're Wildes," Luca snapped. "That's sufficient reason."

Alessandra leaned back on her hands. "I hate to tell you this, *mio fratello*, but so are we."

"We were raised by our mother."

"So were they. By more than one mother, if you want to be accurate. And just in case you didn't notice, not a one of them had anything good to say about our father last night."

"Do not call him that!"

"È quello che è," Bianca said.

Matteo nodded. "*Si.* It is what it is. We all know that."

"*I* know that the Wildes were raised by a general," Luca said, "and we were raised by a man who pretended to be a spy."

"He is the same man," Alessandra said.

"And he is a liar. A fraud. A bigamist."

"*Si*. He is a scoundrel."

"Don't call him a scoundrel," Bianca said. The others looked at her and she shrugged. "It's too polite a word. It makes him sound charming."

Matteo walked over to his sister and affectionately ruffled her hair.

"She's right," he said. "If there is one thing General John Hamilton Wilde is not, it is charming."

"Agreed," Luca said. "And neither is this place, this El Sueño. I would like to leave here as soon as possible."

The Bellinis all nodded in agreement.

"We did what we came to do," Luca added. "The Wildes know about us. We know about them. Now let the man who sired us all live with the results of his deception. Let him try to explain it."

"He tried last night," Alessandra said. The Bellinis gave her sharp looks. "Well, it's true. All those hours of explanation. His life story. The twin brother who died—"

"In an accident of his doing," Matteo said coldly.

"He tried to make up for it by leading the life his brother had been destined to lead," Bianca said.

"*Cristo*!" Luca threw out his hands. "Are you actually defending him?"

"I'm simply trying to make sense of what happened."

"What happened," Luca said, "is that he married an American woman as well as our mother. Two marriages. No divorces. He lied to our mother, lied to us…"

"He lied to everyone, *si*, but it doesn't help to be bitter. We need to accept the truth, painful as it may be, before we can move past it."

"My sister, the psychologist."

Bianca shot to her feet. "A little more psychology and a little less pork-headedness would not hurt you, Luca."

Matteo snorted. Bianca, Alessandra and Luca flashed him irritated looks.

"Sorry," he said, "but it's pig, not pork."

"Pig," Alessandra said, "pork, what's the difference? This is a ridiculous argument. We confronted our father with the facts. We confronted his American children with the same facts. It's time to go home."

Everyone murmured agreement.

"In that case," Luca said, "give me time to shower and dress, and we'll meet out front in fifteen minutes. *Va bene*?"

"*Va bene*," the Bellinis said, and after quick, very Italian exchanges of double-cheek kisses, they all trooped from the room.

* * *

It was a holiday weekend.

An American holiday, to be sure, but still, it was a holiday.

Normally, Luca would have worn jeans and a T-shirt, but it suddenly seemed important not to appear casually dressed in this, the home of his father.

The home of his enemies.

So he ran a razor over his face to get rid of the dark stubble that shadowed his cheeks and jaw, showered quickly, dried off and took a dark grey Brioni suit from his small suitcase. A crisp, custom-made white shirt, black onyx cufflinks, a navy silk tie, black loafers made for him by a shoemaker in Firenze, and he was ready for the drive to Dallas and the private jet that awaited the Bellinis.

One final glance in the mirror.

Good. Fine. He looked like a man who was the king of his own world, and wasn't it amazing that though there were those who called him that, this was the very first time he'd wanted the designation?

Luca straightened his tie, put on his watch, dumped yesterday's clothes in the suitcase and zipped it shut. He picked it up, strode to the French doors, grabbed the handle…

And frowned.

What in hell was he doing? Was he really going to sneak out of this house? It was not his, but he had every right to be here.

Damn right, he did.

Luca turned on his heel, marched to the guest room door, opened it and stepped out into the hall.

Last night, he'd been too drunk to look at the house. Really look at it, beyond seeing that it had walls, ceilings and floors.

Now, he saw that the rooms in this wing were built around a second story loft. An enormous skylight in the cathedral ceiling let in the morning sun; a floating staircase made of maple and wrought iron led down to a vast open area below.

Clearly, this part of the house was an addition. The main structure had to be at least one hundred years old. This wing, obviously meant for guests, was very different from the original house though it blended with it. Not an easy thing to accomplish, Luca knew, and gave a grudging mental salute to the architect or builder who'd designed it.

He was an architect himself. He knew how difficult it could be to blend the new with the old.

He went down the stairs, his footsteps beating a loud tattoo as he descended. A square Oriental carpet—very old, very handsome—lay centered against the maple floor. The walls were whitewashed, highlighted with brilliant splashes of modern art. Was that a Jasper Johns? An O'Keefe?

The Bellini in him tried to find fault with what he saw—the design of the wing, the materials, even the paintings and carpet—but the architect in him had no choice but to admire it.

Luca's mouth twisted.

The last thing he wanted to do was admire anything about the Wildes.

He quickened his pace, entered a narrow gallery that he faintly remembered would lead into the main house...

And heard voices.

Men's voices. Women's. People talking over each other, the sounds strident despite some deep-in-the-heart-of-Texas softening of vowels and consonants.

His steps slowed.

The Wilde clan was meeting, no doubt to discuss what to do with the Sicilian interlopers.

He considered making a quick trip into the room on his right. A glance told him that it was the dining room and, *si*, they were all standing around, not sitting at, a big cherrywood table.

One detour and he could tell them exactly what they could do, not with the Bellinis but with themselves.

But why would he do that?

If they wanted to pick apart the Bellinis, let them. Nothing they said would change the facts and he was not the least interested in making them see the truth, that *they* were in the wrong, not he and Matteo, Alessandra and Bianca.

The Wildes were the offspring who had commanded all their father's time and energy, not the Bellinis. They were the ones he had spent holidays with, the ones who had celebrated birthdays with him.

Not that he gave a damn about any of that. Sentimental nonsense, all of it.

It was the principle that mattered, the fact that the general had created two families and had ignored one in favor of the other, ignored one woman in favor of the other.

Luca snorted.

The man had been a bigamist, and Angelica Bellini had deserved so much more than that…

"You going to stand out here and eavesdrop the rest of the morning?"

Luca blinked. The three Wilde brothers stood glowering at him from the entrance to the dining room faces hard, arms folded over their chests, legs apart.

He glared back.

He could feel his heart pumping.

They looked angry as hell, ready for a fight, and that was fine with him. He was ready to take them all on, beat the crap out of the men, tell off the women, brush off his hands and walk away.

"Why would I eavesdrop?" he said coldly, "when you do nothing but talk nonsense?"

Three pairs of eyes narrowed.

"The man has a nasty attitude," one Wilde brother said.

"Maybe he needs to be taught a lesson," said another.

"Maybe. And if he does, who better to give it to him than us?" the third said, or would have said, but a voice behind Luca cut his words short.

"Big talk," Matteo growled. "But then, that is what Texas is all about, is it not? Big talk. Little action."

The Wildes stepped forward. Luca tossed his overnight bag into a corner. Matteo's shoulder brushed his as he moved up to stand beside him.

"Oh, for heaven's sake! Grow up, all of you, and try to act like adults!"

The five men looked at the woman who had just spoken.

Blonde. Blue-eyed or perhaps green; it was difficult to be sure at this distance. She was a Wilde, Luca knew, although from the way she looked, she could as easily have been a Bellini.

It was a strange thought to have in the middle of what was clearly going to be war, but there was no denying that the Wildes and the Bellinis resembled each other. The men were tall, dark-haired, lean and muscular, their eye color ranging from green to blue. The women were slender, fair-haired, their eye color also ranging from green to blue.

The similarities made Luca feel…uneasy.

"Keep out of this, Jaimie," one of the Wildes—Travis?—said.

"The hell she'll keep out of this," a second Wilde sister said.

"Emily. We know you mean well—"

"Do not," the third sister said, "*do not* take that tone with us, Caleb!"

"Jesus H. Christ! Lissa, you sound just like a woman. We're talking about honor and you're talking about tone."

The three sisters stepped forward, faces flushed, eyes flashing.

"She's talking like a what?" the first sister asked. "Like a woman? Is that what you said, Travis?"

"Come on, James. You know what I—"

"And what, precisely, does this have to do with honor, Jacob?" the second sister asked.

"Don't you get it? These—these Italians—"

"Sicilians," Luca heard Bianca say and despite the heat of the moment, it was all he could do not to turn and hug her. "We are Sicilians."

"And American," Alessandra added. "Thanks to our father."

"Your father," Caleb Wilde said, his mouth turning down at the corners.

"*Si*. Our father. He was American."

"You talk about him as if he's dead."

"He is very much alive, as you well know. It is in our hearts that he is dead."

"And where is he this morning?" Bianca asked. "Has he run away like the coward he is?"

"You've got that right," Jake Wilde said grimly. "The SOB is gone."

Silence descended on the group, what Luca would later think of as a meaningful silence. Matteo broke it by clearing his throat.

"Assuming one likes the idea of being American, it is the one decent thing he did for us."

Luca folded his arms and grunted.

"I take it," Travis said coldly, "that was a 'no.'"

"What's wrong with being American?" Jake demanded.

Luca gave an expressive shrug.

"Nothing, I suppose." His smile was a bright and phony as a bank of neon lights. "It's the Texan part that we can live without."

"Listen, Bellini—"

"No. *You* listen, Wilde—"

"Goddammit!"

Lissa Wilde marched into the rapidly shrinking space between the Wildes and the Bellinis. Her face was flushed, her posture was tree-trunk straight, her mouth a thin line. "Stop it," she said. "Just stop it and look at yourselves!"

Grudgingly, Luca took the advice.

Amazing.

Ten flushed faces.

Ten rigid postures.

Ten mouths that looked as if they'd been drawn by slashes of a pen.

Ten sets of hands on ten pairs of hips.

Cristo!

Two sets of brothers, two sets of sisters. Alike not only in looks, but in body language. In temperament.

And with a common bond.

Hatred for the man who had sired them.

Was that why they were so close to blows? Was it safer to turn their anger on each other than on the man who had brought them to this ugly moment?

"Just look at us," Lissa said, as if she'd read his mind. "I mean, *look* at us! Are we all crazy?"

"Liss," Caleb said, "honey, we know you mean well, but—"

"Listen to how he speaks to her," Bianca said softly to Alessandra. "As if she is a child to be soothed."

Alessandra raised one eyebrow.

"*Si*. He speaks to her as Luca and Matteo often speak to us."

Emily lifted her chin. "It's probably how overbearing brothers everywhere speak to their younger sisters."

"Hey," the Bellini men said.

"Hey," the Wilde men said.

The Bellini sisters pushed past Luca and Matteo and joined Lissa. Emily and Jaimie did the same.

"This," Jaimie said, "is ridiculous. We're acting as if we're enemies, but we're not."

"You didn't think that way last night," Jake Wilde said.

"Neither did you," Luca growled, looking at Bianca and Alessandra. "You didn't even think that way this morning."

"Well, we've had time to rethink the situation," Bianca said. "Is that not correct, ladies?"

Five heads in varying shades of blond nodded in agreement.

"And what we think," Jaimie said, "is that there's no logical reason for us to be enemies."

"None of this was our doing," Alessandra said.

"We thought we were his children," said Bianca. "His only children," she added.

"And we thought the same thing," Emily said. "Who'd have dreamed he was—he was—"

"A bigamist," Lissa said grimly. "Just spit it out. The bastard's a bigamist!"

"Exactly," Alessandra said. "A fooking—pardon my language—bigamist."

"Fooking," Jaimie said, and giggled. "It's just so right. To describe dear old dad, I mean."

The women all laughed. The men just looked at each other. The atmosphere in the room was changing. Was that good… or bad?

"He lied to us all," Emily said.

"Well, yes. But especially to us."

Emily raised her eyebrows. "What does that mean?" she asked Bianca. "That he lied especially to you?"

Bianca shrugged. "You know."

"If I knew, I wouldn't ask."

"Holidays. Birthdays. That kind of thing."

"You mean, he spent them with you."

"Of course not! How could he, when he spent them with you?"

"What? He was never with us!"

"Trust me," Alessandra said grimly, "he was never with us, either. He was always too busy, spying to save the world."

The Wildes sisters smiled. After a couple of seconds, so did the others.

The atmosphere in the room underwent another subtle change. Hands dropped from hips, mouths relaxed, faces took on a kind of ease.

"It would seem he treated us all with indifference," Luca said, after a minute.

"He was probably afraid to spend too much time in any

one place. He might have said something that would give the game away."

"It is not easy to be a cheat," Matteo said. "And a liar." He tucked his hands in his trouser pockets. "That endless it-wasn't-my-fault story he told us last night. How he was torn apart by his brother's death, how his father blamed him for it, how he tried to set things right by living the life his brother would have lived and, oh yes, in the process, he made a fool of our mother."

"Of ours, too," Travis said.

"You need to know that our mother was a good woman," Bianca said. Everyone turned toward her. "Her name is—was—Angelica. She was a wonderful person, a devoted mother, and her sole mistake was believing the lies told her by that—that *stronzo*, your—*our* father."

"What does that mean? *Stronzo*?" Jake demanded.

"It means—"

"It means 'asshole,'" Emily said. Luca's gaze flashed to her. She smiled tentatively, lifted her shoulders in a little shrug. "I'm good at languages."

"He is, indeed, an asshole. And a *bastardo*."

"Wrong," Caleb said. "He's not a bastard. Look around you, Luca. There are ten of us in this room, hell, *ten* of us, and we have the same father." He gave a choked laugh. "Dear old dad isn't the *bastardo*. We are. Maybe not all of us, legally, but the word suits us better than it suits him."

"*Bastardi*," Emily said. They all looked at her. She blushed and spread her hands in front of her. "Sorry."

"No," Jake said, "don't apologize, Em. There's nothing wrong with getting the syntax right..."

There was a communal groan, followed by laughter. It was obviously a Wilde family joke, but even Luca found himself on the verge of a smile. Then his smile faded.

"You were not happy to see us last night."

"Well, no," Travis said. "Did you expect us to be? What if we showed up in Italy—sorry, Sicily—walked in on you four and said, 'Hey, guess what? Your old man is our old man.' Would that have set off cheers?"

Luca gnawed on his bottom lip.

"No," he said slowly, "but—"

There was a tick of silence. Luca looked from one Wilde to the other. They still looked angry, but now he understood that their anger was not meant for him.

And his anger was not meant for them.

The enemy was John Hamilton Wilde.

Four star general. Or brilliant government spy. Take your pick. Whichever you chose didn't matter, because they were one and the same man—and that man was the enemy of them all.

"And you say he's gone?" Luca said. "Do you know where to?"

"No idea," said Jake.

"Headed back to DC, maybe," said Travis.

"He probably figures he won us over with that dog-and-pony show last night, that endless drivel about the mistakes he made when he was a kid, how the life he led never felt as if it were really his," Caleb added.

"You know," Emily said carefully, "I mean, not that I'm excusing him or anything…" Every eye in the room fixed on her. Her chin lifted. Bianca had that same habit, Luca realized, that uplifted, defiant chin. "I'm just saying, it's a sad story when you think about it."

"There is some truth to that," Bianca said, just as carefully.

"*Old Yeller* was a sad story," Lissa said coldly, "and I had a lot more sympathy for the dog than for our father."

"Old Yeller?" Alessandra asked.

"Dog saves family. Gets rabies. Bad ending."

"At least the dog did something heroic. Our father is nothing but a—"

"—coward," Matteo snapped. "It's the reason he was never honest with any of us or with our mothers."

The three Wilde brothers murmured their agreement. So did Luca. And, as he looked around the room, he felt the knot in his belly easing.

Five men. Five women. Strangers until last night. In actuality, strangers still and yet—and yet, they were not strangers. Anyone observing them would surely see that they were not strangers at all.

They were sisters and brothers, joined by blood.

It was the first time he had permitted himself to see it that way.

Learning that your father had a secret family across the ocean, that he had other children, another wife, was hard.

To accept that truth was even harder.

Once he, Matteo, Alessandra and Bianca had done so, they'd stopped thinking of themselves as Wildes. Actually, Luca and Matteo had given up the name several years ago, long before they'd learned their father's secrets, but not calling themselves Wildes didn't change the fact that they were Wildes, every one of them.

Luca considered saying that aloud, but perhaps it was too soon. Perhaps it was enough that they were not snarling at each other anymore.

He wasn't a fool.

He had no illusions, no thought that the ten of them would gather around a campfire any time soon and sing *Kumbaya* the way he'd seen people do in an American movie when he was a kid. Years of bitterness still separated them; it would take time to overcome that.

"You know what would make me feel better?" Jake said. "If he just admitted that he wronged us instead of trying to justify what he did."

"Yes," Travis said. "If he just said, okay, here's the truth…"

"He can't handle the truth," Luca said.

It was vintage Jack Nicholson, only with the faintest possible Italian accent. It startled the Wildes. Hell, it startled Luca. He hadn't meant to joke, but—

Caleb chuckled.

Travis grinned.

Jake and Matteo smiled.

Emily, Jaimie, Lissa, Bianca and Alessandra laughed out loud.

And, to his own amazement, so did Luca.

It felt great to laugh, as if a heavy weight were easing from his shoulders.

"Not bad," a voice drawled. "That Nicholson bit, I mean. You want a part in my next movie, I might be able to fix you up with something."

Luca frowned.

A tall guy was coming toward him. There were other people walking into the room, as well. Three women. Two men besides this one…

But he knew this one.

Not knew him. Recognized him. The voice. The face. The slight limp.

"Nick Gentry," the guy said.

"The actor?"

Nick smiled. "Lissa's husband." He held out his hand. Luca could almost hear all the indrawn breaths. A handshake? Surely, it was far too soon for that…

"Take it from me, dude," Nick said softly. "You only hurt yourself by hanging on to the past."

The past, Luca thought. A past that no one in this room had created.

"Luca Bellini," he said, and clasped the hand that had been extended to him.

* * *

It turned out that Lissa had been up at dawn, baking blueberry muffins.

"When in doubt, eat," Jake said, smiling across the dining room table at his sister.

Bianca tore off a piece of muffin and buttered it.

"I'd love your recipe. These are so good… What?" she said indignantly, when Matteo snorted.

"Our Bianca collects recipes as some people collect stamps. She loves to own them, but she's smart enough not to try and use them."

Everyone laughed, even Bianca.

Luca reached for his coffee.

Amazing.

There was the buzz of conversation all around the table, Wildes talking to Bellinis, Bellinis talking to Wildes, Wilde spouses joining in.

The women were more at ease than the men.

He understood that.

Men were warriors. Women were peacemakers.

Here he was, seated right next to Jake, and after a handshake, they'd yet to say more to each other than "pass the sugar."

Okay. Time to change that.

Luca cleared his throat and looked at Jake.

"So," he said briskly, "you manage El Sueño?"

Jake nodded. "Yeah. I have my own place, too, but what I do for the one spread is pretty similar to what I do for the other."

"Spread?"

"Ranch." Jake reached for his coffee. "Of course, my ranch is nothing like this."

"Two hundred thousand hectares, yes?"

"If two hundred thousand hectares is half a million acres, yup, that's El Sueño."

"There are countries smaller than that."

Jake laughed. "I'm sure there are."

"It must be quite a responsibility. Managing such a property."

"It's like any other corporate structure. I have people

working for me who I trust. They handle a lot of the day-to-day stuff. Well, everything but the horses."

"*Si*. I saw your horses in the paddocks out back."

"You saw some of them. There are more running free in the hills for the summer."

"Morgans?"

Jake raised his eyebrows. "Among others. You know horses?"

It was Luca's turn to shrug. "A little."

"Why do I get the feeling *a little* really means much more than that?"

Luca smiled. "Well, I have what you would call a ranch. In Tuscany. I breed Arabians."

"Magnificent animals."

"Does your brother breed them, too?"

Luca laughed. "Matteo is into a different kind of horsepower. His passion is Lamborghinis. No, the horses are mine."

"Are horses your business?"

"A hobby. I spend whatever free time I can manage at the ranch, but it's never enough."

"What do you do, then?"

"I design. And build."

"Build? Houses, you mean?"

"Houses, hotels, commercial properties. In fact, I've just opened an office in Manhattan."

"Ah. You should talk to Marco. Em's husband. He's in that same field."

"Marco? Do you possibly mean Marco Santini? I know the name. He has a fine reputation."

"Marco did the guest wing you guys stayed in last night."

"Are you two talking about me?"

Luca and Jake looked toward the other end of the table. Marco Santini, Emily's husband, smiled at them.

"We were," Jake said. "Luca's a builder, too. He says he's heard of your terrible reputation."

Luca grinned. "Don't listen to him," he said. "Of course I've heard of you."

"Actually," Marco said, with a little smile, "I have heard of you, too. A fellow Sicilian, a man who owns one of the biggest construction companies in Europe…"

"How nice for you both."

The female voice, though low-pitched, even husky, cut through the pleasant conversational buzz.

All heads swiveled toward the door where a woman stood, hands on her hips, legs apart. She was tall—five nine, five ten, Luca thought as he stared at her.

Hell.

A man would have to be dead not to stare.

She was beautiful.

Long, straight, lustrous black hair pulled back from her face. Eyes the color of the Mediterranean. Cheekbones that could cut glass. An elegant nose above a full mouth.

His glance dropped lower.

The rest of her was as stunning as her face.

High breasts pressed against a white T-shirt. Curved hips cradled by faded jeans. Long legs that ended in what seemed to be the sole deviation from her no-nonsense look: chestnut leather boots with heels so thin and high no cowboy in his right mind would ever have worn them.

"Shit," Jake said under his breath, but he smiled politely as he rose to his feet. "Good morning, Cheyenne."

Cheyenne? Was she Native American? What Luca knew of American Indians he'd learned watching Western movies as a kid. The high cheekbones. The slight arch to her nose. Perhaps she was.

And… He frowned. Was there something familiar about her? No. There couldn't be. Any man who'd met her before would surely remember the encounter.

Every man in the room was staring at her. Then, as if on signal, they scraped back their chairs and rose to their feet.

The woman ignored them. Instead, she cast a deliberate look at the grandfather clock in the corner.

"Morning? It's almost afternoon."

Luca glanced at the clock. It was barely ten.

"Yeah. Well, I'm sorry I'm late, but—"

"You were due at my place an hour ago. I have a full schedule today, but I went out of my way to accommodate you."

Jake blinked. "*You* went out of your way to accommodate *me*?"

"Uh, honey," Jake's wife, Adoré, said quickly, "why don't you introduce—"

"I can introduce myself, thank you," the woman said, her tone making a mockery of the polite words. "I'm Cheyenne McKenna, and I sincerely hope the rest of you have heard of an invention called the telephone. You know. A thing that makes it possible to contact someone and say 'Sorry, I'm going to be late.'"

"Okay," Jake said tightly, "okay, Ms. McKenna, that's e—"

Adoré shot to her feet.

"Everybody," she said brightly, "Cheyenne bought a piece of land a few miles east of our place. The old Sweetwater Ranch? Anyway, we met in town and got to talking and it turns out that she's going to run horses—Arabians, wasn't it, Cheyenne—and the Sweetwater's barns and outbuildings need work and she said she had some questions about what could and couldn't be repaired and I said, well, my husband knows all there is to know about ranches and horses and barns and that I was sure he'd be happy to drive over to check things out and make some suggestions and..."

Her words trailed away. She flashed an imploring look at her husband. He sighed, his expression softened, and he went around the table to her, tilted her face to his and kissed her gently on the mouth.

"It's okay, honey," he whispered. Then he straightened up and looked at Cheyenne McKenna. "So," he said briskly, "tell you what. Why don't you join us, have some coffee while I—"

"I had plenty of coffee, thank you very much, while I waited for you."

Jake's eyes turned icy.

"Listen, Ms. McKenna—"

"I have a better idea."

Everyone stared at Luca. *Cristo*, if it were possible, he'd have stared at himself.

What was he doing?

The answer was that he was walking toward Cheyenne McKenna. She watched him approach from under a sweep of dark lashes almost too full to be real, but he'd have bet they were real.

As real as the rest of her.

That attitude.

That mouth.

That body.

A tightness formed low in his belly.

Ridiculous.

He had not been with a woman in a while. Still, he was not some teenaged idiot with an out-of-control libido. He was only trying to ease a tense situation. That was all. Things were difficult enough at El Sueño this morning without adding this nonsense to it.

"And who," the McKenna woman asked coolly, "are you?"

Despite her height, despite the nosebleed-high heels, she had to tilt her head back to look at him. He liked that. Liked that she had to give up a little of her arrogance in deference to him.

"I am Luca Bellini."

Her smile was lethal. "Am I supposed to be impressed?"

"I know something about construction as well as ranches and horses."

She took her time looking him over, head to toe and back up again. He knew what she saw: a man in a four thousand dollar suit, a man she was sure had never had dirt under his fingernails or horse manure on his custom-made shoes.

"I believe there is an American adage," he said softly. "Never judge a book by its cover."

"And?"

"And, rather than take Jake from his breakfast, I'll go with you and look at your property."

"There's another old saying, Mr. Whatever-You-Said-Your-Name-Is. Talk is cheap. And," she said, waving him off as if he were a pesky housefly, "I'm not in the mood to play games with a make-believe carpenter or cow—"

She caught her breath as Luca wrapped his fingers around her wrist.

"You have a short memory, Ms. McKenna. My name is Luca Bellini. I am not a make-believe anything." His hand tightened on her, just enough to draw her closer. "And if I choose to play a game, I am the one who issues the invitation."

The people gathered at the table had gone silent.

They were all staring.

Staring at her, Cheyenne knew.

She felt all those eyes on her as surely as she felt the pressure of Luca Bellini's encircling fingers on her wrist.

She'd made a fool of herself.

She knew that.

Bursting in here the way she had…

The housekeeper had politely suggested she wait in the living room, but Cheyenne, angry as hell—unreasonably angry, though she had not wanted to admit it—had brushed past her and said she was tired of waiting

Well, she was. But that really had nothing to do with the Wildes.

It had to do with her and her life, and why she'd decided to let her anger out on people who had no part in any of it was beyond her.

So what if she'd waited an hour for Jake to show up? Really, did she have anything else to do?

Not anymore. No deadlines. No shoots. No interviews.

Her time was her own.

Another adage and a bad one. Who wanted their time to be their own? People needed to have commitments. Things to do. Places to be. That was one of the reasons she was buying Sweetwater Ranch. She needed to feel as if she had purpose, dammit, and because she was on shaky ground when it came to that, she'd taken it out on these absolute strangers.

And on this man.

His hand still clasped her wrist.

She looked up, and their eyes met. His were blue, so blue they were almost black. He had what her makeup stylist would have called a Roman nose. His mouth was full; his chin was square and had an almost indiscernible cleft.

She came from a world filled with handsome men, but this man wasn't handsome. He was beautiful in the way a hawk or a wolf is beautiful, as if there were a tightly contained wildness in him, a kind of savagery.

Something hot hummed through her blood.

The sensation shocked her. It had been a long time, a very long time since anything or anyone had made that happen.

Logic warned her that the smart thing to do was turn down his offer, but it had been an equally long time since she'd paid attention to logic.

"Very well," she said. "I accept your offer."

"What offer is that?"

"The one you made. To take a look at my land."

"Are you asking me to look at your land, Ms. McKenna?"

How subtly he'd changed the meaning of her words, she thought, and smiled.

"One more adage, Mr. Bellini. Nothing ventured, nothing gained."

Luca laughed. He walked back to where he'd been sitting, picked up his mug of coffee and drained it dry. Then he put down the empty mug.

"How can I turn down such an enticing offer?" he said, and he followed Cheyenne McKenna from the room.

CHAPTER TWO

ONCE OUTSIDE THE house, Luca started toward the car the Belllinis had rented at the airport. Cheyenne McKenna headed for a bright red pickup.

"I have a car," he said.

"Trucks do better on these roads," she replied, yanking open the driver's side door and getting behind the wheel.

He hesitated.

He didn't like being a passenger. Not in cars, not in life, not in anything.

Women always sensed that, or maybe they liked it. Whatever the reason, if he rode in a woman's car, she always tossed him the keys

The man was in command, the one who decided on speed, route and destination. That was the unspoken agreement.

Apparently, Cheyenne McKenna wasn't aware of it.

He thought about telling her that he wanted to drive, thought about how she'd have to provide him with directions and how ridiculous that would be, even assuming she agreed, and instinct told him that she wouldn't.

"Well?"

He looked up. She'd reached across the cab and flung open the passenger door. "You up for this or not?"

Attitude, and in spades.

He considered turning around and going back into the house, but that was probably what she wanted.

What she expected.

She was impudent, and in-your-face rude.

But it was amusing, especially after the tension of last night.

She stood up to him, and women never did. They were invariably eager to please, almost pathetically so.

"Make up your mind, *signore*. Are you getting in, or have you changed your mind about what I'm sure is your considerable expertise?"

Changing my mind would probably be smart, he thought…

And he got into the truck.

"Fortunately for you," he said, "I have not."

She laughed.

He slammed the door behind him, she turned the key, hit the gas and the truck practically stood on its rear wheels as it shot down the mile-long gravel driveway to the road.

* * *

She drove fast enough to make the scenery blur, and gave no ground for the endless bumps and dips in the gravel. She swerved once, but that was to avoid a coyote that shot out ahead of them.

When they reached the sooth-surfaced main road, it was that American phrase—pedal to the metal.

Luca would have been surprised at anything less.

He took his Ray-Bans from his inside jacket pocket, slipped them on and glanced at her.

Everything about her said that she didn't believe in taking the easy way. The safe way. She was impetuous, outspoken, arrogant, hot-tempered…

And gorgeous.

And there it was again, that whisper in the back of his brain that said they'd met before.

He thought about asking her if they had. No. He wouldn't do that. Even though he'd mean it, the line was so old it was a bad joke.

Besides, he had an excellent memory. You had to have a good memory when you spent your time talking numbers with clients.

If they'd met, it would come to him.

For now, he'd concentrate on watching her. The way her one hand rested on the steering wheel and the other lay in her lap. The proud profile. The determined set of her jaw. He couldn't see her eyes—she'd slipped on a pair of oversized dark glasses—but he could admire her mouth, the fullness of it, the slight overbite.

She was stunning. And interesting. An enigma. So much temperament, such disdain for what most people would call simple civility.

She was, in a word, a puzzle, and he'd always been fascinated by puzzles.

Dammit.

Luca folded his arms and shifted his long legs under the dashboard.

Be honest, man.

What she was, was a woman he wanted to take to bed.

He'd only known her for, what, fifteen minutes? Still, he was fantasizing about having sex with her. He wanted her beneath him, his hands cupping her ass, her mouth lifted to his, her legs wrapped around his hips, all that impudence giving way to submission as he took her.

One thing he'd learned early in life was that it didn't take long to know you wanted a woman. Pheromones, hormones, whatever, you saw the right woman and the message went from your brain straight to your balls.

Luca frowned.

Still, what was with him and this fixation on a stranger? He came across beautiful women all the time and he often considered what they'd be like in bed—he was a man, after all—but this was a little overdone.

Or maybe not.

He sat back, looked straight ahead and thought about his life these last few months.

Sex was probably what he needed to make a full return to sanity

Ever since his mother's death, he'd been immersed in a quagmire of ugly secrets and even uglier realities.

For a long time, he and Matteo had suspected that their

father was not a government spy. That he led some sort of secret life in the United States. And after looking through a box of old documents when they'd had to make some necessary repairs to the house they'd grown up in, they'd come to the conclusion that their parents' marriage might not have been legitimate.

Still, they hadn't delved too deeply into things.

They'd wanted to protect their mother as well as their sisters.

They thought they had kept their suspicions from the girls, but the day of their mother's funeral, Bianca and Alessandra confronted them. They said they'd long suspected their father was keeping some dark secret and they'd demanded to be part of whatever it took to find the truth.

The following weeks had been spent untangling years of lies, of illusions. They'd devoted their days and nights to the search for facts.

The fact that their father had never really been married to their mother had been the worst shock of all.

Luca had been in the midst of opening his offices in New York. He'd set all that aside. Except for staying in contact with his administrative staff in Rome and his people in Manhattan, he'd pretty much abandoned his own existence. No dinners with friends. No long weekends at his Tuscan ranch.

In other words, when had he last been with a woman?

He actually couldn't remember. Truth was, he'd all but given up noticing that women existed.

No wonder he couldn't stop thinking about sex.

About Cheyenne McKenna.

He gave her one last appraising look from behind the anonymity of his Ray-Bans. Then he turned his head and focused his gaze on the outsized Texas landscape rolling past the windshield.

Cheyenne McKenna—and wasn't that one hell of a name—Cheyenne McKenna was attractive. Under other circumstances, he'd have been interested in seeing where things went. He suspected she might feel the same. He'd sensed a little buzz between them and he was never been wrong about those unspoken messages, but he was expected in Manhattan this evening.

He had no time for sex, or at least for what sex meant to a woman. Drinks. Dinner. Conversation. All the little games that went into an affair, no matter how brief. He was down with that, with seduction, but the last thing he had time for right now were those frills.

So he'd do precisely what he'd offered to do.

Take a look at her land, ask some questions, make some suggestions…

A tree that had been long-ago split by lightning loomed on the side of the road. Cheyenne McKenna turned the wheel hard and zipped past it onto a narrow strip of gravel road. The truck hit a bump and all but flew into the air. The instant of weightlessness would have been enough for him to have banged his head on the roof if he hadn't been wearing his seatbelt.

"Sorry."

She didn't sound the least bit sorry. If anything, she sounded pleased. He shot her a narrow look. Had she deliberately taken the turn too fast?

"I should have warned you this was going to be rough."

He was certain of it now. She'd spotted that gully and

accelerated on purpose. She was playing with him; she'd written him off as an urban cowboy, and she was having fun at his expense.

Luca felt that tightening low in his belly again.

If only he had the time…

But he didn't, so he said nothing as a handful of buildings came into view and when she slowed the truck, he hardly waited until she shut off the engine before he undid his seatbelt, flung open this door and stepped into the hot Texas morning.

* * *

In some ways, Sweetwater Ranch reminded him of El Sueño,

Endless meadows stretched toward a distant set of hills, low and peaceful under the sun's fire. The grass was a rich, brilliant green. The house itself was built on a low rise.

That was where the resemblance to El Sueño ended.

The El Sueño house was a mansion.

This house was a disaster waiting to become a wreck.

The roof was shot. So was what had once been a huge brick chimney. The porch hung askew, as if it were clinging to the house by metaphorical fingernails. Almost all the windows were gone. The massive front door was tightly closed as if to safeguard the place.

A bad joke.

There was nothing here to safeguard, and Luca made that clear with a blunt statement.

"This is a disaster," he said.

"In its present state," Cheyenne replied.

"Let me rephrase that. The house should be razed."

"I have no intention of having it destroyed."

"It is unsafe."

"It's unlivable, not unsafe."

Luca sighed. "Perhaps I'm not making myself clear. The house is not worth salvaging."

"It is."

"Dammit, Ms. McKenna…"

"The house was built in 1842. It's withstood blizzards, hurricanes and tornadoes. It even survived an influx of Yankee soldiers during the Civil War. It's salvageable, Mr. Bellini, and I want it salvaged."

Luca looked at her. Her head was up; her eyes blazed. Her lips were set in a firm line.

He wondered what it would take to soften those lips. To have them part in sweet, eager anticipation of his kiss.

Dio!

A muscle danced in his jaw.

When he got to New York, it might be smart to cancel that business meeting and spend the evening with a woman. He knew a lot of people in the city; he'd met several women at parties and charity functions over the last months. He was certain it would not be difficult to find one who'd be more than happy to spend some time with him.

Clearly, his celibacy needed to come to a swift conclusion.

"Did you hear me? I know the house needs work, but—"

"Stay here," he ordered, and he took a cautious step onto the porch.

"The inside needs work, too, and—"

"A shocking revelation," he said grimly.

He was almost at the door when he heard her footsteps behind him. He swung toward her and caught her by the shoulders.

"Perhaps it is *you* who did not hear *me*. I told you to stay where you were."

The look she gave him could have brought on a new Ice Age.

"Do not tell me what to do, Mr. Bellini."

"Then do not behave foolishly, Ms. McKenna." Luca's eyes narrowed as he looked down into hers. "I have to fly east later today and I won't be able to do that if I'm stuck here, waiting for an ambulance to arrive."

Her teeth flashed in a smile that drove the temperature down another ten degrees.

"Such charming concern for my welfare. I'm touched."

"Just stay where you are while I take a quick look around. Do you understand?"

She wrenched free of his hands, folded her arms and glared at him. He figured that was as close to a 'yes' as he was going to get and he crossed the porch and stepped cautiously through the door.

Surprise, surprise.

The floor seemed sound enough. He squatted down, rubbed away some leaf litter and ran his hand over the wood he'd exposed. Oak. And, under layers of time and dirt, undoubtedly handsome.

He took his handkerchief from his breast pocket, wiped his hands and got to his feet. He looked up. The ceiling rose a full two stories; an enormous crystal chandelier hung from it. Another surprise. The chandelier seemed intact.

He moved further into the house.

The wide staircase to his right hadn't been that lucky. Same as the porch, it seemed to be clinging to the house for its very life.

He took a step back, and bumped into Cheyenne McKenna.

"Dammit," he said, swinging toward her, "didn't I tell you to stay outside?"

"I'm not good at taking orders," she said, "or haven't you figured that—"

A dark shadow swooped down the decrepit staircase. She gave a little cry and Luca caught her by the shoulders and pulled her toward him.

"A bat," he said.

She gave a quick little laugh.

"It took me by surprise."

"That's the thing about bats. They almost always take you by surprise."

"I'm not really afraid of them."

"No. I didn't think you would be."

"I don't believe in all those old wives' tales. You know, that bats will get into your hair…"

It was an inane conversation.

Equally inane was the fact that he was still holding her. That she was still letting him hold her. That he could smell her shampoo or maybe it was her perfume, something that reminded him of wildflowers, and it seemed to be scrambling his brain.

Her pupils were wide and dark. Her lips were parted. Her breathing had quickened....

And then she stepped back. Or he let go of her. Perhaps both things happened at once. Either way, they moved apart. She went out the door. He waited a couple of seconds before following.

The sun, blazing down from the cloudless sky, was very, very hot.

Cheyenne turned toward Luca.

"Well?" she said briskly, "what do you think?"

"I told you what I think." He sighed. "But it isn't what you want to hear." He hesitated. "I haven't seen the second floor."

"Neither have I, but the realtor said that it probably needs—"

"Work. *Si.* I am sure that it does." Luca shrugged his shoulders. "The house can be rebuilt."

"You see? I told you it could be!"

"Understand me. It can be rebuilt. I'm not making that recommendation, and that it can be rebuilt is not the same as it being salvageable."

"What's the difference between the two?"

"Money," Luca said briskly, as he started downhill toward the outbuildings. "It will cost you more to rebuild than to tear the house down and start from scratch." He frowned as the barns and sheds came into better view. "As for these buildings..."

"The first barn, that big one, is fine," she said as she hurried to keep up with him. Her legs were long, but she was having trouble matching his stride. The gentlemanly thing to do was to slow down, but he was not in the mood to behave like a gentleman.

"I'll determine that."

"I don't like your attitude, Mr. Bellini!"

"You are not paying for my attitude, Ms. McKenna, you are paying for my expertise." Luca stopped outside the first barn. "In fact, you are not paying me at all, which is even more reason that I don't have to put up with *your* attitude. Am I making myself clear?"

Her face flamed.

"That's enough," she said sharply. "I'm taking you back to El Sueño. Jake can come here instead of you."

"He can. But he'll tell you the truth, just as I am." Luca's smile was all teeth. "And after you finish explaining that you aren't interested in the truth, he'll shake your hand, wish you well, and say goodbye."

She glared at him. Then she marched past him into the barn.

He hesitated. Then he thought, what the hell. She was his ride back to El Sueño. He might as well see this through.

This time, she was right. The barn was in excellent condition. It was old, probably older than the house, but the timbers were strong and the floor, walls and ceiling were all intact. The structure needed a good cleaning, but not much beyond that.

"How many horses will you keep?"

"I'm not sure. Ten. Twelve. Why?"

"You can easily put in stalls for that many."

They moved on to the other buildings—the second barn and several storage sheds.

All had to go.

Even what remained of the paddocks was a joke. The rails and pickets still standing looked as if a kid could topple them with a touch.

The bottom line was that Sweetwater Ranch was what an American client of Luca's had rightfully called a money pit after Luca had explained the cost differences between gutting and rebuilding a summer house outside Florence, or putting up one that was new.

Cheyenne McKenna had already made herself clear on how she felt about that.

The best Luca could hope was that she had paid for the land, not what stood on it. Not that it was his money; he just hated to see anybody scammed by a snake oil salesman passing himself off as a realtor.

Finally, they'd seen everything. They headed for the truck.

He would tell her, one last time, something she didn't want to hear, but he'd built his career and reputation on honesty, starting a decade ago when he'd started Bellini Design and Construction on a shoestring. Now, the company was worth millions, but honesty was still its cornerstone.

Damn, it was hot!

Luca peeled off his jacket—why in hell he hadn't done that sooner was beyond him—undid his shirt cuffs and collar, loosened his tie, pulled it off and dumped it and his jacket into the truck.

Then he looked at Cheyenne McKenna.

She was feeling the heat, too.

Her hair was damp.

Straight as it was, tiny tendrils curled delicately at her temples.

Her T-shirt was damp, too. It clung to her like skin. Was

she wearing a bra? He could see the faint outline of her breasts through the cotton.

He could see the sweet thrust of her nipples.

She was a desirable woman. Even a fool would see that, but so what? He didn't like her.

He liked his women soft, comforting and accommodating. This woman would never be that. She would always be a challenge and why would a man want a challenge in his bed? Challenges were for boardrooms.

Still, she would be interesting. For an hour. A night. Not more than that—she would surely become an irritant fairly quickly—but for a little while, she would be…

Interesting.

She had turned away from him; she stood in profile as she looked at the house and all his logic fled.

What a sight she was!

Eyes narrowed in concentration, hands on her hips, feet apart, head tilted back. Every part of her, all her intensity, was focused on that ruin of a house.

Was she that focused when she was with a man?

She would be, if he were that man.

He knew things that would make her universe contract until he, and what he was doing to her, were all that mattered…

Dio. He was going to embarrass himself if he kept this up.

Luca shifted his weight, frowned and cleared his throat.

"This place," he said brusquely, "is a mess. Did you actually see it before you bought it?"

She looked at him as if he were an idiot. What did it matter how she'd bought it? The property was hers. It had nothing to do with him.

The problem was that he just couldn't seem to keep quiet.

"Or did you purchase it, sight unseen, after finding it advertised in the back of a magazine published by the rich for the rich?"

She folded her arms.

"Published by the rich for the foolish," she said with sugar-sweet sarcasm. "Isn't that what you mean?"

"What I mean," he said, "is that you wasted your money. Aside from the one barn, there are no sound structures."

"I already knew that."

"Then, why...?"

"I don't see that as any of your concern."

No sarcasm this time. Her tone was frigid. She had put him in his place, and she had every right to do so.

Still, it angered him.

He wasn't accustomed to being talked to this way, as if he were a peasant and she a queen. It angered him, too, that even though he liked her less and less, he wanted her more and more. There was something about her that demanded conquering in the most basic, most primitive way.

Hell.

What did that say about him?

He had been raised on his father's tales of warriors who had raided their way across Europe; his mother had done her fair share, telling stories of Roman legionnaires whose blood flowed in their Sicilian veins.

As boys, he and Matteo had played soldiers, using branches in place of swords.

As men, they played on a different kind of battlefield, wielding power and money rather than swords.

Luca knew the adrenaline rush that went with facing down a business opponent and bringing him to heel. It was the same kind of rush that went with finally bedding a woman he wanted, but he'd never felt this, the desire to take a woman, this woman, in his arms, bear her down into the grass, ignore her protests as he undressed her, as he touched her everywhere until, at last, she wound her arms around his neck, pleaded for him to finish what he had started, to make her his, make her want only him, cry out only for him….

Shocked, appalled at the ferocity of the primitive images, at the sudden rush of blood to his groin, he turned away from her, grabbed his jacket, jammed his tie in a pocket and got back in the truck. She did, too, and they headed for the road.

She drove the way she'd driven before, fast but with complete control. He suspected she was someone for whom control was a necessity.

He was the same.

She was stubborn. Or determined, depending on your point of view.

So was he.

They were more alike than different, and yet she had seized command of the situation. Of him. Of their relationship. A business relationship, certainly; still, she was dominating it.

He was, literally and figuratively, simply along for the ride.

There had to be a way to turn things around. He was not a male chauvinist—not really—but a man was a man and a woman was a woman. It was the normal course of things. He needed to reestablish that.

Luca cleared his throat.

"We passed a café on our way here, just where we got off the main road. If you take the turnoff ahead..."

She zoomed past the turnoff.

His jaw tightened.

Minutes went by. They were nearing another turnoff. A billboard loomed ahead. *Fancy's Home Cookin'. Biscuits 'n Grits Like Mama Made.* Not much of a recommendation. Biscuits were all right. Grits were an alien food product. And his own mama had been among the world's worst cooks, but what did any of that matter?

"How about this place?" he said. "*Fancy's Home...*"

Zip. They flew past the sign and the turn-off.

Luca folded his arms over his chest.

"Exactly where are we going? Because I have to get back to El Sueño. My brother, my sisters and I are flying to—"

"You're related to the Wildes."

A statement, not a question. He frowned. No way was he ready to discuss the ugly intricacies of the Wildes' connection to the Bellinis and the Bellinis' connection to the Wildes.

"You all resemble each other."

"Do you recall what you said when I asked why you'd bought that ranch we just left?"

She looked at him.

"I said it was none of your concern."

"An excellent answer to an unnecessary question."

"Actually, you didn't ask why I'd bought it, you asked if I'd been stupid enough to buy it out of an ad."

"I didn't say you were stupid."

"You didn't have to. And you haven't answered my question. Are you and the Wildes cousins or what?"

"Or what," Luca said. "And I repeat, it is none of your concern."

"Why are you so uptight?"

"Why am I so what?"

"Upright. Tense. You look as if you're about to explode."

Enough, he decided. A quick check in the side view mirror confirmed that theirs was the only vehicle in sight. No chance of an accident—and, after this, no chance that he might explode.

He reached across the console, wrapped his hand around the steering wheel and wrenched it to the right.

The pickup swerved toward the shoulder, and she gasped.

"What are you doing? Are you crazy? We'll roll over!"

"We will unless you stop fighting, let go of the wheel, and slow down."

"The hell I will! This is my tr—"

"Do it or regret the consequences!"

She called him a name. Under other circumstances, it would have made him laugh. Then she lifted her hands from the steering wheel and took her foot from the gas pedal.

The truck bounded onto the gravel shoulder.

"Slow down," Luca ordered.

She braked.

The pickup rolled to a stop.

Silence, unbroken except for the tick-tick-tick of the cooling engine, filled the cab.

Luca undid his seat belt and turned to her.

"You want my advice? Here it is. Unload that property as quickly as you can. Sell it at a loss if you have to, but that's better than paying taxes on something that should be left to die on its own."

She undid her seat belt, too, turned toward him and folded her arms over her breasts. Not 'over.' Not exactly. The angle at which she'd crossed her arms lifted her breasts, made them an offering, and his damnable body wanted to respond to it.

Determinedly, he locked his gaze to hers.

"I have no wish to sell, Mr. Bellini. Get that through your head."

"In that case, be prepared to spend…" He went through a list of repairs mentally, years of experience coming to his assistance, added a handsome amount to cover what undoubtedly would be problems as yet unknown, reached into his jacket pocket for the small notebook and pen he always had with him, and scribbled a number. "Be prepared to spend at least this, Ms. McKenna, and quite possibly a lot more."

He held the out the notepad.

She took it from him.

Their fingers brushed and sexual awareness became almost a palpable presence. He knew that she'd felt it, knew it by the way her eyes widened, by the way she caught her breath.

IIis heart thudded.

Hers had to be thudding, too. He could see the sudden leap of her pulse in the hollow of her throat.

Their eyes met. Held. Then she took another breath and looked at the seven figures he'd scribbled.

"I've done a little Googling," she said. "This is probably

accurate."

"Yes. It probably is." Her hand was still holding one edge of the notebook. His hand held the other. Once again, the tips of their fingers brushed. This time, he could damn near feel the sizzle. "Cheyenne." She looked up. Her eyes were more than blue. They were almost midnight black. "This is not about facts or figures or numbers," he said, in a voice so raw and low he barely recognized it as his own.

The notebook tumbled to the floor.

Luca caught her hand, brought it to his mouth. His lips closed on her fingers; he sucked them into the heat of his mouth and she made a sound that brought him fully, almost painfully erect. Then he let go of her hand and reached for the handle of his door.

"What are you doing?"

"I'm going to drive," he said. "There's got to be an inn or a motel nearby."

"There's a motel a couple of miles ahead, just before the next town." Cheyenne reached for the ignition key. "We can be there in five minutes." The tip of her tongue swept over her bottom lip. "Two minutes. I'll drive fast," she said, and laughed.

"No," Luca said. "I'll drive."

She ignored him. Instead, she checked the mirror, then pulled back onto the road.

Goddammit.

Why did he care which of them drove?

It didn't matter.

The hell it didn't.

It mattered, just as it mattered when they pulled into the

motel parking lot and she walked ahead of him toward the door marked *Office*.

"Wait a minute," Luca growled. She kept moving. He caught up to her, grabbed her wrist and spun her toward him. "I'll get us a room."

"Fine."

She said it in a way that made him feel as if he'd just suggested something stupid and she'd been generous enough to acquiesce.

It infuriated him—but not enough to keep him from dragging her into his arms, right there in a very public place, and claiming her mouth with his.

It was a kiss made up of heat and passion, teeth and tongues. He was on fire when it started and by the time it ended, he was blazing like the prior night's Fourth of July fireworks.

He let go of her, taking some small satisfaction in the way she looked, her face all flushed, her eyes bright and glittery, her lips parted and trembling. He leaned in, kissed her again, nipped her bottom lip. Then he strode to the office.

He was back a minute later, a key in his hand.

He took her elbow, led her to an outside staircase, down a corridor and to a door. The room was clean, but that was all you could say for it. There was no charm to it, nothing attractive or handsome.

It almost stopped him.

He had not taken a woman to a place like this since he was eighteen.

But when he turned to face Cheyenne, he saw that she had already shut the door.

Toed off her boots.

Pulled her T-shirt over her head.

She was wearing a bra, but it was sheer. Her breasts, her nipples, were clearly visible.

She reached for the clasp on her jeans. He caught her hands and stilled them.

"I just realized… I don't have a condom."

"I'm on the pill."

She undid her jeans. Shimmied them down her legs. He wanted to tell her to slow down, that he would undress her, that he would set the pace, but seconds later she was naked.

And he was burning to possess her.

She reached for the buttons on his shirt.

He batted her hands away, damn near tore off the shirt and the rest of his clothes and then they tumbled onto the bed, her hands on him, his on her. She pushed him on his back and straddled him.

"Wait," he said, or would have said, but she lowered herself on his swollen penis, slowly, slowly, so slowly that he hissed with pleasure as he clasped her hips and guided her home.

She rocked against him. Once. Twice. Three times.

And came.Fast. Too fast. Not too fast for him—he had never been as ready to come in his life—but surely, too fast for her.

She moaned. Rocked against him again, and he let go and came so hard that he felt as if he'd been caught up in a whirlwind.

She started to roll off him, but he wrapped his arms around her and brought her down against his chest.

"You can let go of me," she whispered.

It was what women always said, or words to that effect, as if letting the woman you'd just fucked lie sprawled on top of you was some sort of burden.

Generally, he'd wait a minute or two, then roll to his side with the woman in the curve of his arm because the truth was, lying this way wasn't really comfortable. Even when a woman was slender, you could feel her weight bearing down on you.

This time, though, he didn't feel anything except the warmth of Cheyenne's skin, the whisper of her breath. His arms tightened around her; he stroked her hair, stroked his hand down her spine.

It took a while until he felt her muscles relax.

Her breathing slowed, grew more even.

She was asleep.

Too bad, because he wanted her again with him in charge, with things moving slowly. Slow caresses. Slow kisses. Soft whispers telling him what she liked, how she wanted to be touched and taken because he'd yet to take her.

The truth was, she'd taken him.

Not that he had any objections, he thought, biting back a yawn.

He liked sexually assertive women, but he also liked to conquer.

It was male. Purely, basically male…

Luca yawned again.

His lashes fluttered, drooped.

He was asleep.

* * *

He didn't sleep long.

A few minutes, maybe a quarter of an hour. He woke lying on his belly, still naked, still on top of the bedspread.

Sunlight streamed over him.

They had never closed the curtains.

Quite a show, had someone been standing outside, he thought, and smiled.

He rolled to his side. No Cheyenne. She was probably in the bathroom. Maybe in the shower.

He smiled again at the thought of surprising her there, joining her under the spray, cupping her ass and drawing her back against him.

Soaping his hands and filling them with her breasts.

He hadn't even tasted her breasts. Her nipples. He knew they were a dusty rose in color, beautiful and sweet-looking. They'd taste sweet, too.

His erection was instantaneous.

So was his bone-deep need to be inside her.

Luca sat up. Swung his legs to the floor. Padded to the bathroom and knocked at the closed door.

"Cheyenne?"

No answer.

He knocked again.

"Cheyenne?"

She might not hear him, if she was in the shower...but if she were, wouldn't he hear the sound of running water?

A disquieting thought stirred inside him. He said her name once more and turned the knob.

The door swung open on an empty room. Just to be certain,

he drew back the vinyl shower curtains.

Nothing.

His mouth thinned.

He left the small room, walked through the bedroom, peering into corners as if he might locate her in one of them.

He didn't, of course.

She was gone.

Her clothes were gone.

The only sign that she'd been there was a note scratched on the thin memo pad the motel had provided.

Sorry, but I have an appointment in Dallas. I checked—there's a phone number for a cab service in the directory on the desk. And thanks for your help.

The initial C was scrawled below.

Could a man actually feel his blood pressure threatening to burst his arteries?

Luca stared at the note.

At that *thanks for your help*.

What was that supposed to mean? His help with her plans for Sweetwater Ranch? Or what had happened here. In this room. In this bed.

She'd had an itch and he'd scratched it.

Was that the 'help' she was talking about?

H, made his hand into a fist, then dropped the crumpled pad on the carpet.

His head was pounding. Pounding!

He thought back over the years, to other times he'd been angry. Times he'd been furious. The worst had been when he'd found out that his father was a bigamist, that he'd created four bastard children.

And even then, his anger had not been like this.

He could feel it rising within him, a black cloud of pure rage, wiping out all logical thought, all civilized behavior.

"Bitch," he said. "Fucking bitch."

He told himself to calm down. To take it easy. To be reasonable…

"Goddammit," he snarled, and he reached for the ugly lamp on the ugly table beside the ugly bed, wrapped his hand around it, yanked its electric cord free of the socket and hurled it at the wall across from him.

It shattered into dozens of pieces.

That, at least, was a start.

Then he took a deep breath. A series of deep breaths.

He took his trousers from the floor, pulled his cellphone from his pocket and punched a button.

Matteo answered on the first ring.

"Luca? Where the hell have you been? We're already on the road, heading for the airport."

Luca spoke calmly.

Yes, he said, he'd figured that. He apologized for not returning to El Sueño. Something had come up, he said, his mouth thinning at the ugly pun.

"I'll meet you at the airport," he told Matteo. "Yes, fine, I'll be there in plenty of time."

"Did you finish with the McKenna woman?" Matteo asked.

"No," Luca said, still calmly, "no, I haven't finished with her."

He disconnected. Took a hundred dollar bill from his wallet and left it on top of the lamp shards. Then he pulled out another hundred and placed it on a pillow on the bed.

He phoned the cab company. Took a fast shower. Dressed. And as he paced outside the motel, waiting for his taxi, he thought how much truth there had been in what he'd told Matteo.

He wasn't finished with Cheyenne McKenna.

Not by a long shot.

CHAPTER THREE

HE REACHED THE airport in time.

Not that it really mattered.

The Bellinis were using a private jet; there was no particular schedule to adhere to other than everyone having agreed they wanted to be in New York by nightfall. Matteo and Luca had business functions they had to attend; Bianca was going to a lecture, and Alessandra, as usual, was mysterious about it all.

He made his way down the aisle of the luxuriously appointed Dessault Falcon 50 EX and took a seat. His sisters moved past him to a pair of loveseats in the plane's midsection. Bianca took an iPad from her oversized purse; Alessandra took a copy of *Vogue* from hers. Matteo chose a seat and opened his laptop.

Luca took out his iPhone. All he could recall about tonight's commitment was that it involved some kind of charity. He sighed. The last thing he was in the mood for was being in the company of people whose common bond was that they were rich.

Perhaps his P.A. had included some information about the evening in an email.

"Takeoff in two minutes, folks," the pilot's disembodied voice said. "Please fasten your seat belts."

There was nothing from his P.A.

He probably wasn't being fair to the glittering crowd that would attend tonight's whatever. His P.A. accepted or declined invitations to such things on his behalf; she'd been with him almost from the start of Bellini Construction—he'd dropped the 'Wilde' from his name the day he'd turned twenty-one.

He trusted her judgment.

If he was attending a dinner or a cocktail party or an auction for some charity, it was surely one with a good cause. Jessica had probably filled him in on it, but the craziness of the past couple of days had driven everything else from his head, which wasn't like him at all.

He prided himself on being organized. On being logical.

His mouth thinned.

There'd been nothing organized or logical about his behavior today…

Forget that.

Today was history.

Concentrate on tonight.

Tux or dark suit? Dark suit. He hated the stodgy formality of tuxes, always half-expected somebody to come up to him and say, *you look good in that tux. Where'd you rent it?* even though his tux was custom made.

The fact was, his family had been raised knowing they had

to spend every *lira* and euro with caution. Had their father's money gone to the American family he'd acknowledged? Did it really matter?

Maybe Bianca was right.

What was the sense in condemning the children for the sins of the father?

All six of the American Wildes had determinedly made it on their own. They'd worked themselves through school and attained success through their intelligence and determination.

There would be people like that at tonight's whatever-it-was, people with money but with good instincts. Oh, there'd be the usual contingent who'd want to show the world that they were part of the fabled one or two percent, but most of them had a genuine interest in Doing The Right Thing.

Some few might even hope that an act of charity might cleanse their souls of past transgressions.

Still, he'd bet not one of them had transgressed as he had today.

The shabby motel room. The quick, no-emotion sex with a woman who was a stranger…

And, *Dio*, what was wrong with him?

Sex with a stranger? He'd done that before. Once at a masked ball in Venice, another time at a dinner high in the clouds at a Manhattan penthouse.

Exciting, each time.

As for what had happened today…

No emotion? There'd been plenty of emotion. Hunger. Heat. And release.

He was a man, not a boy. Consensual sex of any kind was

not a sin.

The jet was picking up speed.

He could feel the plane gathering itself for takeoff, for that power-pulsing climb that would leave the earth beneath its wings.

What had happened between him and the McKenna woman had been like that. The urgency. The rush. The sense of leaving all reality behind. Two people who'd just met, who had treated each other with cold removal…

But there'd been nothing cold about what happened in that room.

The sex had been like fire. Like flame. He had burned for her and he knew damn well that she had burned for him.

She used you.

Well, so what? They'd both gotten what they wanted.

She'd taken control of everything, from start to finish.

Yes, and what about it? He wasn't a male chauvinist. He believed in gender equality.

Most men he knew would have been elated. Dammit, *he* should have been elated! A beautiful woman had driven him to a motel, torn off her clothes and his, and ridden him into ecstatic oblivion.

Still, there was something incredibly hot about a woman losing control under the stroke of a man's hand. He thought about what it would be like to undress her with slow deliberation, to watch her eyes blur as he bared her, to hear her moans as he slid his hand between her thighs and felt her turning slick and wet for him…

No.

If he were with her now, he'd take her fast and hard, never mind those images of slow seduction; he'd tear off her jeans, her panties, bend her over the table, push himself into her again and again until she wept for mercy, for release, for him…

"*Merda!*"

Matteo looked up. "You okay?"

"Fine," Luca said. "I'm fine."

The hell he was!

The plane was big for a private jet, but not big enough for what he needed. A long walk. A five-mile run. A workout that would shut down his head, his hormones…

His insanity.

He unbelted, rose from the leather chair, went to the bar and poured himself some Johnny Walker Blue. Back in his seat, he sipped at the Scotch. Maybe it would ease the knot of anger lodged in his gut.

Luca turned his head and stared out the window.

The view was perfect. Pale blue sky. Cottony clouds.

Except, all he could see in his mind's eye was Cheyenne McKenna as she must have looked when she rose from the bed, her expression dismissive, her interest centered on dressing as quickly as possible without waking him so she could sneak away from that small, barren room.

Away from him. From the possibility of his waking and wanting another performance, because that was what the entire incident had been, a performance, a woman wanting quick sex, no strings attached…

His hand tightened around the glass of whisky.

"Luca?"

Wham, bam, thank you ma'am, twenty-first century style.

"Luca!"

He turned toward Matteo. "What?" he snarled.

Matteo raised his eyebrows.

"You hold that glass any tighter, you'll bust it."

"What in hell are you talking about?"

Matteo jerked his chin toward Luca's hand.

"Your knuckles," he said quietly. "They're white."

Luca followed his brother's gaze. His fingers were so tightly wrapped around the glass that he could feel them cramping. Deliberately, he relaxed his muscles and put the glass on the small table beside him.

"I guess that's what happens when a man finally gets his hands on good Scotch," he said with what he hoped was a smile.

"I take it that your morning with the McKenna woman was…interesting."

"What's that supposed to mean?"

"Hey! At least growl before you bite my head off. It meant exactly what I said. That your visit with her was probably interesting."

"It wasn't a visit. I offered to stand in for Jake. She accepted." Luca heard the sharpness in his voice. Carefully, he picked up the glass and took a drink. The whisky was warm, smooth and soothing. "And that was it."

"It was even money on which one of you would make it through the morning alive," Matteo said, grinning. "Devoted brother that I am, my money was on you."

"Yeah. Thanks."

"Was the property any good?"

"The land was okay."

"The buildings?"

"One good barn. The other outbuildings, the house—all write-offs."

"The house isn't worth repairing?"

"Not if you're sane, no."

"That bad, huh?"

"That bad."

"How'd she take the news?"

Luca took a long swallow of Scotch. "Not well. She has a mind of her own."

"Uh huh. We kind of figured she'd give you a rough time."

Luca looked at his brother. "Were Cheyenne McKenna and I a topic of conversation after we left?"

"No," Matteo said quickly, "of course not."

"But you talked about me. About me going with her."

"Hell, dude, I'm not part of whatever's biting you."

Luca felt a muscle jump in his cheek. He raised his glass. It was empty. He got to his feet, went to the bar and refilled it.

"Sorry. I'm tired, that's all. Still feeling the effects of last night, I guess."

"Yes." Matteo leaned into the aisle and looked back at his sisters. Both had fallen asleep, Bianca with her iPad on the floor beside the loveseat, Alessandra with her magazine open and forgotten in her lap. "The girls are completely exhausted," he said softly.

"It was one hell of a night. And I have to admit, I never imagined it would end with us breaking bread with the Wildes."

"Breaking blueberry muffins, you mean."

Luca smiled. “She’s a good cook, that Lissa.”

“She is.” Matteo paused. “They’re nice people. And, like it or not, they’re our brothers and sisters.”

“Half-brothers and half-sisters. But I’m not ready to think of them that way.”

“To be honest, I’m not quite there, either. But it’s a truth we can’t walk away from.”

“A biological truth. The rest will take time.”

Matteo nodded. His email program pinged; frowning, he read the note that had just appeared, typed a quick reply and looked at Luca again.

“One of my clients is divorcing his wife. I told him I don’t like to handle divorces.”

“No. Why would you? All that drama.”

“Exactly. A man loses his grip on reality, says ‘I do’ and pledges his love forever. A few years later he comes to his senses, realizes he’s made a terrible mistake…and the only ones who benefit are the lawyers.”

“Unless the man is the world-famous spy-and-general, John Hamilton Wilde.” Luca sighed. “Sorry. Let’s forget about him for a while. So what did you tell your client?”

“That I’d take the case.” Matteo shrugged. “I’ve known him for years. I couldn’t bring myself to tell him ‘no,’ especially when his greedy, soon-to-be-ex will try to take him for every cent he has.”

Luca raised his glass to his brother. “Who would have known that a lawyer could have a heart?”

Matteo smiled, set aside his computer, rose to his feet and went to the bar.

"And a bank account. Some legal eagle will benefit from this mess. It might as well be me." The brothers laughed. Matteo poured himself a drink and went back to his seat. "So, after you left, Jake told us he had never seen the ranch the McKenna woman bought, but he didn't expect it would amount to much. He said the place had been on the market for a couple of years and he'd heard it was because it would take a big infusion of cash to make Running Water, whatever it's called, operable."

"Sweetwater," Luca said, and took another mouthful of whisky.

"Right. Sweetwater. A good name. At least there's something sweet about the lady."

But there was more than that that was sweet about Cheyenne McKenna. The feel of her skin. The scent of her hair. The taste of her mouth.

"Besides her looks, I mean."

Luca grunted. "She's okay."

"Okay?" Matteo rolled his eyes. "Did you not see that face? That body? Definitely a woman made to… What's the matter?"

"Nothing," Luca snapped. "Nothing at all."

"I only said—"

"I heard what you said! Is that all you can think about? Sex?"

"*Dio!*" Matteo shot a glance at their sleeping sisters. "Keep it down," he hissed.

"Yeah. Sorry."

"So what will she do with the property now that you've told her it's a disaster waiting to happen?"

"How would I know?" Luca tipped the glass to his mouth and downed the remaining whisky. "Dynamite and a bulldozer was my advice."

"And?"

A quick shrug of the shoulders. "And, she doesn't take advice very well."

"You think she'll rebuild anyway?"

"I just told you, I don't know."

"If she does, will she contact you?"

Luca rose again, walked to the bar, and reached for the bottle of Scotch. His head was buzzing. Well, no. Not really buzzing. A shot of Scotch wasn't enough to make a man drunk—unless all he'd had to eat in the past umpteen hours was half a blueberry muffin and a belly full of bile.

Grim-faced, he put his empty glass on the granite countertop, then walked back to his seat.

"Luca? Do you expect to hear from her?"

"No," he said flatly.

"Will you contact her?"

Luca looked at Matteo.

"Didn't you hear what I said? If I don't expect her to get in touch with me, why would I get in touch with her?"

"I don't know. I just thought, you know, she's a good-looking woman."

"The world is full of good-looking women."

"True, but this one—"

"I have work to do," Luca said sharply. He picked up his iPhone and turned it on. "Surely, you do, too."

"Bianca said she seemed familiar."

"Who?" Luca said impatiently, as if he had no idea what his brother was talking about.

"Cheyenne McKenna. Bianca said—"

"Do you think we could stop talking about a woman none of us will ever see again?"

Matteo gave him a long, searching look. Then he tossed back his drink, set the glass aside and opened his computer. Seconds later, he was engrossed in reading and responding to the emails that had accumulated in the last couple of days.

Luca tried to do the same thing, but it didn't work.

He was back in that cheesy motel room, his head filled with X-rated images.

And anger.

Why?

They'd had sex, and she'd left. So what? Why was he so pissed off?

She used you.

Back to that again. Well, so what? They'd both gotten what they wanted.

She'd taken control of everything, from start to finish.

Yes, and what about it? He wasn't a control freak. He wasn't into domination.

He wasn't.

But he wanted to dominate her. He wanted to take charge, demand that she give herself to him, not just give herself but submit to him…

Every muscle in his body had turned to stone.

Basta! Enough of this nonsense.

He picked up his phone again, called up his emails and scanned them. There were messages from his various project managers, a note from a friend who would be travelling from

Rome to New York in a couple of weeks, but most of the emails were updates and reminders from Jessica. He had a lunch appointment Wednesday with a client for whom he'd built homes on the Costa Brava and in Connecticut; the *Wall Street Journal* wanted an interview; he had been invited to a weekend in Bermuda and he'd yet to respond.

And here was the information about tonight's appointment.

He frowned.

He was expected at a fundraising dinner. Drinks at seven-thirty, dinner at eight, black tie, blah blah blah.

Black tie. A tux, then. Hell. Maybe he could get out of the commitment. Quickly, he texted his P.A.

Re tonight: OK just to send a check?

She texted back just as quickly.

Not OK. You bought a table for 8.

Luca sighed.

Name of charity?

Horse Sense.

What?

Horse Sense. An Equine Therapy Program.

An image flashed through his head. A horse. A couch. A shrink taking notes.

He almost laughed.

But no, not funny. He knew how some horses were treated.

So he sighed again and texted *OK*. A charity for animals. There were worse ways to spend an evening. Sitting in his penthouse, replaying the day's events would surely be one of them.

Kindness to horses was a much better alternative.

By the time the event was over, he'd have forgotten all about Cheyenne McKenna.

The plane gave a delicate bounce.

"Sorry, folks," the captain said. "Just a little turbulence."

Indeed, Luca thought. Just a little turbulence.

Then he re-opened his email inbox and got to work.

* * *

Cheyenne McKenna was on one hell of a tough bike ride.

What made it even tougher was that on her stationery bike, it was a ride to nowhere.

Just like her life.

Sweat dripped from her face, soaked her tank top and shorts. Her hair, piled in a knot on top of her head, was a soggy mass. Her thighs burned; her calves felt as if the muscles were tying themselves into knots.

Eye of the Tiger blasted through her earphones.

Had blasted through them.

She'd hit the stop button on her iPod twenty minutes ago so she could devote her attention to the flat screen TV hanging on the wall ahead of her, while Dr. Will imparted his daily dose of wisdom to the masses.

Cheyenne watched Dr. Will for the same reason she suspected most people did: so they could look at the idiots who came on the program and instantly feel better about themselves.

Right now, an otherwise-normal looking woman was sobbing over some mistake she'd made a decade ago.

Dr. Will let her rant for a while. Then he handed her a box of tissues, looked into the camera and said, in hushed tones, that they'd be back after the break and while they were gone, he wanted her to put things in perspective.

"You made a mistake," he said, "and yes, you embarrassed yourself. But it's time to put that behind you and move on."

The screen faded to a deodorant commercial, but before it did, the camera took one last shot of the woman's face. She was still sobbing, but now she was looking at the doctor as if his advice might save her.

Cheyenne snorted.

How good could his advice be if he didn't know enough to shave off his foolish-looking mustache and beard? Surely, a couple of million viewers must have told him that by now.

He'd look a hundred percent better.

All men looked better clean-shaven.

She'd never been into guys with mustaches. Or beards. She'd never been into any kind of facial hair.

So how come she could still remember that faint dark stubble on Luca Bellini's jaw, the sexy look of it but, mostly, the feel of it against her skin as he'd kissed her breasts?

She pedaled faster.

Actually, she'd been pretty sure he'd shaved just that morning, that he was simply the kind of man who came by that I-just-tumbled-out-of-bed look naturally.

Lots of the guys she'd worked with over the years cultivated that look, the sexy male model thing: five o'clock shadow, smoldering eyes, long muscled bodies, husky voices…

And there he was again, front and center in her head. Luca

Bellini, gorgeous and naked in that bed.

"Idiot," Cheyenne said briskly.

She left Dr. Will and the sobbing woman to each other, switched on her iPod, turned up the sound and pedaled even harder until, finally, the only thought in her head was that it would be a miracle if she could survive five more minutes on the bike, but she always thought that and she always survived it.

You didn't get to the top of the modeling world by being a wuss.

Not that she was at the top anymore.

Prinnng!

The timer went off.

Gasping, she killed the iPod and yanked the headset buds from her ears. Dr. Will was casting his grave look at a different woman who was weeping over a different mistake, but his advice was the same.

"I know," he said. "You made a mistake, you embarrassed yourself, but—"

"But," Cheyenne said, her voice mingling with his, "it's time to put that behind you and move on."

It didn't take a degree to do this counseling stuff. She'd figured that out years ago. All you needed was a sorrowful expression, a deep voice, and a solid line of bullshit.

Enough, she decided, and she grabbed the remote, aimed it at the TV and blasted Dr. Will into infinity. Or eternity. Or wherever it was TV pitchmen went when a remote sent them scattering because Dr. Will, doctor title or no, was a pitchman.

And she was soaked to the skin.

Cheyenne plucked a towel from a small bench, blotted

her face and arms, dumped the towel on the bench again and marched through her Soho condo to the kitchen. There were half a dozen small bottles of water in the fridge; she took one, unscrewed the top and guzzled down the contents.

You made a mistake, you embarrassed yourself, putting it behind you and moving on was not just an option, it was the only thing to do.

The problem was that every now and then, what you'd done tagged along with you like an annoying clown, sticking its thumbs in its ears, waggling its fingers and going *la la la* 24/7.

Cheyenne opened the cabinet under the sink, tossed the empty bottle into the recyclable bin and slammed the door, hard. The mood she was in, the solidity of the *thud* was nice and reassuring.

As for moving on… A fine concept. But what did you do next? Wait for a little time to pass, right? Once it did, the mistake would be history.

A logical realization, but it didn't make her feel any better.

How could it? she thought as she entered her bedroom, peeled off her clothes, dropped them in a soggy heap on the floor, and headed for the shower.

A mistake.

"Ha!" she said.

What a pathetic way to describe what had happened this morning—and was it really only this morning that she'd gone to bed with Luca Bellini?

"Give it a break, McKenna," she said as she stepped inside the shower stall and turned on the overhead spray.

She hadn't 'gone to bed' with him. She'd jumped his bones.

Fucked his brains out. A man she didn't know. Didn't like. They'd spent, what, two hours together, arguing and snapping at each other and, wham, next thing they were in a motel room they might as well have rented by the hour.

"Dammit," she whispered, and felt heat rush to her face.

How about by the minute? Because she'd gone at him like a bitch in heat. Fast. Greedy. No preliminaries and then the final touch. That note. God, that note.

Cheyenne turned on the side sprays, closed her eyes as the water beat against her aching muscles.

The only thing she hadn't done was leave him a fifty-dollar bill for cab fare.

Was that what happened when you hadn't had sex for a while? For more than a while?

"For months," she said aloud. "Be honest, McKenna, at least with yourself. You haven't been with a man for a long time."

She hadn't planned it that way. It was only that none of the guys she knew seemed terribly interesting. They rarely did. She knew what it looked like from the outside, a woman moving in a world of sexy-looking male models, but the truth was that it was a world of shiny egos and fragile dispositions, and being out with a man who couldn't pass a mirror without looking at himself grew old pretty fast.

Besides, she'd always had a removed attitude about sex. She wasn't shy about it—it was a normal human need, which, given everything that had happened in her life, sometimes still struck her as a surprise, but yes, when the time and the man were right, she didn't hang back. And yes, she liked to take the lead. Nothing wrong with that, either.

But she didn't have sex with strangers. And no matter how you looked at it, Luca Bellini was a stranger.

She sighed, tilted her head back and gave herself up to the soothing cascade of warm water.

At least she'd never have to see him again, so who cared what he thought? Who cared what any of them thought, from the photographers who had once asked only for her and now acted as if they were doing her a favor when they shot her, to the designers who had once fought have her on their catwalks and now had to be convinced to hire her, to her agent, dammit, her very own agent who'd told her, bluntly, that putting up with the temper flare-ups of a Naomi Campbell was one thing; tolerating the increasing control issues of a Cheyenne McKenna was quite another.

The first thing got publicity.

The second put you on everybody's shit list.

Besides, she didn't have control issues.

Just because she knew what lighting was best for her hair and skin, what makeup would show whatever she was modeling to its maximum advantage; just because she had a better eye for color than most photographers, a firmer grasp of how to accessorize than many designers…

Just because she'd had sex with a man she'd damn near raped…

"Oh for God's sake, McKenna!"

Back to that.

And it was ridiculous, thinking that way.

A woman couldn't rape a man. And even if it were possible, she had surely not raped the Italian. He'd been a more than willing participant in their steamy encounter. That finger-sucking thing in her truck, and then that kiss in the motel parking lot…

That kiss had sent a river of fire racing through her blood.

His erection, pressing into her belly.

His arms, hard around her.

He'd almost carried her to that motel room and once they were alone, when she'd unzipped his fly, he'd sprung into her hands, his flesh hot, swollen, eager.

"Stop it," she whispered.

She was turning herself on, just remembering.

Why had the sex with Luca Bellini been so thrilling?

He was gorgeous, yes. He had a wonderful voice, that little accent thing. She'd liked that he was big and lean and hard-bodied, that he was taller than she was, even in those silly cowboy boots she'd worn—worn deliberately, because she'd expected to spend a couple of hours with Jake Wilde and she'd met Jake so she knew he'd tower over her and she didn't like that, the feeling she got when she had to tilt her head back to look at a man's face, that sense of giving a man some kind of power over her, and how come instead of not liking that she had to do that to look at Luca's face she'd—she'd found it a turn-on?

Was it that he'd stood up to her? Men never did. They were always as eager as puppies to please her. To impress her.

Bellini hadn't tried to impress her at all.

In fact, she was pretty sure he hadn't liked her any more than she'd liked him.

All he'd wanted was to get inside her panties.

Which was what she'd wanted, too.

Okay. So those things made him a little different, but they didn't explain why the sex had been so hot.

A possibility nibbled at the edges of her mind, one she didn't like, but one of the things she'd always believed in was honesty. With herself, anyway.

Cheyenne let the water wash away the last vestiges of shampoo.

She'd had the feeling that he'd held back. That he'd wanted to take her instead of letting himself be taken. Well, nothing unusual in that. There was almost always that to contend with, a man who'd let her do her thing and then try to take over, but she never let it happen and they were cool with it.

Bellini hadn't been cool with it.

She'd sensed that need in him. The hunger to reverse their positions, to pin her beneath him and ride her as a stallion rode a mare.

But she wasn't into me-Tarzan-you-Jane sex.

That was why she'd sneaked out of the room while he slept, because she'd known that things would be different once he woke, that he would not tolerate having control wrested from him again, and the amazing thing was that the thought had not so much frightened her as it had…

As it had excited her.

"Crazy," she said, as she shut off the shower. Totally, completely crazy.

Why would a woman want to be taken? Want to give herself up to a man's touch, his body, his control? Why would a woman want to bend to a man's domination? To anyone's domination?

Been there, done that, thank you very much—and what

was the point in reliving what had happened hours ago with a stranger in a cheap motel room?

Dr. Will was right about one thing.

What mattered was getting on with your life.

And she was doing exactly that.

The ranch in Texas. That was getting on with your life, wasn't it? Maybe she wasn't in such demand as a model anymore. So what? She'd made a fortune, a veritable fortune starting when she was seventeen, and she'd had the brains to invest it wisely. She was twenty-nine now, and she had one huge pile of dough.

Cheyenne wrapped herself in an oversized bath towel and stepped onto the heated bathroom floor. She dried off briskly, hung the towel on the rack and reached for her hairbrush.

She had not spent her money on drugs or clothes or bling. No fancy cars. No Manhattan townhouse.

Instead, she'd turned it over to the smartest broker she knew and she'd watched it grow.

The result was that she owned this condo as well as a small house on a lake in upstate New York where she kept her beloved pair of Thoroughbred horses.

She'd purchased them on a whim—amazing, because she wasn't given to whims, but she'd been on a shoot at a horse farm in Kentucky and a stable hand had spoken casually about a pair of horses kept in a small barn by themselves. He'd said that they didn't win races, that one had some kind of hoof problem and the other was off its feed.

"Bad investments," the guy had said, and shrugged.

"So what happens to them?" Cheyenne had asked, because, right away, she'd had a bad feeling.

"The owner will cut his losses."

"How?"

"Best of all worlds? Sell 'em to a riding academy. Otherwise, who knows? Dog food factory. Or maybe, you know, they're insured for a lot of money." He'd given her a sideways glance. "Sometimes, horses like them just, you know, they just get real sick…"

"Would the owner actually…"

The guy had looked at her as if she were an idiot. And she had to be, to ask the question. The answer was, he would. Of course, he would. She knew that better than anyone. There'd been a horse in her childhood, a sad, broken-down creature, her best friend, her only friend…

An hour later, she'd been the owner of a pair of horses. She'd shipped them to her place in upstate New York.

And fallen in love with them both.

She'd gotten them excellent veterinary care, hired a boy who loved horses to look after them. She'd spent every possible weekend with the animals, nursing them back to good health, winning their trust and, in turn, trusting them in ways you could never trust people. The horses calmed her, it was as simple as that, and when she'd stumbled across an article in a magazine about equine therapy, even though she'd discarded as pure BS all the mumbo jumbo shrinks proposed for dealing with emotional trauma or childhood disorders or whatever you wanted to call simply not sucking it up and getting on with life, the idea that working with horses could help troubled kids made sense.

Having Baby in her life when she was a kid had helped her.

Not for long, but for a while.

Cheyenne switched on her hair dryer, bent at the waist, brushed and dried her hair until it was a fall of shiny black. Then she stood straight, pushed the slightly damp locks away from her face, and stared at her reflection in the mirrored wall.

Her appraisal was dispassionate, that of a pro for the product she sold.

A long, lean body. Up-tilted breasts. Curved hips. Long legs.

Her hair was straight and glossy, her cheekbones razor-sharp. She had thick, sooty lashes, a nose that was, as one photographer had gushed, more interesting than perfect, and a wide mouth above a determined chin.

The body was Mama's: a small-town beauty queen who ended up with a pocket full of failed dreams.

The rest was her father's: a reservation Romeo with failed dreams of his own.

Not that she'd ever seen her father, but in her sober moments, that was how Mama had described him. Black hair. Thick lashes. Proud nose. Full mouth.

"Fell for him while I was workin' in a diner near Fort Laramie," she'd said in her whiskey-rough voice. "Easy on the eyes. Looked like Cochise musta looked in his day."

Cheyenne had heard the Cochise comparison endless times and when she was ten or eleven, she'd foolishly pointed out that Cochise had been an Apache and her father, according to Mama, had been Cheyenne.

Mama, drunk as usual, had backhanded her.

"Smart ass kid," she'd said.

"Oh, sweetie," she'd sobbed the next day when she saw

Cheyenne's black eye, "I'm so sorry," but by then Cheyenne had learned apologies were meaningless whether they were for beatings or for being warned to make Mama's latest boyfriend happy…

"What in hell are you doing?" Cheyenne demanded of her reflection.

That was all history.

She had escaped Wyoming, escaped Mama, escaped the life she'd been born to and created her own life, one that she, alone, controlled.

And she was wasting time.

The *Horse Sense* fundraiser started in less than an hour. The timing was bad—she'd stayed in Wilde's Crossing a day too long—but until almost the last minute, she'd toyed with the idea of baling on the fundraiser and then she'd realized no, she couldn't do that. The *Horse Sense* board was counting on her to greet guests and convince them to open their wallets and give generously to the foundation.

She knew she wasn't a real supermodel anymore, but nobody outside the business did.

She had to get dressed, look glamorous, and get into the mood to be Cheyenne McKenna, whose face had graced magazine covers.

Plus, she wanted to see the expressions of the people on the *Horse Sense* board when she told them she was giving them a ranch and she'd foot the cost of reconstruction.

Just thinking about it made her smile.

She took a dress from its hanger, a long fall of silk in shades that ranged from the palest blue to the deepest sapphire, and let it slither down over her head.

No thong. No bra. No panty hose. Not with a dress like this. No accessories except a pair of deep blue Manolos with icepick heels, and a rhinestone clip to hold her hair back from one side of her face. Add a flick of black-as-midnight mascara. A dusting of blusher on her cheeks. A slick of bright red lip gloss.

Cheyenne looked in the mirror and smiled.

She looked the way she was supposed to look. Like a million bucks. Like a magazine ad. Like everyman's dream come to life.

Would she bring in lots of donations?

She hoped so.

And then, just as the doorman phoned to tell her the limo that had been sent for her was waiting at the curb, she had one last, unexpected thought.

What would Luca Bellini say if he saw her like this?

Would he lift her in his arms, carry her away, strip the dress from her and do all the things men wanted to do to women? Those things that gave men power and made women helpless. Touch her breasts. Put his hand between her thighs. Clasp her wrists, push her against a wall, force her to accept his domination?

She waited for the rush of nausea that always accompanied such images…

And felt, instead, breathlessness, a melting of her bones, a sensation of heat low in her belly.

Cheyenne gave herself a mental shake.

Then she grabbed a small silk purse, tucked two hundred bucks, a comb, her keys, her iPhone and her lip gloss inside, and set off to face the world.

CHAPTER FOUR

WHY HAD HE ever agreed to host a table tonight?

It was the last thing in the world Luca felt like doing.

Of course, when he'd made the commitment he hadn't known he'd be flying back from Texas that same day after confronting what had turned out to be his father's second family—or his first, depending on your point of view.

Most of the time, when he was approached to donate to an event that involved the rich and powerful dressing up to impress the rich and powerful, he'd explain—politely—that he'd be unable to attend, but he'd be happy to write a check or sponsor a table, meaning he'd pay the fees for whatever number of guests could be seated at it.

That always made everybody happy.

Somehow, he'd forgotten to make those plans clear to the person chairing tonight's event.

Not a problem, he told himself as his driver pulled the black Mercedes to the curb.

He would put in an appearance, say all the right things, shake all the right hands and after a couple of hours, he'd say goodnight and go home.

Luca checked his watch, then leaned forward.

"Two hours, Aldo—unless I can get away sooner."

"I'm as near as your cell phone, sir."

Luca nodded. Aldo had been with him for years, long enough to know that his boss didn't like formal functions any more than he liked having doors opened and closed for him, so he sat quietly behind the wheel until Luca stepped from the car and walked briskly to the hotel through the small crowd that had gathered to gawk at possible celebrity sightings.

Tourists, the lot of them, Luca thought with mild disdain.

No true New Yorker would gawk at a celebrity, much less acknowledge the presence of one. Luca might have been born in Italy, but he held dual American and Italian citizenship; he had attended Columbia University; he'd lived in the city, first in student housing, then in rented apartments on and off for years before buying his condo. He considered himself a native son to the marrow of his bones, which was one of the reasons he was not impressed by events like this.

The doorman smiled politely, the door swung open and Luca stepped into the marble and gold lobby.

It was handsome, though not something he would choose to be associated with professionally—it was too fussy for his tastes, but he could appreciate the care and expertise that had gone into its design and creation.

Ahead, at the foot of three wide marble steps, a discreet sign listed the evening's events.

The *Horse Sense* ball and banquet was in the Skytop Room, on the hotel's sixtieth floor. It was a spectacular room with a spectacular view. He had been to events there many times before, and he knew the space was big enough to accommodate several hundred people.

He bit back a groan as he stepped into an elevator that would whisk him directly there.

There would be endless hands to shake, endless small talk to be made, endless business contacts to make and renew, and, *Dio*, he knew all too well how many women would end up in his path.

He was an eligible bachelor in a city of too few eligible bachelors.

He should have brought a date to run interference.

Cheyenne McKenna, for instance.

One look at her beside him and the competition would have known enough to stay away, and wasn't that a foolish thought? He had not taken her address or phone number. She hadn't given him the chance to do so.

And why in hell was he back to that?

The elevator doors opened. He stepped from the car and straight into a wall of noise. Loud voices, coming from the expensively dressed crowd. Loud music, coming from a band on a stage at one end of the huge room.

His belly knotted.

He'd told Aldo he'd stay for two hours, but that had been a mistake. He was not in the mood for this. He'd put in a long day. A difficult day. There was still time to turn around, get right back in the elevator and…

A hand clasped his shoulder.

"Luca! Great to see you."

Another hand reached for his.

"Bellini. How've you been? We need to do lunch this week, talk about a new project I'm considering in Tribeca."

Too late. He'd just have to get through the evening, or at least a piece of it.

He smiled, nodded, shook hands, was all but smothered by drifts of perfume competing for attention as Manhattan's most elegantly-dressed women rose on their toes to press their cheeks to his.

And, as he'd known they would, the not-terribly-subtle attempts at matchmaking started almost instantly.

"Luca? Have you met my…"

Daughter. Niece. Sister. He had met them all at one time or another. Or perhaps he hadn't. Either way, he said the right things, smiled the right smiles…and kept moving, his destination the bar at the opposite end of the room.

He'd almost made it when he heard a feminine shriek and a bejeweled hand grasped his arm.

"Luca!"

The hand and shriek belonged to Alene Beresford, wife of the CEO of a small, elite hotel chain—and, he now remembered, the Chair of tonight's fundraiser.

Alene was a born do-gooder, always looking for a new cause that would get her name in the *Times' Sunday Styles* section. True to form, she had a photographer in tow and before Luca could object, Alene plastered herself against his side and beamed for the camera. She was dressed to kill in what was surely a couturier gown in a pink so bright the color hurt Luca's eyes. Her hair was a shade of red that would never appear in nature, and the skin of her face was so taut that he had an almost overpowering urge to try and bounce a coin off it.

An image of Cheyenne McKenna, exquisite in her jeans and T-shirt, her face bare of makeup, her hair drawn back in its no-nonsense braid, swam into his head.

What would she have worn for an evening like this? Something simple, he was sure of it. Something silky, long and diaphanous. Something that would complement her natural beauty…

"Luca, darling," Alene said, "I was starting to think you weren't going to show up!"

"Alene," he said, smiling politely. "I said I'd be here, didn't I?"

"Yes, darling, you did." She lifted her eyebrows. At least, she made the attempt, but whatever had frozen her face in its awful parody of eternal youth wouldn't permit much more than a quiver. "And I must say, I was delighted! We all know that having you put in an appearance is quite a coup!"

Luca smiled again. By the end of the evening, the muscles of his face would surely ache hurt from an endless succession of phony smiles.

"Well, here I am." Someone jostled him from the rear; someone else stepped on his toes. "Although," he heard himself say, "I'm afraid I can't stay for the entire evening."

"Oh, you'll change your mind when you see the marvelous people I've seated at your table."

"I'm sure they're interesting, but I have an early morning appointment."

"Luca. Darling boy, tomorrow is Saturday."

Okay. The smile was already starting to become painful.

"I know, Alene, but—"

"Everyone deserves a day off, even you!" Alene batted her lashes and leaned in. "Besides, I'm counting on you to keep tonight's honored guest happy." Her voice dropped to a dramatic low. "I'm not supposed to tell anyone yet, but we just learned that she's not only going to be our poster child for *Horse Sense*, she's going to give us an incredible gift!"

"How generous," Luca said politely.

"Indeed it is! She's giving us a horse ranch so we can expand our work. Isn't that wonderful?"

Wonderful indeed, Luca thought grimly. Had he been transported into a universe in which people gave away ranches the way circus clowns gave away balloons?

"In Texas."

"What about Texas?"

"The ranch, silly man! It's in Texas. It needs some work, of course."

Luca narrowed his eyes. A ranch? In Texas? No. That was impossible.

"And, naturally, we'll need your professional advice. Luca? Are you listening to me? We'll want your advice."

"Where is this ranch located?"

Alene rolled her eyes.

"You're not paying attention! I just said. In Texas."

"Where in Texas?"

"Oh, for goodness sakes, how do I know that? It's just in Texas, Luca. You can ask Ms. McKenna for the specific—"

"Who?"

"The donor's name is McKenna. Cheyenne McKenna. Our new spokeswoman…or is it spokesperson? I'm never sure which is PC, though I doubt if Cheyenne would—"

"Cheyenne?" he said. "Cheyenne McKenna?"

"Yes. The model. Do you know her? I'm sure you know her face. Her picture is everywhere. Well, almost everywhere." Alene looked around, then leaned close again. "Not as much lately, it would seem. There've been rumors. About her career. That it's on the skids, but it doesn't matter to us. Not too much, anyway. She's still famous. And that's what matters."

Luca wasn't listening. He was thinking back to what Matteo had said, something about one of their sisters suggesting that Cheyenne seemed familiar.

"…the perfect face to publicize our cause. Well, you can see for yourself. Not from here, though. This crowd…" Alene clasped Luca's arm and drew him across the room. "There. See? That wall, darling. That's Cheyenne McKenna."

Luca stared at the display of photos, all done in stark black and white.

All magnificent, thanks to the subject matter.

Thanks to Cheyenne.

In one, she stood beside a white horse, her hand resting on the animal's arched neck. In another, she held the reins of a black stallion as she led him down a hillside. There were half a dozen other photos of her with what seemed to be the same pair of horses, riding them bareback, feeding them from the palm of her hand, stroking their muzzles as the animals closed their eyes in ecstasy.

He understood that ecstasy.

He had felt it this morning as Cheyenne had ridden him to a mind-blowing orgasm.

"Well? What do you think?" Alene said. "Will she help get us noticed? Will Cheyenne McKenna do what we need?"

What Cheyenne McKenna was doing was certainly not what he needed in a public place, turning him inside out, firing a hunger so raw, so savage that he could feel his cock turning to stone.

The lies he'd told himself rose like bile in his throat. Telling himself that he was over her, that he didn't want her… Every nerve ending in his body mocked him. What they'd done had not been anywhere near enough. He wanted her again, his way, not hers, wanted her begging for him, pleading for his possession, a willing slave to his every need, every demand, every desire…

"Luca? What do you think?"

Say something, he told himself fiercely, but how could a man say something intelligent when his body had taken control of his brain

"That face. That body. Add in the ranch she's giving us and we'll be off to a tremendous start. I mean, we're such a new charity…" Alene giggled. "Just look at you! You're speechless. Well, I can't blame you. This is just superb news, isn't it?"

Luca cleared his throat.

"Superb," he said.

"And I've put her at your table, you lucky man, so you can

ask her about the ranch. She hasn't told us much. Well, we really haven't had time to talk. She was away, you see, but now that she's back—"

"Alene," Luca said quickly, "this—this thing about a ranch… It's not what I do. I'll be happy to recommend someone, but—"

"Good evening."

A male voice boomed through the ballroom. Conversation ebbed, then died; people turned toward the stage and applauded the white-haired man, microphone in hand, who beamed down at them.

"Thank you for that warm welcome, and let me extend an equally warm welcome to you and to what we hope will become an annual tradition, a celebration of horses, kids, and the wonders that can happen when you mix the two together. For those of you who don't know me…"

Polite laughter greeted that statement.

"I'm your host, Jonathan Beresford. My lovely wife, Alene, is the genius who planned this amazing evening. Alene? Darling, where are you? Come up here and help me thank all these good people. I'm afraid our guest of honor is a bit late, but she's phoned to assure us that she's on her way. Until she arrives, Alene will tell you all about our wonderful new project."

"I have to go," Alene hissed as she pressed her lips to the air beside Luca's cheek. "See you later, darling. And remember—we're counting on you to help us get this project off the ground."

"No. Alene, wait—"

Too late.

Alene Beresford had slipped through the crowd.

* * *

Luca did the same.

There was no reason to stay, no matter what Alene said.

He had paid thirty-five thousand dollars to sponsor a table. That was his act of charity for the night. He could leave now and no one would question it. People understood that the Luca Bellinis of this world had full schedules and were often called away on a moment's notice.

"Excuse me," he said as he made his way through the crowd and toward the ballroom doors. "Sorry. Coming through."

Why would he want to spend the evening sitting beside Cheyenne McKenna, pretending to engage in polite conversation?

They had nothing to say to each other.

They hadn't had anything much to say this morning, either. They'd shared a moment of mindless sex, and even if his libido was willing to make a fool of itself over the memory, his intellect wasn't.

He was out of here.

He'd phone Aldo, get into his car, make a couple of calls, arrange to meet someone for a drink at the *Rose Bar* or perhaps *The Top of the Standard*. That writer he'd met last week, maybe, the one with the cute little laugh. Or that blond banker…

He frowned as he reached the elevators.

What was he doing? Running away? From a woman? He, who had never run from anything in his life? Not from his mother's hot temper or his father's cold withdrawal, not from the priests' beatings at his Sicilian boarding school or from those given by the upscale bullies at the Yorkshire prep school he and Matteo had been sent to when they'd proved 'difficult.'

He'd never run from anybody or anything and now he was going to run from a woman because he couldn't seem to look at her without getting an erection.

"Pathetic," he muttered.

The doors to one of the elevators slid open.

"You going down?" a guy next to him asked.

Luca shook his head.

"No. No, *grazie*. I, ah, I changed my mind."

He turned away, crossed the hall to the men's restroom and opened the door on a sea of gold and marble. A white-jacketed attendant greeted him with a polite smile. Luca was not in the mood for a smile. He was not in the mood for attendants: he had never understood why a man was not expected to pluck his own towel from a basket of towels, use it and dispose of it without help.

Still, he returned the smile.

It was not the attendant's fault he had a job like this any more than it was the man's fault that he, Luca, had almost behaved like an asshole.

He chose a stall, went inside it and turned the lock.

Run? Ridiculous. Why would he run?

What he was going to do was find his table, sit down, eat a meal, chat politely with the others seated with him and yes, that included Cheyenne McKenna, who would surely chat just as politely with him.

That was what civilized people did.

He waited a few seconds, flushed a toilet that didn't need

flushing, undid the lock, emerged from the stall and went to the sink. He washed his hands, said *grazie* to the attendant when he handed him a small white towel, dried his hands, dropped the towel on the counter, fished out his wallet and gave the attendant a ten dollar bill.

He did the things normal people did in a normal world and, as he'd expected, doing those things helped him feel grounded and focused and calm…

Until he left the restroom and found himself face to face with Cheyenne herself.

* * *

Cheyenne had arrived almost twenty minutes late.

Her taxi had run into traffic.

A snarled knot of vehicles on West Houston had eaten up precious time. She'd taken advantage of it to phone Alene Beresford and tell her about the ranch. She'd intended to tell her later tonight, but why wait?

Alene had squealed with delight.

"The board has to give official approval, of course," she'd said, 'but they'll be thrilled, Cheyenne, absolutely thrilled! And I have the perfect man for you to talk to about this. I'll change the seating, put you at his table… Oh, this is wonderful news!"

Talking with someone was the last thing Cheyenne felt like doing tonight, but she appreciated Alene's enthusiasm. Her dinner companion would probably be a *Horse Sense* board member, and this talk wouldn't be anything like the one she'd had with Luca Bellini because that hadn't been a talk at all, not even the part that had involved Sweetwater.

It had been a debate.

He'd opposed everything she'd wanted, except for the sex, and by the time the cab finally pulled up to the hotel, she'd been wondering what had ever impelled her to bother with his assessment of the place at all, let alone have sex with him.

All he was now was an uncomfortable memory.

Alene's assistant had greeted her at the elevator, hand outstretched.

"Quick! Come this way. No, not through the ballroom. The introductions have already started. I'm supposed to take you through the back, to the stage."

"Sorry," Cheyenne said. "The traffic—"

"Alene told me. Just go straight onstage. Johnny Beresford just called her to the mike. You have a couple of minutes until she gets there."

Cheyenne barely had time to run her hands through her hair before she was standing in the glare of lights with Alene.

"Ladies and gentlemen, the fantastic Cheyenne McKenna," Alene said, and the crowd applauded

Cheyenne smiled brightly and responded by saying how happy she was to be there.

Untrue, of course, because her already not-so-great mood took a further downward trajectory at the sight of all those people staring at her as if they wanted a piece of her for their own, but she reminded herself of why she was involved in this, of how important the goals of *Horse Sense* were, and she smiled and waved and said it was the Beresfords who were fantastic.

Eventually, Alene's husband announced that the buffet was open and those who'd yet to pick up their seating cards should please do so, blah blah blah.

Alene put her arm around Cheyenne's waist, moved her away from the mike and asked if she wanted to make the announcement about her gift tonight or hold off for a press conference the next morning.

"Your choice," Cheyenne said.

"Well, we might get more mileage if we hold off until people are tweeting about tonight's party," Alene said, "but that doesn't have to keep you from talking about the ranch with the man I told you about. He's a famous architect."

Cheyenne looked at Alene. Such simple words, but they sent a whisper of unease dancing up her spine. Silly, of course. The world was full of men who were architects.

"But we don't want to commit to one tonight, Alene. New York must have dozens of architects who could work with us on this."

"Trust me, darling. This is the guy we want. Assuming we can get him, that is. He's probably got enough jobs to keep him busy from now through the next century, but he's like every other man on the planet—he won't be able to resist a pretty face. You just turn on the charm and I'll bet you'll have him eating out of your hand." Alene chuckled. "Not that he isn't pretty charming himself. He's got more money than Fort Knox, he's amazingly good looking and on top of all that, he's very, very talented."

Alene still had her arm around Cheyenne's waist; they were going down the few steps that led from the stage to the ballroom floor. Cameras and cellphones were pointing at them; Cheyenne kept her smile in place, something she'd learned to do early in her career, but it was getting more difficult to maintain.

That strange sense of unease was growing.

"What's his name?"

"There's *Vanity Fair*," Alene whispered. "Give them a big smile."

"Alene. What's his name?"

"The photographer from *Vanity Fair*? I can't recall."

"The architect. The man you're hoping I'll meet."

"No worries, darling. You'll meet him. I put you at his table. Oh, look! Is that Annie Leibovitz? It is! Fantastic. Let me introduce you."

"I've met Annie," Cheyenne said impatiently. "Just tell me the name of this architect."

"Annie! Yoo hoo!"

"Alene. The architect. Who is he?"

"Luca. Luca Bellini."

Cheyenne had felt her heart rise into her throat. No, she'd thought, no, no, no! The last person she wanted to deal with tonight was the man she'd been with this morning. As for working with him… The idea was laughable. Except, laughable was the wrong word. She would never, not in a million billion years, work with Luca Bellini.

And, sweet Jesus, there wasn't a way in hell she was going to explain that to Alene Beresford or anybody else.

"Yoo hoo, Annie!"

"Alene."

"Annie. Over here."

"Alene!"

"Cheyenne, for heaven's sake, what are you doing? If we can get Annie Leibovitz to agree to do a shoot for us—"

Cheyenne dug in her heels. Not easy, when they were five inches high, but she did it. Alene Beresford almost stumbled.

"What are you doing? Annie Leibovitz is right over—"

"I know. I see her. But—but I have to—to check my makeup. My hair."

"You look gorgeous!"

"Not for a famous photographer, I don't." Cheyenne stepped back. "Where's the ladies' room?"

"Out in the hall, across from the elevators, but really, Cheyenne—"

"I'll be right back," Cheyenne said, flashing a brilliant smile.

Cheyenne all but forced her way through the crowd. Everybody wanted to say hello; everybody wanted a photo or a selfie. A sea of smartphones waved ahead of her like grass in a Sweetwater meadow.

She kept smiling. And moving.

The hell she'd be right back.

Finally! There were the elevators. Dammit, people were waiting for them. She couldn't just stand around. Luca was here, but where, exactly, was that? No way did she want to run the risk of finding out.

The restrooms were right were Alene had said they'd be.

Perfect.

A quick detour into the ladies'. Kill a couple of minutes so that one or two elevators could arrive, get into one, take it to the lobby, get into a cab and phone Alene while she headed downtown. *Sorry,* she'd say, *but I came down with a headache.*

It wasn't a foolproof plan—Alene would be ticked off—but it would have to do.

The restroom attendant was watching her.

Cheyenne went to one of the marble vanities. Opened her little purse. Took out her lip gloss and ran it over her mouth.

And checked her watch.

Surely, two or three minutes had passed.

She capped the gloss, put it away, fumbled a ten-dollar bill from her purse and dropped it into the glass bowl on the vanity. Then she looked in the mirror, made sure she looked cool and collected—amazing, what years of working before a camera could do—and went to the door.

Good. Excellent. Nobody was waiting for the elevators.

She pasted a professional smile to her lips. Walked out of the restroom. Closed the door behind her…

Just as the door to the men's room opened.

And Luca Bellini stepped into the corridor.

CHAPTER FIVE

LUCA RECOVERED FIRST.

"Cheyenne," he said politely.

"Luca."

She was polite, too, but he could see her struggling to stay that way. Good, he thought coldly. She had every right to be uncomfortable.

What she had no right to be was so incredibly beautiful.

There were scores of women here tonight. They were all impeccably groomed, coifed and gowned.

He'd brought women he'd been involved with to functions like this. He had a general idea of what it took for a woman to make an appearance at a glittery charity event.

Paying the bills, *grazie a Dio*, did not involve knowing all the details, but he knew enough to be aware that those details included hair appointments, nail appointments and time spent with makeup artists, and that all those things followed hours spent choosing the most elaborate gowns and shoes and everything else that would never mean a damn to a man, but would be vital to a woman.

Unless everything about Cheyenne was an artful illusion, he doubted that she'd put in more than a few minutes getting ready for tonight.

It wasn't that she didn't look beautiful.

She did.

Her hair was loose and flowing, drawn back on one side by some kind of clip.

Her face glowed, the skin almost a dusty gold, her mouth a sexy red, her lashes dark and long.

Her gown was blue, half a dozen shades of blue. The neckline left most of her shoulders bare.

Kissably bare.

The fabric looked silky; just looking at it made him want to feel its texture between his fingers.

It skimmed her body. Breasts. Waist. Hips. Thighs. It hung in a way that was demure even as it hinted at what lay beneath: breasts he had yet to taste, though he knew they would be sweet on his tongue; hips seemingly made for his hands to grasp; that hot delta between her firm thighs.

The gown was artfully slit from hem to thigh. Each time she moved, he caught a glimpse of tanned flesh.

His body went rigid.

He was on the verge of a monumental erection, the kind he hadn't had in public since he'd learn to control his body's needs at the age of sixteen.

The possibility of making a fool of himself was bad enough. Even worse was the realization that it was she who would make a fool of him, just as she had done before.

No, he thought coldly. That was not going to happen.

"What a surprise."

"Yes," she said. "I was thinking the same thing."

He almost laughed. Her eyes were like pools of ice, her tone glacial, but she was smiling as politely as he.

And no wonder, he thought, as he caught the glow of a flashbulb from the corner of his eye. They were on display, a pair of actors trapped in a bad play, and she wouldn't want ugly publicity anymore than he would.

"Yes," he said, "isn't it? When Alene told me you were here, I was…dumbstruck."

"Such a nice, old-fashioned word. Dumbstruck."

"Ah. She told you, too."

"A few minutes ago."

His smile tilted. "And you came looking for me."

Her laughter was the kind no man ever wanted directed at him.

"You wish."

Such disdain. Such hauteur. Such ego. It was enough to change his plans.

"Yes, I do. You saved me the trouble of looking for you."

He'd surprised her. He could see it in the swift narrowing of her eyes.

"You were looking for me?"

Another flashbulb went off. He looked in its direction, saw the camera, saw a couple of cellphones aimed at them. Still smiling, Luca closed the couple of inches separating them and clasped her elbow.

He felt her stiffen. She was going to jerk free, or at least she was going to try, and there was no way he'd let that happen.

Deliberately, he tightened his grasp.

"Lights, camera, action," he said, very softly, bending his head so that his lips were almost at her ear. "Or don't they say that in your world?"

"Whatever you think you're doing, Bellini?"

"What I'm doing is saving your ass, McKenna. Put that ego of yours away and trot out what little you know of good manners. In other words, smile and look as if you're thrilled to have found me…unless, of course, you want to be on every cheap gossip blog by midnight."

She glared at him. Then he saw her throw a quick look over his shoulder, saw knowledge of their growing audience register in her eyes.

"Shit," she whispered.

He laughed. "I couldn't have said it better myself."

"Oh, Luca," she said gaily, "that's so amusing!"

She threw back her head and laughed. He imagined dipping his head lower and pressing his mouth to the elegant curve of her throat.

It was an image he didn't need right now, and he forced it out of his head and replaced it with a grin.

"I thought you'd like it," he said.

Then, still holding her elbow, he led her through what was now a fair-sized group of gawkers, into the ballroom and to his table.

* * *

There were six other people seated with them.

Two psychiatrists and their spouses, plus a portly man and his seemingly anorexic wife.

The shrinks—one male, one female—were politely reserved.

The portly man was effusively friendly.

"Jim Holland," he said. "From Staten Island. This is my wife, Verna."

Luca shook hands all around. So did Cheyenne. He searched for a conversational gambit, thought of saying that though he'd lived in New York, on and off, for years, this was the first time he'd met someone who actually lived on Staten Island, but caution suggested that might not go over well.

Besides, he didn't need a conversation starter.

He had the only one that mattered, seated next to him.

Cheyenne was what everyone wanted to talk about; she was the person they wanted to talk to. Not even the evening's entertainment—a famous rock band and its even more famous lead singer—were enough of a distraction to change their focus of attention.

They all recognized her. Even the shrinks seemed excited to meet her—or, at least, as excited as Luca figured people who spent their lives trying to seem unflappable could get.

"I saw you on one of those huge Times Square billboards," one of them said.

"Oh, yes," his wife added. "In that soap ad. What was the brand?"

"Gardenia Body Shampoo," Cheyenne said politely.

Gardenia Body Shampoo. Luca remembered the scent of her naked skin. Was that what she'd smelled of? Gardenias?

"And you did those jeans ads," Verna Holland said. "I bought a pair." She gave a nervous laugh. "Of course, they didn't look on me the way they'd looked on you."

Nothing would look on any woman the way it would look on Cheyenne, Luca thought, although what she'd always look best in was her own naked skin.

"I heard a rumor that you're donating your ranch in Tennessee to the organization," Shrink Number Two's husband said.

"Texas," Cheyenne said, smiling politely.

"Do you raise horses?"

"No, I don't."

"You have a ranch, but no horses?"

Cheyenne's smile tilted. Luca saw that the conversation was making her uncomfortable. Good, he thought coldly. Let her be uncomfortable.

"I don't breed horses, but I do own two."

"Ah. On your Tennessee ranch?"

"It's Texas. And no, I don't have—"

The lady shrink put her hand over her husband's.

"Are you interested in equine therapy?"

Cheyenne seemed to hesitate. "It's an interesting field."

"What I mean is, do you have a personal interest in it?"

"Now, Beverly," the shrink's husband said, smiling broadly, "don't pry."

"I'm not prying. I'd never pry. I'm just curious, is all. Equine therapy is a relatively new field and no one seems to have a firm set of statistics proving whether or not it's effective over the long term. I thought, if Ms. McKenna had actually experienced it, her opinion would be interesting."

Cheyenne's smile had grown fixed. She seemed more than uncomfortable; the word that came to mind was desperate.

Good, Luca thought again or, at least, that was what he wanted to think, but there was something in her eyes, a trapped expression…

He put his napkin on the table, rose to his feet and drew back her chair.

She looked up at him.

"They're playing our song," he said briskly.

He figured the odds were good she'd tell him they didn't have a song or that she'd sooner dance with a hippopotamus, but she got to her feet and said, "Yes, they are."

He took her hand and led her onto the dance floor. She went into his arms, but she kept what felt like the length of a football field between them.

He wasn't going to tolerate that.

She stiffened as he drew her closer.

"Try looking like you're enjoying this, McKenna."

"Our song?" she said.

Luca had no idea what the band was playing. Now, he listened. And then he laughed.

"*Say Something*."

"I just did."

"The song. It's called *Say Something*. Seems appropriate, don't you think? Especially the first line. 'I'm giving up on you.'"

Her face was turned up to his. For a couple of seconds, her expression didn't change. Then she smiled.

She had an amazing smile.

"I wouldn't have picked you for a man who knew much about popular music."

Luca turned her in a slow circle.

"I would not have picked you for a woman who would permit the blathering of fools to bother her."

She tried to draw back, but he wasn't going to tolerate that, either.

"Relax," he said softly. "Feel the music."

They moved together slowly for a few minutes. Then she sighed.

"I hate when people pry."

"They wanted to know more about you."

"Why?"

"Why?" Luca said, surprised at her naïveté.

"Yes, why. Why would they want to know more about me? I'm a stranger to them."

"You're not. At least, that's how they see things. You've been in their homes, on their television sets, in the magazines they read."

The music had changed. *Midnight*, by Coldplay. The song was as slow and plaintive as the last one. It suited what he felt, suited the feel of having her in his arms. His hand slid down her spine, settled just at its sweet indentation. He lowered his head a little, enough so he could smell the light scent of her skin and hair.

If they were alone, he thought, if they were alone…

"That they've seen me pretending doesn't entitle them to ask me personal questions."

Her answer puzzled him.

"Pretending?"

"It's what models do."

He turned her again. The floor was crowded; they had little space to maneuver in. That was fine with him. It meant he could keep her close.

"That's an interesting way to put it. That what you do is pretense."

"What else would you call it?"

"I don't know. Acting, perhaps."

"It's the same thing."

Dio, she felt wonderful in his arms.

He didn't want her to feel wonderful. He didn't want to think about how perfectly her body fit his.

And he sure as hell didn't want to think that the time they'd spent in that motel had been pretense. A meaningless exercise of body and brain, her cries, her flushed face nothing but an act.

An act he'd bought into, same as he was buying into it now.

Except, goddammit, he wasn't.

He turned her again. And again. They moved into a tiny area that, for the moment, was all their own.

"It is unreasonable to expect strangers to know when you're being real and when you're not."

"It doesn't matter what strangers think."

"An interesting philosophy."

Maybe the tone of his voice suggested something. She pulled back, but only as far as his encircling arms would permit.

"Thank you for getting me away from the table," she said, "but I'm fine now. I'd like to go back and get my purse and—"

"And run."

"I'm not running, Mr. Bellini. I'm simply going home."

"Mr. Bellini. Such formality from a woman who shared my bed this morning."

Color swept into her face.

"I knew it wouldn't last," she said.

"Oh, it lasted," Luca said, deliberately misunderstanding her. "It would have lasted even longer if you hadn't run."

"I was referring to your pathetic show of courtesy," she hissed. "I should have known it was meaningless."

"What about your pathetic tendency to run? Is that what you always do when the stakes get too high?"

She stopped moving.

"I'm going back to the table."

"Is that the reason you sneaked out of my bed? Because the stakes got too high?"

"It was a motel room bed, and I am done with this!"

Oh, she was full of fury! Eyes flashing. Mouth trembling. Pulse beating in her slender throat like the heart of a trapped songbird.

She was exquisite and—and, *Cristo*, he wanted her. Here. Right now. He wanted her more than he had ever wanted a woman in his life.

"Were you afraid of showing honest emotion, of giving up that act, that need to take control, to take charge, to run the show?"

She lifted her hands, formed them into fists and punched them against his shoulders.

"Let go of me!"

Luca grabbed her fists.

"Or were you afraid I was going to ask you a personal question? Something like, what's your phone number? Where do you live? Or, even worse, may I see you again?"

The music changed. Now, it was something fast and hot. Couples were moving around them, dancing, laughing, and she was struggling against him. Maybe people thought they were dancing. Maybe not. He didn't give a crap.

"You insulted me," he said in a low voice. Until that instant, he hadn't realized that that was the heart of the problem. Now, he did.

"I insulted you?" She laughed. It was not a pleasant sound. "What's your problem, Bellini? Do the women you screw usually stay around, applaud and write reviews?"

Why did her use of that word, screw, make him angry? Never mind the reason. It did. Everything about her made him angry, and he'd be damned if he'd let her avoid this confrontation.

"The women I screw, as you so delicately put it, don't creep off as if they're leaving the scene of a crime."

"LET GO!"

He tugged her to him. It was easy. He outweighed her, outmuscled her. She fell against him, breasts, hips, thighs.

"Actually," he said in a low, harsh voice, "you overestimated yourself, *bellissima*. We had a good time. It was over. It was a relief to find you gone. I'm not much for saccharine goodbyes and—*Merda*!"

Her stiletto heel was like the strike of a knife against his foot.

She looked up into his eyes and batted her lashes.

"Oh," she said sweetly, "did I step on you? I'm so sorry—What are you doing? Bellini! Bellini! Damn you, let go!"

He'd have sooner have let go of an asp poised to strike.

Hand wrapped tightly around her wrist, fingers digging into her flesh, Luca all but dragged her through the crowded dance floor, out the door and into the empty hall, though he wouldn't have given a damn if it had been packed with partygoers. He pushed her back against a velvet-flocked wall.

He was angry. Angry? He was furious and he had been ever since the morning.

This time, he wasn't going to let her get away.

She owed him.

For insulting him. For angering him.

For denying him what he'd needed in that motel room.

He could see the wildness in her eyes, the passion, and even as the civilized part of him asked him what in hell he thought he was doing, the savage part of him knew.

He wanted her.

Not because she was fighting him although yes, all that fire was part of it.

He wanted her because he had not had enough time, enough of her… And because he wanted her on his terms.

Submissive.

No. Not submissive.

Responsive.

He wanted her responsive. To him. Only to him. He wanted her to beg for release. To do whatever he asked of her.

He wanted to take her to bed and dominate her.

He wanted things he had never before wanted from a woman, and even as he tried to understand what was happening to him, he saw the change in her as she struggled against him, as her body brushed his.

He saw the fire turning to a flame that would consume them both.

He said something in a low, rough voice, clasped both her wrists in one hand and pinned them against the wall, high over her head.

"No," she panted.

Too late.

His mouth came down hard on hers. His tongue sought entry and when she wouldn't provide it, he sank his teeth into her bottom lip, hard enough to draw a moan of passion or pain from her throat.

Which was it? He didn't know and it didn't matter.

What mattered was that she bit him back—and then she groaned and opened to him and her taste was hot and sweet, and now there was no doubt that she wanted what he wanted.

This.

This kiss. This explosion of heat. This rush of blood as they moved against each other.

Yes, he thought, yes, *Cristo*, yes.

He ran his free hand down the length of her, from her throat to her breasts to her belly.

"Luca," she sobbed, "Luca…"

Her gown was slit to the thigh. He slipped his hand under it, and felt only skin.

She was naked.

No panties. No thong. Nothing between his hand and the elegant curve of her hip, the delicacy of her belly, the silken softness of her dark curls.

Another minute, he was going to explode.

"Open for me," he whispered.

She gave a little sob.

Parted her legs.

He put his hand between her thighs.

She said his name and he kissed her, deep and hard.

And cupped her. Stroked her.

She screamed into his mouth and came against his palm. Hot. Wet. All for him. Only for him.

His vision blurred.

He reached between them for the zipper of his fly. All he had to do was free himself, push her gown up, thrust into her. Make her come and come and come.

Sanity, a cold kind of sanity with a cruel edge, stopped him.

He let go of her wrists. Took his hand from the hot dampness between her thighs. And stepped back.

"No," she whispered. She was trembling. "Luca…"

He was trembling too, but that didn't matter.

He dug into his pocket, took out his iPhone, hit a button, his eyes never leaving hers.

"Aldo," he said. "A woman will be coming down to the lobby in a couple of minutes. She is dark haired. Tall. Very beautiful. Flag a taxi for her. No, I won't be with her. Thank you, Aldo." He put the phone away. Took out his wallet. Pulled out two hundred dollar bills and held them out. "That should cover cab fare."

Cheyenne looked from his face to his hand. She snatched the bills from him, tore them in half and let them tumble to the floor.

"You're being foolish," he said calmly. "As you pointed out, your purse is back in the ballroom."

"You are," she said, her voice shaking, "you are despicable!"

"I'd have left you instructions on how to find a taxi," he said, "but this seems more efficient."

The blow, when it came, was hardly surprising. He'd been half-expecting it and he'd braced himself for it; still, the force of it made his head snap back.

"Good night, Ms. McKenna," he said. "And thank you for an interesting interlude in an otherwise dull evening."

Later, thinking back, he was sure she'd have hit him again, but just then the doors to one of the elevators slid open. A man and a woman stepped from the car, he in a tux, she in a glittering gown, her arm looped through his. They were laughing, but their laughter stopped as soon as they saw the scene before them.

"Oh," the woman said.

It was, Luca thought, the only intelligent comment possible.

He knew what they saw.

Him, his color high, his breathing rapid, his clothes disheveled.

Cheyenne, her hair wild around her face, her eyes like black pools, her mouth pink and swollen from his kisses. He saw the stricken expression on her face and his gut twisted.

The right thing to do was step in front of her. Shield her from the strangers' curious glances. After all, they'd just been making love…

His heart hardened.

They hadn't been making love. They'd been doing exactly

what they'd done this morning

No. Not quite. They'd fucked this morning, he thought with icy precision, but he'd deliberately kept that from happening this time.

The desire to protect her vanished.

The elevator doors started to close. He moved forward quickly and jammed his hand between them.

"I believe you were waiting for an elevator," he said calmly.

Cheyenne's eyes flashed with fire. It made her even more beautiful. He wanted to drag her into his arms, carry her into the car and finish what he had started.

Instead, he smiled politely and motioned her forward.

For the first time in his life, he understand that old expression, *if looks could kill.* If they could, he'd be dead on the spot.

Head high, she swept past him into the car and pressed the button for the lobby. The doors closed. He took a steadying breath before he turned around.

The man and woman were watching him the way snakes might watch a mongoose, fully aware that polite appearances could mask the worst possible intentions.

"Enjoy your evening," he said pleasantly, and he opened the door to the fire stairs and took out his phone as he started down.

"Aldo," he said brusquely. "The brunette. When you flag her a cab, give the driver a couple of hundred dollars. If she won't let you do that, drive her home yourself. What do you mean, what if she protests? She *will* protest, Aldo. You are to ignore that and see to it she gets safely home. Do you understand?"

Halfway down the stairs, he paused. Her purse. Was it still lying on the table in the ballroom? Surely, her keys were in it.

He thought of going after it…and then he remembered the morning, how she'd used him, how she'd treated him tonight, as if he were part of an unfortunate memory she preferred to forget, and he kept going, straight to the lobby.

Wherever she lived, he thought coldly, she had a doorman. A superintendent. A building manager. Someone would let her into her apartment. Besides, it wasn't his problem.

When he reached the lobby, he was still telling himself that he'd done nothing more than Cheyenne had deserved.

Then why was a voice deep inside him whispering *liar*?

CHAPTER SIX

ALDO AND THE black Mercedes were waiting at the curb.

"I take it the lady wouldn't let you drive her home," Luca said as he got into the rear seat.

Aldo nodded, checked his mirror and pulled into traffic. "That is correct, sir."

Luca sat back, arms folded, mouth thinned. Of course, she wouldn't let him drive her home. No surprise there—but her reaction to the offer irritated him, which was ridiculous. Why would anything she did irritate him? Wasn't he supposed to be feeling good at having evened the score?

"So, you saw her into a taxi instead."

His driver hesitated. "Not exactly."

"What does 'not exactly' mean?"

"She refused to go with me, or to get into a taxi. She said she was perfectly capable of walking."

"Walking?" Luca's voice rose. "Walking where?"

"To wherever it is she lives, Mr. Bellini," Aldo said uncomfortably. "She didn't say."

"And you let her go?"

"Sir, I couldn't stop her." The driver cleared his throat. "She was—she was very determined. What she said…What she said made that clear."

"Dammit, I'm not in the mood for games. What, exactly, did she say?"

"She told me precisely what I could do with my offers. What you could do with *your* offers. She said I was to be sure and give you that message." Aldo's eyes met Luca's in the mirror, then skidded away. "Sir."

Luca almost laughed. He suspected her message had been crisp, clear and to the point.

Still, this wasn't a laughing matter.

She had left without her purse. He'd known women who tucked a couple of bills into their bras, but she hadn't been wearing a bra.

She hadn't been wearing anything under that gown.

Just her lush body.

And then, his caressing hand.

Luca felt his throat constrict. If he shut his eyes, he knew that he'd be back in the hallway. That he'd know the sweet taste of her mouth. The feel of her body pressing against his. The heat of her burning against his palm.

He shuddered.

This was not a time to turn himself on.

It was a time to wonder how the woman he'd forced into the night without so much as a penny was going to get home, because one way or another, he *had* forced her out of the hotel; there was no getting around the truth.

And he didn't even know where 'home' was.

Two blocks away? Ten blocks? For all he knew, she lived in the financial district. Or in Brooklyn. He thought of her in that gown, her body so elegantly outlined, and then there were those icepick heels, sexy beyond belief, but impossible if you had to manage a purposeful stride, and a purposeful stride was what you needed to guard against the predators that hunted on some of the city's streets.

She was alone and vulnerable, and it was all his fault.

Idiota, he thought grimly, and he leaned forward.

"Did you see the direction in which she went?"

"She headed downtown. At least, I think she did, but there was a lot of traffic and—"

"Turn around. Go back to the hotel."

"Sir?"

"I said, go back to the hotel. Immediately!"

Aldo glanced in the mirror, saw his employer's face, nodded, and all but stood on the brakes as he turned the wheel. Horns bleated as he made a U turn across two lanes of traffic.

When they reached the hotel, he pulled the Mercedes to the curb. Luca was out of the car before it had stopped.

One of the Skytop elevators was waiting in the lobby.

"Miracle of miracles," he muttered, stepping quickly into the car and jamming his finger against the *up* button. "Come on, come on," he said as the elevator made its climb. The doors slid open and he hurried into the ballroom and started across the dance floor.

"Luca!" Alene Beresford stepped away from her husband and caught hold of Luca's arm. "Are you having a good time?"

"Alene. I'm very busy right now."

"I hope you and Cheyenne are getting along."

"Yes. No. We are…" Luca cleared his throat. "Do you know where she lives?"

"Cheyenne?"

Cristo, he had no time for this!

"Yes. Do you have her address?"

"I don't, no. She lives downtown somewhere, I think…or maybe in midtown. Why not ask…" Alene gave a sly laugh. "Oh, I get it. You want to send her flowers as a surprise. Really, that's so charm—"

"Excuse me, Alene," Luca said, pulling his arm free of her hand. "I'm in a hurry."

"You still haven't told me how the two of you are—"

Luca hurried to his table. Everyone looked up and smiled.

"There you are," one of the shrinks said pleasantly. "We were beginning to wonder what—"

"Sorry," he said, though he knew that the way he scooped up Cheyenne's purse and ran back the way he'd come made it clear he wasn't sorry at all.

The elevator was still there.

He got in and opened the bit of silk as the doors closed.

Cash. A tube of lipstick. A comb. A set of keys. A phone. That was it. Nothing else. No I.D., no driver's license—

Wait.

He turned on her cellphone, pressed a button and brought up her phone number, but what good was that to him? It was virtually impossible to associate cellphone numbers with addresses.

Perhaps she also had a landline. Lots of people had both. He did. He could only hope that she did, too.

Through the lobby. Out the doors. Into his Mercedes, where he dropped her phone in his pocket and took out his own.

"Where to, Mr. Bellini?"

Luca shook his head. Dialed 411. Telephone information. Asked for a phone number for a Cheyenne McKenna in Manhattan.

He waited. And waited.

"Operator?"

"Yes, sir. I'm sorry."

Luca felt his heart sink.

"How about trying C. McKenna?" He knew that women often didn't use their full names for telephone directories on the assumption the ruse offered some protection. "Or try Brooklyn. Or—"

"There is a Manhattan number, sir. But it's unlisted.

"Unlisted?"

"Yessir."

Luca all but pumped his fist in the air.

"Well, I need it. The address, not the number."

"Sir. Unlisted numbers are—"

"Did you hear me? This is an emergency."

"I am not free to give you that information, sir."

"I just told you, this is—"

Click. The line disconnected.

Luca glared at the phone as if the fault were its and not his.

Now what? He had an attorney on retainer; the attorney surely could recommend a private investigator who could get him Cheyenne's address. Or Matteo could recommend someone. He was certain that all lawyers had such connections—but by then, hours would have passed.

He tapped his cellphone against his knee.

He needed somebody who could bypass all the legitimate channels through which information flowed. Somebody who knew how to get information no one else could get…

"Caleb Wilde," he said softly.

He had done background checks on all the Wildes.

Jake, the rancher, had been a fearless helicopter pilot who'd spit in the face of a cowardly superior officer, done what he knew was his duty and returned home a hero in the eyes of everyone but himself.

Travis, the financial genius, had been a hotshot who'd flown jets and had never met a situation he couldn't control until he fell in love with a dying woman.

Caleb, the lawyer, had originally been recruited into a government agency so secret that only a handful of people high in the D.C. power structure knew of its existence, let alone its alphabet soup name.

Over breakfast, he'd overheard Matteo and Travis swapping quick stories about their siblings.

One of Travis's stories had involved Jennie, the wife he obviously adored, and the miracles his brothers had done for him and for her.

Jennie had been sick, he'd said. Dying. But she'd lived, and it was because of them.

Jake's connections with other wounded warriors had led them to a cure.

"But that was useless, unless we found Jennie. She'd run away, see, and..." Travis had cleared his throat. "Caleb found her. Nobody else could have done it so fast, but Caleb had all the right contacts and he located her in less time that it takes to tell the story."

Luca narrowed his eyes.

Caleb was the man he needed.

But to ask a favor of his half-brother, of a man he still could not think of without a quick rush of anger...

Besides, this wasn't a life or death situation.

This was simply a situation in which a woman dressed for a glittery party rather than the sometimes mean streets of the city was almost certainly out there on her own, heading in any one of a hundred different directions, and all because he'd been so fixated on getting even with her for what she'd done that morning that he'd behaved like a heartless fool.

Luca turned on his phone, brought up his contact list, found Caleb's number and tapped it.

* * *

Caleb answered on the first ring.

Luca could hear a woman's voice in the background, and the sound of a crying baby.

"Yes?" Caleb said, a little impatiently.

"Caleb. It's Luca. Luca Bellini."

"I know that. Your name came up on my screen. Listen, Bellini, if this is about your findings—"

"What findings?"

"The property you checked out for Jake. Sweetwater Ranch? You might want to talk with him. Or with the McKenna woman's lawyer. See, I'm not her—"

"It isn't about the ranch."

The baby's cries escalated.

"Bellini. Luca. Look, I'm kind of busy here…"

"It's about the woman," Luca said. "Cheyenne McKenna. I need her address."

Silence. Even the baby's screams stopped.

"I don't understand."

Luca could feel his face burning.

"I can't explain. I mean, I could, but…" He took a deep breath. Exhaled slowly. "We had a, uh, a falling out. She, uh, she walked away. It's late and it's not safe for her to be alone."

"A falling out? At Sweetwater? You're still there?"

Cristo, why had he thought this was a good idea?

"Bellini? Where are you?"

"In Manhattan. So is she."

The baby's cries began again. "Shh, sweetheart," Luca could hear a woman say. "I know teething hurts, but—"

"What I mean," Luca continued, "is that we bumped into each other. At a party. We quarreled… Look, I don't have time to go into details. We had an argument, okay? I told my driver to take her home, but that didn't happen and now I'm concerned because she's out there, alone at this hour and—and—and—" Hell. Another breath. Another expulsion of air. "If I give you her phone number," he said grimly, "would you be able to get her address for me? Would you be willing to do that?"

This time, the silence was absolute.

At first, he wondered if Caleb had heard him. Then, he wondered if he'd heard him and hung up.

"Never mind," he said, just in case Caleb was still on the line. "I never should have—"

"What's the number?"

Luca shut his eyes with relief and rattled it off.

"I'll get back to you in ten minutes."

In the end, it took five. Caleb phoned, gave him the address, wished him luck…and, mercifully, asked no other questions.

"I owe you," Luca said stiffly.

If they'd had a video connection, he'd have seen Caleb grinning.

"Yeah, dude, you do. Someday, I'll want the whole story."

Upset as he was, Luca barked a laugh.

"Don't hold your breath," he said, and after quickly running Cheyenne's address through his head and becoming even more concerned when he realized how far downtown she lived, he instructed Aldo to head south. "Slowly," he added, and hoped against hope that she had, by some miracle, found a way to get home without making the journey on foot.

* * *

He had almost despaired of finding her when, suddenly, he spotted her just passing under a street lamp.

"There she is," he said sharply. "Pull over."

Aldo turned the wheel hard toward the curb.

She'd gotten much further than he'd anticipated. He supposed, from her point of view, that was the good news.

The bad was that she'd left the glitzy upper realm of the east side behind and she was now walking through what he suspected a realtor would call a transitional commercial area.

Her pace was steady and brisk, head high, arms swinging as if there were nothing unusual in a woman wearing what was probably a five thousand dollar evening gown going for a solitary nighttime stroll.

That she'd made good time was at least partly because she'd taken off the lethal stilettos. They dangled by their straps from her left hand.

The street was not crowded.

There were only a few pedestrians, and none gave her more than a curious glance. Only tourists were ever naïve enough to stare. New Yorkers wouldn't have made eye contact with Saint Peter and a choir of angels on a Manhattan street.

Evidently, there were only New Yorkers walking here tonight.

Cheyenne was fine.

Angry—Luca could tell that from the imperious angle of her chin. Determined—her stride assured him of that. But untouched, as far as he could see. No bruises. No signs that she'd had to struggle with predators.

Even as the thought went through his mind, a posse of men materialized from a dark doorway a few yards ahead.

Cheyenne saw them; Luca could tell because her steps

faltered, but only for a second. Then she quickened her pace.

Aldo was maneuvering the Mercedes into a tight parking space. Luca was not about to wait. He flung his door open.

"Cheyenne!"

Either she didn't hear him or she'd decided to ignore him. He shouted her name again, hurried out of the car and onto the sidewalk.

The men spread themselves in a lazy line ahead of her. There were eight of them. *Cristo,* eight!

Cheyenne kept moving.

"Hey, baby," one of them said. Another made a smacking sound with his lips.

Cheyenne showed uncertainty for the very first time. Her steps slowed; her spine stiffened. Her gaze raked the line and Luca knew she was searching for a way around or through it.

He also knew that there was none.

"Cheyenne," he said quietly.

"Cheyenne," one man said. "What kind of fuckin' name is that?"

The others laughed.

Luca did a quick assessment. They were in their early twenties, and they were big. They were also drunk. Or high. Maybe both. Even at a distance, he could smell beer and weed.

"Cheyenne," he repeated. "Come to me."

"Ooh, Cheyenne," another man said in a mincing voice, "ooh, baby! Come to me."

They laughed again, and closed into a loose semi-circle around her.

Luca could feel his adrenaline pumping. He moved toward

her.

"Get behind me," he said in a low voice.

She flashed him a look that suggested he was crazy even to suggest it.

"Dammit, woman, get behind me!"

Cheyenne switched one of the stilettos to her right hand. She held it with the long, sharp heel extended, brandishing it the way Luca had seen men in Sicily hold knives when they were ready to fight.

"One of you fuckers takes another step," she said, "you'll wish you were never born."

"Oooh," the men said, in mock terror.

"The lady's gonna kill us."

"Yeah. With her shoe."

The comments drew snickers of laughter.

"You touch me," Cheyenne said, "I'll take your eyes out."

More laughter.

Luca made a sound that was closer to a growl than anything else. He wasn't sure if he wanted to applaud the lady for her balls or turn her over his knee and spank her for her foolishness.

"Cheyenne," he said, "dammit, get over here!"

"Lookit him," one of the men said, "the tough guy in a fancy suit!"

"Hey, tough guy," another said. "You lookin' for a phone booth so you can pull off that suit and turn into Superman?"

The men roared with laughter. Then the biggest of them took a step toward Luca.

"What you gonna do, Superman? Huh? What you gonna do?"

There was no laughter now. No snickering. The mood was hard and vicious, and Luca knew there was no way this could end well unless Cheyenne did as he'd ordered, but she was completely ignoring him.

By now, Aldo was standing beside Luca.

Two against eight. Bad odds, but Aldo had been a soldier in what he sometimes described as another life, and Luca had fought his way through two boarding schools and, for kicks, worked out on a speed bag a couple of times a week.

Besides, he had the blood of Sicily in his veins.

"Cheyenne," he said, "get in the car."

Maybe there was something in his voice. Maybe it was the ever-tightening circle of men. Whatever it was, Cheyenne looked at Luca for the first time. Then she looked at her tormentors.

"*É*šk⌧seeséhotame," she said, and spat at the one who seemed to be their leader.

His shoulders hunched. "What you call me, bitch?"

Luca was wondering the same thing, but this wasn't the time to ask. This was the time for action.

"Aldo," he yelled, "the car."

Aldo took off, running. Luca stepped forward, drew back his fist and landed a blow directly on the punk's jaw.

It was a good shot. Damn near perfect, the still-rational part of Luca's brain acknowledged in admiration.

The man dropped like a stone.

The others stared at Luca. At their fallen leader. At each other. Then one of them yelled "Get him!" but by then, Luca had grabbed Cheyenne's hand and started running for the

Mercedes. He shoved her into the back seat, climbed in and shouted "Go!" at Aldo, who gunned the engine.

The car shot away from the curb.

Luca looked back. Then he and Aldo exchanged glances in the mirror.

Both men grinned.

"Nice job, boss," Aldo said.

"Nice job?" Cheyenne sputtered. "Nice job?" She made a fist and punched Luca's shoulder. "Damn you, Bellini! I was doing fine by myself!"

Luca sighed. "You're welcome," he said dryly.

"Did you hear what I said?"

"I heard. I also heard you say something to those hoodlums. Esko..." He looked at her. "What was that?"

"I called him a pig. In Cheyenne."

Luca raised an eyebrow. "You speak Cheyenne?"

"I speak maybe a dozen words, and don't change the subject. What gave you the right to interfere?"

"Too bad you don't speak Italian."

"What?"

"If you did, I'd tell you that you were *pazzo*. Hell, I'll tell it to you anyway." His voice rose. "You're crazy if you think a shoe could hold off eight stoned fools."

She glared at him; he glared back. Finally, she swung away, folded her arms and stared straight ahead.

"How did you find me?"

He gave a lazy shrug.

"We didn't. We were en route to my place and there you were. Pure good luck."

He caught Aldo's eyes in the mirror. Poker-faced, Aldo looked away and concentrated on the road.

"Really?" she said sweetly.

"Really. Don't flatter yourself by thinking otherwise."

"No. Why would I do that? Just because you live in that building on Fifth Avenue and 75th…"

She caught herself, but it was too late. A glance told her he was looking at her the way a cat might look at an especially interesting canary.

"You researched me?"

Until this moment, he'd seen the *Times* doing a piece on the building and naming him as one of its residents only as a violation of his privacy. Now, he saw it as fascinating.

Cheyenne gritted her teeth.

She thought about denying it, but what was the point? She *had* researched him. She always Googled the people she met—it wasn't about him, personally. You just couldn't be too careful in this world…

Okay. It *had* been about him, personally, but why wouldn't a woman want to know more about a man she'd slept with?

So she sat back, arms still folded, eyes still straight ahead, and wondered, now that there was time to wonder, if the sharp pain in the sole of her left foot meant she had stepped on a piece of broken glass somewhere back in the 50's.

"I checked," she said, making it sound like a careless act, "yes."

"Because?"

"Because if it turned out we lived anywhere near each other, I wanted to be prepared for the distinctly unpleasant possibility of bumping into you." She shot him a nasty look. "Too bad I didn't Google what charities you'd been dragged into supporting."

"Nobody dragged me into *Horse Sense*." Well, it was the truth. He'd stumbled into it, but that wasn't the same thing. "I've always supported animal welfare organizations... What's so amusing?"

"Is that what you think *Horse Sense* is? An animal welfare charity?"

"I don't think it. I know it."

She laughed again. He didn't like the sound of that laugh.

"What's so funny?"

"Nothing. Nothing at all."

A lie. He knew it, but he wasn't going to plead for an answer. All he'd do was take her home and deliver her safely to her door.

"Aldo has your address as 55 Sloane, off West Houston," he said curtly. "Is that correct?"

"It's correct. How do you know that?"

"I looked you up in the phone directory."

"You couldn't have. My number is unlisted."

He shrugged again.

"Take it up with the telephone company."

She was silent for a moment. Then she looked at him again.

"What you did tonight..." She poked out her bottom lip and blew a breath over it. How could something so simple make his belly tighten? "It was contemptible."

He leaned forward, pressed a button and the privacy screen slid into place.

"I was angry."

"Do you always force yourself on women when you're angry?"

"I did not force myself on you. And I wasn't talking about what we did. The sex."

"The sex." Her tone was cruel. "That's a charming way to describe rape."

He could feel his anger growing.

"I no more raped you tonight than you raped me this morning, McKenna. We both wanted what happened."

She stared at him. Why deny it? She *had* wanted him, both times, but that second time, in the hotel…

That had frightened her.

He had overwhelmed her.

Possessed her.

Controlled her.

She didn't like to be with men that way.

Which was why the hot excitement she'd felt in that hotel corridor made no sense. The hunger that had all but consumed her. The memory of his hands on her, heating her blood, even now…

"I can read your eyes," he said in a voice gone husky.

"Good. Then you can read my disgust at what you did."

A nerve jumped in his jaw. "You're right. I'm disgusted at what I did, too."

"I'm glad you admit it. Forcing me into sex—"

"I'm talking about letting you flee the hotel without considering that you had no money for cab fare. But you were foolish. Worse than foolish. Refusing my driver's offer to take you home or, at least, to get a taxi for you…"

Her chin rose.

"Did you actually think I'd accept anything from you?"

His mouth curved in a thin parody of a smile.

"Would you have preferred a note?"

Her face colored. "I don't know what you mean."

"Give me a break. McKenna. You know exactly what I mean."

"The note I left you was perfectly polite."

Luca folded his arms over his chest. "'Sorry, but I have an appointment in Dallas,'" he said tonelessly. "'I checked—there's a phone number for a cab service in the directory on the desk. And thanks for your help.'"

Her mouth opened, then closed. The color in her face heightened. Good. He was glad her own words made her uncomfortable.

"As I said, the note was perfectly acceptable."

"Finding a note instead of the woman I'd just made love with was a little… disconcerting."

"Sex."

"Excuse me?"

"We had sex. We didn't make love."

"That's an unusual distinction. Most women—"

"I am not 'most women.' I have a healthy attitude toward sex. Actually, it's the same attitude men generally have. I find sex pleasurable, but I don't see a point in confusing the needs of the body with society's need to pretty it up by clouding it with supposed emotion."

Luca stared at her.

"Do you really believe that? That emotion and sex are separate things?"

"I know it."

"Then I feel sorry for you, *bellissima*. Emotion is, or should be, the best part."

"You misunderstand. There's emotion in sex, of course. Pleasure, fulfillment, satisfaction... All of that is part of the experience."

"The experience." Luca smiled tightly. "An interesting choice of words."

"You miss the point. The act of sex... I have nothing against the experience, but—"

"Is it always the same for you? What you call 'the experience.'"

Where was this conversation going? And why was she letting it happen? This was far too intimate a topic to discuss with a man who was still little more than a stranger.

"This is a foolish discussion."

"I don't think so."

"Well, I do. Asking me these questions—"

"Why do you turn away from me? Am I getting too close to some sort of truth?" Luca grasped Cheyenne's shoulder. "Look at me. Look me in the eye."

"Leave me alone!"

"No. I don't think so."

His hand tightened on her. She was sitting close beside him. A long lock of dark, silky hair lay against her cheek. One move, and he could press his mouth to it. He could do more. One touch, one kiss was all he'd need to shatter that wall she'd built around herself. She would go into his arms and he would make her admit that sex was more than a man and a woman seeking carnal pleasure.

A horn blew, and the car stopped short. Cheyenne gasped, reached down and grasped her foot.

"What's the matter?"

She shook her head. "Nothing."

"Dammit, woman, don't lie to me!" Luca leaned forward. His hand swept over hers. "Did you hurt your ankle?"

"No. It's my foot. The quick stop… I must have dug my toes into the carpet, and there might be a little cut or something on the bottom of—"

In a series of swift motions, Luca switched on one of the rear compartment lights, turned her toward him and lifted her foot into his lap.

"Let me see."

"That isn't necess—"

"Your foot is bleeding!"

"It's just a cut."

"When did it happen?"

"I don't know. A little while ago. And it isn't a big…What are you doing?"

A foolish question.

What he was doing was wrapping her foot in a pristine white handkerchief he'd pulled from his jacket pocket.

"Aldo," he said over the intercom, "we need a hospital."

"Are you crazy? We do not need a hospital! When I get home, I'll wash it and put a bandage on it and—"

"When was your last tetanus shot?"

"Oh, for heaven's sake!"

"Aldo. The Mt. Sinai emergency room."

Cheyenne clucked her tongue. "I don't need a tetanus shot.

I had a booster last year, before we did a shoot in Belize. Would you please let go of me? I do not need your help."

"Shut up, McKenna."

"Goddammit! You cannot talk to me this way. You cannot order me around. You are not in charge of me. *I* am in charge of me, and—"

Luca silenced her with a kiss.

"It's time you relinquished authority to someone else," he said in a low voice. He kissed her again, and when the kiss ended, he looked deep into her eyes. Then he told Aldo that they were not going to her apartment.

They were going to his.

CHAPTER SEVEN

LUCA SAID SHE couldn't walk.

"Not until I've cleaned that cut and made sure there's no glass in it," he said as he carried her from the car, past a doorman who greeted him as if he was accustomed to the sight of one of the famous building's most famous residents marching through the doors with a woman in his arms, past a concierge who showed the same bland reaction.

A private elevator took them to Luca's duplex.

"You can put me down now," Cheyenne said.

He didn't answer. Instead, he carried her up a winding staircase, through an enormous bedroom and into a huge marble bathroom.

"Stay there," he said, lowering her carefully onto a *chaise longue* that faced a handsome fireplace.

"Really, Bellini, if you'd just point me at the washcloths and bandages…"

"Cheyenne. Do not move."

"I don't take orders. Not from anyone."

He bent down and kissed her. Lightly. Gently. She wanted to slap him…or maybe just to wind her arms around his neck.

Sweet Jesus, he was confusing the hell out of her. Why was she letting him behave this way?

Nobody was in charge of her except her.

She'd taken her life in her own hands when she was thirteen.

No more enduring Mama's drunken rages. *You get out here, goddammit. You show your face or when I find you, I'll beat the shit out of you, girl!*

No more enduring the upswings that invariably followed. *Sweetie, you know I didn't mean it. Gimme one more chance, baby, and I swear, it'll never happen again.*

And no more being nice to…to Mama's 'friends.'

Come say hello to the nice man. He wants to give you somethin' pretty. See? Oh, come on, baby. Sit on the nice man's lap. You'll have fun. And then Mama's voice taking on a knife-sharp edge, her hands digging into Cheyenne's shoulders as she pushed her forward. *You do what I tell you, Cheyenne. Go on. That's it. That's Mama's girl. That's the way.*

And it had been 'the way,' first with what Mama called having fun, then with much more that that, and it had gone on for what had seemed a very long time, until one day, one terrible, awful day…

But something good had come out that day.

Foster care.

It wasn't paradise, but it was lots better than what had come before. She'd worked hard, graduated high school at sixteen and decided to move to New York.

How to get there evolved through trial and error.

She hitched to a town that was a flyspeck on the map and landed a job washing dishes and sweeping up at a horrible little café where flypaper hung from the ceiling and roaches the size of salamanders scurried along the counters. She had no working papers, but nobody asked any questions—and that was a lesson in itself.

After a few weeks, she moved on, working from town to town, café to café, always heading east toward the Big Apple.

It took months. But, at last, she got there.

Except, New York wasn't paradise, either.

In fact, it was a nightmare.

Big. Loud. Dirty. And it turned out you did need working papers or, at least—because she'd always looked older than her years—I.D. Best of all, a social security card.

She got herself a grubby room, not in Manhattan but in Queens, and a job waiting tables in a grimy hole-in-the-wall where nobody asked for her I.D. and nobody spoke English except her and the kid who mopped the always-filthy floors.

His name was unpronounceable; everybody called him 'boy,' but Cheyenne felt bad for him—he was the first person she'd met who seemed worse off than she was—and she learned to say his name or, at least, to come pretty close to saying it.

One day, he whispered to her that she could do better than this job.

"I don't have any I.D.," she said, and he winked.

A week later, she had a social security card and a driver's license. A week after that, she had a job waitressing in a busy coffee shop off Madison Avenue in Manhattan, and one day a guy handed her a tip and his business card and told her to give him a call.

He was gay. Anybody could see that, which was the only reason she hadn't slugged him and had, instead, said "What for?"

"Because," he'd said pleasantly, "your hair is a disaster, you need somebody to teach you that slapping on lipstick is not the right way to do your makeup, you have to drop maybe ten pounds, but your bones are good, so is your height and maybe, just maybe, I can turn you into some kind of a model."

Her life had not been the same since that moment.

Professionally, she'd reached the top. Until recently, anyway, when the idiots who ran the world she now lived in had decided she'd gone too far in taking over, but really, how could you go too far when you knew what was best?

Her personal life? As far as she was concerned, it was fine.

People said she was closed off, but that only meant she chose her acquaintances with care. Why wouldn't she? They said she didn't trust anyone. Yes, and what fool did?

As for men…

Men said she was difficult.

They said she was a control freak. Or that maybe she had OCD. Or maybe it was something else. The bottom line, they said, was that she didn't understand relationships.

Wrong.

She understood them, all right. She understood that women were expected to acquiesce to whatever a man wanted, in bed and out, and that was so not a problem because early on, she'd discovered that what she wanted from men, in bed and out, was to go her own way.

Especially in.

She was human. She had needs. Every now and then, she fulfilled those needs. With men who liked her attitude and if they didn't, so what? She didn't see them again. In fact, that was the best way to treat sex. As a basic need. As a one-time thing.

She never went back for more.

She looked up as Luca came through the door carrying a small basin and a washcloth. He'd discarded the jacket of his tux and loosened his tie. The sleeves of his white shirt were rolled back, exposing his forearms: muscular, tanned, and lightly dusted with hair.

How could a man look so masculine and so beautiful at the same time?

Her belly tightened.

No.

She never went back for more. One man, one woman… That wasn't her thing.

So how come she'd had sex twice today, okay, almost twice today, with this man, a man she didn't even like?

The question was jarring. That he was kneeling before her, reaching for her foot, was even more jarring.

Cheyenne jerked her foot away.

He reached for her foot again. She tried to pull it back, but he was stronger and instead of letting go, he propped her heel on his thigh, tilted her foot and peered at the sole.

"It's a cut," he said.

"Thank you for that brilliant diagnosis, Dr. Einstein."

He looked up, a smile playing over his lips.

"Better that than Dr. Frankenstein."

She almost laughed. Good thing she didn't. Laughing would have been a big mistake.

"What are you doing?"

"I'm going to clean the cut," he said as he wrung out the washcloth. "Your foot is dirty."

Her eyes narrowed. "You try walking on a Manhattan sidewalk and see how clean your feet will… Hey!"

"Does that hurt?"

"Yes, it hurts! Stop pinching me!"

"I'm not pinching, I'm squeezing. I want to be sure there's nothing stuck in the cut. Gravel or glass, maybe."

"I can check for myself," she said, tugging her foot free of his hands, grabbing it, angling it, bending over and peering at the cut.

She looked up.

"It's bleeding," she said.

And, just that quickly, the floor tilted, the room spun and the world turned grey.

"Hell," Luca said gruffly. He caught her by the shoulders and she sagged against him.

"I'm fine," she said in a tiny voice.

"Yes," he said, even more gruffly. "I can see that. Take a deep breath. Again. And no, do not try to sit up, dammit! Keep your head down."

She did as he'd said. What choice did she have? If she sat up, he'd win the argument over who was and who wasn't in charge.

But, God, she felt like a fool. Such a ridiculous thing, to go woozy at the sight of blood. She wasn't a coward, and only cowards reacted to things like that.

She shuddered.

Luca felt it happen, the delicate tremor that went through her, just as he felt the soft exhalation of her breath against his throat.

His arms tightened around her. He held her that way for a long minute, her body warm in his embrace, her heart thudding against his heart.

Then he frowned, drew back and he held her away from him with the impersonal concern of a good Samaritan—which was, after all, his part in this scenario.

Why would it be anything more?

She was not a woman who expected tender gestures, nor was he a man to offer them.

"Better?" he asked, his tone brisk.

She nodded, but he doubted if that was true. Her face was pale; he suspected she was only now reacting to what had happened on the street. Delayed shock, or something close to it.

For a heartbeat, he almost drew her close again. Fortunately, logic overcame that flash of inexplicable foolishness.

He set her back on the loveseat and got to his feet.

"I'll get a bandage for your foot. And a cold compress."

She nodded. What was the point in arguing? The best thing to do was regain her strength and get the hell out of here.

She was tired. That explained everything. Tired from the endless day and the long walk that had grown more and more wearing as the neighborhood went from busy and upscale to less crowded and more commercial and then to the last couple of blocks where everything inside her shouted, *You're a fool!*

Such stupid pride! You should have accepted a ride home. At least flag down a cab and once the driver gets you to your building, tell him he's just going to have to wait five minutes while you go inside and get his fare.

But before she could, those men had stepped out of the shadows and she'd prayed she could tough it out and then, like a miracle, Luca had appeared.

The truth was, she'd have been in deep trouble without him. She hated knowing it, hated admitting it, even to herself. She wasn't made for the pathetic, damsel-in-distress routine. She absolutely hated it. The sense of helplessness, the admission that she was powerless….

Luca was back.

He knelt before her again and swept the hair away from the nape of her neck. A cool cloth replaced the brush of his fingers.

A small sigh escaped her throat.

"Good?"

"Good." She hesitated. Then she looked up at him from under her lashes. "Sorry about that," she said, hoping she sounded contrite and even a little embarrassed, the way anyone might after the foolishness of a near-faint over a bit of blood.

He shrugged, all business as he slathered an antibacterial ointment on the cut, then covered it with a bandage.

"Blood has that effect on some people."

"Yes, well, I don't usually—"

"And you're reacting to what happened earlier. It's only natural."

His certainty infuriated her. They had come into each other's lives only hours ago. What gave him the right to make decisions and now judgments on her behalf?

"Enough," she snapped, grabbing the cold pack and tossing it into the sink as she rose to her feet. "I'm out of here."

"Don't be ridiculous." He clasped her shoulders. "You're in no condition to go anywhere."

She glared at him. He glared back. Then his expression softened.

"It's not a crime to accept help, Cheyenne."

"Oh, for heaven's sake," she said… And then, to her horror, tears filled her eyes.

Luca muttered something, reached for her and gathered her into his arms.

This was surely the perfect way to end an evening. First, come close to fainting. Then, come close to a complete meltdown.

Not very good ways to impress a man.

Not that she wanted to impress this man.

Not that she'd ever wanted to impress any man.

Accept me on my terms or leave me alone. That had always been the standard by which she lived.

She shut her eyes.

What was wrong with her today? She wasn't herself at all. She hadn't been herself this morning or this evening, and certainly not now.

"It's all right, *cara*."

Luca's voice was low, almost hypnotic. The feel of his arms around her was comforting. She wanted to stay in his embrace, let some of his strength seep into her bones.

"Cheyenne."

She felt trapped. Felt the walls closing in. Her eyes flew open. She pulled back, jerked free of him. The room swayed a little, but she fought hard not to show it and she succeeded.

Just as she'd told him earlier, she was good at acting.

"Thank you for everything, but it really is time I left."

"Not yet."

She could feel her heart racing. He was too close, too tall, too ruggedly beautiful. He brought out a weakness in her that she couldn't quite define except to know it was a weakness and that, in itself, was terrifying.

"Really, I have to."

"I'll drive you home when it's time."

"Luca." She forced a laugh. "It *is* time. It's getting late and—"

"It's just after midnight. Last time I checked, my car had not turned into a pumpkin."

He put his hand under her chin and gently but deliberately urged her face up until their eyes met. He was smiling. And his eyes… Oh God, his eyes! Such a deep blue. Sapphire blue.

A tremor went through her.

"I have to leave, Luca."

"Progress," he said softly.

"What progress?"

"You, calling me by my given name."

She forced a laugh.

"What else would I call you? Really, you have to step aside so I can—"

"You've been calling me 'Bellini.'" His lips twitched. "And other things."

"Yes? Well, I'm sorry about—"

"I'm the one who's sorry." His hand spread over her jaw, cupped her cheek, the slight roughness of his fingertips exciting against her skin. "I apologize for everything, *bellissima*."

"That's not necess—"

"I have treated you badly. Rudely. Unkindly."

His fingers were in her hair threading through the dark, thick strands. All she had to do was turn her face and she could press her mouth to his palm.

"No. I mean, it wasn't your fault. I should have accepted your driver's offer..." She shuddered as he bent his head and brushed his lips lightly over hers. "Don't," she whispered. "Luca. Please—"

"Everything was my fault, especially what happened in the hotel tonight. I admit, I wanted you so badly that I couldn't wait...but I should never have ended it as I did."

"Stop. It's over. Done with. What happened—"

"What happened," he said, "should only have been the beginning. I should have taken a room. Or had my driver bring us here." He lifted her against him, her feet dangling, her belly pressed to his erection. It felt hard and hot and more powerful than any she'd ever known. "I should have been inside you, *bellissima*, deep inside you so that we came together, you flying free even as I held you."

He kissed her, his mouth caressing hers, asking for a response. She wanted to give it. To kiss him back. Or to beat her fists against his shoulders. How could she want both? How could fear and desire be the same?

They couldn't be.

He was confusing her.

Her lashes fell to her cheeks as his lips traced the vein that pulsed in her throat. She moaned. God, she was melting, melting…

“Stop!” Gasping, she tore her mouth from his. “What do you want from me?”

“I want us to do something we have not done, *cara*. I want to make love.”

“We had sex. And I don’t want to have it again. I told you, I want to go home.”

“I don’t want to have sex, either.”

Another kiss. She felt her lips soften and cling to his. What for? This wasn’t about tenderness. It was about need and release.

“What I want,” he said, “is to make love.”

“You’re trying to seduce me.”

His laugh was soft and incredibly sexy.

“I’m trying to enlighten you, *bellissima*. What is there to be afraid of?”

“I’m not afraid,” she said quickly. “I’m not afraid of anything.”

Luca swung her into his arms.

“Prove it,” he said, and silenced what might have been her protest with a kiss.

She sighed at his taste. She had never paid attention to the taste of a man’s mouth before. His was wonderful. Clean. Smoky. He’d ordered champagne for the table at the party, but now she remembered that he’d ordered Scotch for himself. Was this what Scotch tasted like? If it was…if it was…

Her thoughts blurred. It was impossible to think.

She could only feel.

The firmness of his lips.

The strength of his arms.

The thud of his heart.

The whisper of his breath.

Her hands rose. Clasped the sides of his face. There was a tiny cleft in his chin. Stubble on his jaw. She brushed her fingers over it. The slight abrasion was exciting.

How would it feel against her breasts?

"Luca," she said, her voice raw with uncertainty. "Luca, please…"

"Please what, *cara*? All you have to do is tell me what you want."

But that was the problem. What did she want? Surely not this. This feeling of helplessness. Of being overcome.

Of wanting to be taken.

She said his name again.

"Yes," he said, "that's the way. Say my name, Cheyenne. Know who I am. Let me show you how this can be."

They were in his bedroom. Darkness lay in the corners, lay everywhere except for the soft glow of the Manhattan skyline visible across the vast expanse of Central Park.

His bed dominated the room.

It was big. Handsome. A slatted headboard and footboard. Soft-looking black and white pillows.

A bed made for pleasure.

She trembled as he brought her to it.

"Easy," he whispered, kissing her gently as he laid her down on the silk duvet. "Nothing will happen unless you wish it to."

The pillows seemed to sigh as she settled against them.

He gave her a long, searching look, his gaze moving slowly

over her face, her breasts, her belly and her legs.

She moved restlessly.

Why didn't he do something? Come down beside her? Touch her?

"You are the most beautiful woman in the world, *cara*," he said, very softly. "Do you know that?"

She didn't know anything. Not anymore. What game was this? Why was she playing it?

"I want to kiss you again," he said. "Would you like that?"

Yes, oh yes, she wanted his kiss.

"You have to tell me," he said. "You have to ask me to kiss you."

She couldn't. Her lips parted, but the words wouldn't come.

"Say it," he said. "Tell me that you want me."

She whispered his name.

An eternity seemed to slip by. Then he bent and brushed his lips over hers. It wasn't enough, but she couldn't tell him that. Surely, it wasn't enough for him, but he was so calm. It wasn't fair, that he was calm and she was—she was—

He sat down next to her.

Ah.

That was better.

His mask of calm was slipping.

She could see desire in his eyes. In the set of his mouth. A thick strand of dark hair had fallen over his forehead and when he thumbed it back… Was that a tremor in his hand?

The world began righting itself.

He wasn't cool and composed after all; it was an act. He wasn't in command. She was. She always was, and what was that tiny feeling of disappointment all about?

This was the way she wanted things to be.

So she smiled. Sat up against the pillows. Reached for him, for the buttons on his shirt…

He clasped her wrists.

"No."

She laughed. Tugged her hands from his…

His grip on her tightened.

"I said no, *bellissima*."

He read the confusion in her eyes. Such beautiful eyes.

"Don't you want me?"

He turned her hands over. Kissed her palms.

"More than my next breath." He lifted his head. "But I told you, we're going to do this my way."

She laughed. It sounded forced, even to her own ears. She could only hope it didn't sound that way to him.

"Doesn't your way involve taking off your clothes?"

"It involves many things." His voice was low. "The first is that I am the one who establishes the rules."

Rules. His rules. The words made her breathless. She felt a rush of fear—and then a sizzle of heat.

"Luca. We're both adults. Surely we don't have to—"

Slowly, he eased her back against the pillows.

"And rule number one is that I am in charge tonight."

There it was again. That breathless feeling, as if she couldn't draw enough air into her lungs. That whisper of excitement, sighing through her bones.

No. No! How could she possibly want him to be in charge? It was impossible.

"No," she said. She'd meant to sound decisive, but the word was a broken whisper. "I don't want you to make rules for me. You don't know anything about —"

He touched her.

Jus one light stroke of his fingers over her silk-covered nipples, and then his tongue replaced his fingers.

She heard a soft whimper of pleasure. Had she made that sound?

"I'm going to take what I want, *cara*. What we both want."

No, she thought…

Images flashed through her head. Luca, moving over her. His hands, his body, his lips holding her captive.

Captive to his touch, to his kisses, to his slow possession.

A honeyed weakness stole through her muscles. She began to tremble.

"Cheyenne," he whispered.

His hand closed around her breast. She felt the nipple furl, begging for the heat of his mouth.

Her breath hissed between her teeth. What was happening to her? She couldn't possibly want this. To be in his control. To succumb to his commands.

His demands, and her desires.

She whispered his name.

He captured her mouth with his.

It took all his strength to end the kiss, but he knew he had to stop now or he would be lost. His need for her had reached a level of intensity that was almost painful. Another few minutes and he'd let her do whatever she wanted, just as long as it finished with him deep inside her.

"Rule number two," he said, raising his head.

Her eyes widened with shock as his black silk tie replaced his hands around her wrists.

Her heart began to race.

"Luca?"

He kissed her again, hard, deep.

"Luca," she whispered as he drew her arms above her head and fastened the ends of the tie to the slatted headboard.

"Rule number three, *cara*. Tonight, you belong to me."

The words were low, hot, and dangerous.

He straightened up. Ran the tip of his index finger lightly over her mouth. Then he stood and unbuttoned his shirt. Slowly. So slowly. One button at a time.

The shirt hung open.

He tugged it free of his trousers.

She was supposed to do that. Undress him, touch him, make him lose control.

She caught her breath.

He was beautiful. Truly beautiful. His skin was tanned; the muscles in his abdomen stood out in taut relief.

And the way he was looking at her. The set of his jaw. The narrowing of his eyes. The hard line of his mouth.

A whimper broke from her throat.

She was wet. So wet. She was soaked with wanting him, with watching him.

Terror shot through her, a river of icy fear that made her body arc like a bow.

"I've had enough," she said in a high, thin voice.

His smile was full of wicked promise.

"You haven't had anything yet, *bellissima*."

"Untie me." Her voice rose. "Untie me, dammit!"

He got onto the bed beside her. "Not yet."

"This isn't funny. I don't—"

"It isn't meant to be funny, *bellissima*."

Her throat constricted. "Whatever you think I want—"

She gasped as his hand cupped her breast.

"Don't," she whispered.

"Don't what?" He bent to her, closed his lips around one silk-covered nipple. She felt the quick nip of his teeth, the heat of his mouth. A moan rose in her throat. "You have beautiful breasts, *cara*. Have I told you that?"

"Please… Luca. Untie my hands."

"I'm not going to hurt you."

His voice was husky. And lightly accented. Most times, she didn't really notice the accent, maybe because it was barely perceptible, but she could hear it now.

Exotic.

Rough.

Dangerous.

She cried out. Raised her knee to throw him off. He rolled on top of her, angling his body over hers.

"I'm not going to do anything you don't want me to do."

"No! No! This is crazy. I don't want—"

"*Si*. You *do* want, and I'm going to prove it to you."

"How? By making me your prisoner?"

He laughed. It was a sound that spoke of power and pleasure, and she hated it, hated him…

"Get off me. Get off, get off, get—"

"If you truly want me to stop," he whispered, "you have only to tell me so."

His mouth covered hers again and as it did, he slid his hand under her gown, just as he had in the hotel.

Stop, she thought, stop…

But she didn't say the word.

And then it was too late.

His hand moved over her thigh. She heard him catch his breath as he felt her heat, her wetness, all the things that made a lie of her protests.

"Open for me," he said, as he had said before, and she moaned and her legs parted and she sighed his name as he cupped her, captured the essence of her in the palm of his hand.

She wept.

He kissed her.

She wanted to fight him. Keep herself from him, and she struggled against the silken bonds that kept her his captive, but he wouldn't untie her, wouldn't stop caressing her, wouldn't let her hide from the truth as he found her clitoris with his thumb, stroked it until she was sobbing his name against his lips, writhing beneath him, rising toward him.

What had been heat became flame.

She wanted him.

Like this. Exactly like this. She wanted him to take her. Possess her. Overpower her.

Free her.

Not of the silk around her wrists.

Free her of fear. Of the past.

Of herself.

He took his hand from her and she groaned with frustration.

But he wasn't done.

God, no. He wasn't done.

He was touching her everywhere now. Exploring her over her silk gown, his caresses certain and exciting.

She tossed her head against the soft pillows and arched toward him.

She was his. His to do with as he wanted. As she wanted. And what she wanted was more of this, of what he was making her feel.

Of him.

His hands on her naked breasts, his mouth on her nipples. His thigh between hers so she could rub against him.

Most of all, most of all, she wanted him inside her.

She sighed his name.

He whispered hers.

And she said the words, the correct words, the ones that would end this exquisite torment.

"Please," she said, "Luca, please."

He gave a growl of triumph.

His hand closed in the deep neckline of her gown. One sharp tug and he tore it open. The silk parted like the petals of a flower.

Exposing her to him.

Baring her to him.

He bent his head. Her nipples tightened in anticipation. Lightly, deliberately, he tongued one nipple. She cried out; her hips lifted from the bed.

He raised his head. "Do you like that?" he whispered. He

bent to her again. Tongued her again. Blew lightly over her damp flesh.

She raised her head, sank her teeth into his shoulder, tasted salt and sweat and man. Tasted Luca.

Nothing like this had ever happened to her before. She was always in command. It was the only way she could do sex…

He drew the tip of one breast into his mouth. His hand was still between her legs.

She was mindless. Incapable of thought. She could only feel.

His mouth was at her navel.

On the lowest part of her belly.

She gasped when she realized what he was going to do.

"No," she said, but her thighs were opening, opening to him, to his fingers, his breath, his tongue.

His kiss.

She whispered his name.

He sucked on the swollen bud of her clitoris. Lights danced behind her closed eyelids.

She was coming apart. No, she thought, no, no, no…

"Let go," he said, "let go, *bellissima*, and fly with me," but she couldn't, she couldn't, couldn't let go of the earth, of reality, of herself because what would happen to her if she did, if she did…

"Let go," he commanded, and he reached up, undid the silk that bound her wrists.

She sobbed his name and wrapped her arms around him, buried her face in his shoulder and he slid his hands under her, lifted her to him, fused his mouth to hers.

She felt everything slipping away, felt herself flying into the night, and he groaned, shifted his weight between her thighs, and sank home.

CHAPTER EIGHT

LUCA WAS AS much a product of his time as any other twenty-first century male.

He knew the protocols of after-sex behavior, the things women liked.

Women liked to be held. They liked to indulge in pillow talk. They liked to… What was that word? Cuddle. Even the word was awful. It made him think of teddy bears, and who wanted to think about teddy bears at the same time he thought about sex?

On the other hand, what a man wanted most after sex, even terrific sex, was to get up and get on with his life.

He'd once been unfortunate enough to overhear his sisters discussing the topic.

He and Matteo, Bianca and Alessandra had all been gathered in the house they'd grown up in, trying to organize their mother's things a couple of weeks after her death. He'd been heading out to the porch when he heard the sound of Alessandra's voice.

"Men can be so stupid," she'd said. "They think it's only about the big bang."

At first, he'd thought she was talking about an American TV series. Then, just as he was about to open the screen door, he heard Bianca say that one of her psych profs theorized that evolution had designed men to spread their seed as fast and as frequently as possible.

"Women, on the other hand," she'd said in her best academic voice, "were designed to require post-coital relaxation. There's nothing romantic about it. It's just that lying still may increase the odds for pregnancy."

Luca could have sworn he'd felt the tips of his ears redden.

Whoa, he'd thought, and he'd turned on his heel and gotten the hell out of there.

What man wanted to think his sisters knew anything about sex, even when they were grown women?

And what man wanted to think about his sisters at a time like this, when he lay sated in his bed with a woman still wrapped around him…and yes, Cheyenne was wrapped around him, her arms around his neck, her legs around his hips, and *Dio,* he was still inside her and what he was thinking had nothing to do with his sisters and everything to do with their ideas about men and sex, with *his* ideas about men and sex.

Hc could only remember one or two times when getting on with life had not been his after-sex goal.

This was one of them.

What had just happened… It had damn near turned him inside out.

He was an experienced lover. Over the years, he'd had good

sex. Great sex. Mind-blowing sex. As for games… He'd played them before. Every now and then, they were fun. They were exciting.

But this—this had been different.

He hadn't planned to take her this way. Binding her hands. Tearing away her gown. Not permitting her to touch him. Sure, teasing like that could be exhilarating, but what had had changed everything had been her response to him.

He was not given to wasting time philosophizing, but he didn't have to be a student of Zen to know that something had happened to Cheyenne tonight.

And to him.

When her pleas that he release her from bondage had become pleas that he take her in pleasure…

"Luca."

He didn't want to move, didn't want to get up, didn't want to do his usual *that-was-wonderful-cara* thing as reality crept in and random thoughts about tomorrow's appointments, the stock market, the weather, whatever it was that normally filled an idle mind, took over.

All he wanted was to lie here with her in his arms, wait for the world to right itself and then do what they'd just done all over again.

"Luca."

Except, he had to move. She wasn't wrapped around him anymore. Of course, she wasn't. He was probably all but crushing her; he was far too heavy to use her as a mattress even if he liked the feel of her beneath him. Soft curves. Silky skin. The scent of flowers and sex and woman…

"Luca!"

"*Si, bellissima.*" He brushed his lips over hers, rolled to his side and took her in his arms…

Except, he couldn't.

She had rolled, too, not toward him but toward the edge of the bed, clutching the edges of her torn gown to her breasts.

He smiled. Modesty? Now? He laughed softly, reached out, trailed the tip of his index finger the length of her spine.

"Don't," she said, jerking away and rising to her feet.

Luca sat up. There was a world of meaning in that 'don't.'

"What's wrong?"

"Nothing's wrong."

"*Bellissima—*"

"You can give up the *bellissima* routine. It's done its job. Where are my shoes?" Her gaze swept the room. "Didn't I have them with me when we got here?"

So much for cuddling and pillow talk and post-coital whatever it was. Luca swung his feet to the floor, reached for his discarded trousers, got a foot into one leg.

She was already heading for the bedroom door.

"Cheyenne? Wait a minute. Where are you—" *Merda*! He caught his toes in a trouser cuff. "Goddammit," he roared as he recovered his balance, yanked the damned pants on, zipped the fly and went after her. He caught up to her in the hall, gripped her by the shoulders and swung her toward him. "What the hell is this?"

"Let go of me, Bellini."

"Answer me," he growled. "What's going on here?"

"Surely you have the brains to figure it out for yourself."

"Watch that smart mouth, McKenna."

"You watch your hands, Bellini," she snapped, shaking herself like a dog coming in from the rain. "I don't want them anywhere on me, understand?"

"You're good at this."

"At getting trapped by you? So it would seem, but it won't happen again." Another shake. "Damn you, take your hands off me!"

"You're good at running from what you can't face."

"Psych 101. Another of your marvelous skills."

"Funny. I wouldn't have figured you for a coward."

Her eyes, hot and wild, narrowed to glowing slits.

"I'm not going to honor that with an answer."

"One session between the sheets, you came like you never have before, and you bolt."

"Oh, that's charming, Bellini. So poetic. So—"

He kissed her, although it was more than a kiss. It was a claim, a statement that she was his and not all the denials in the world could change that.

Only one problem.

She bit him.

He jerked his head back as her teeth sank into his bottom lip. He stroked the tiny wound with the tip of his tongue and tasted the salty tang of blood. She was staring up at him, her breathing rapid, her cheeks scarlet, her gaze rebellious. Everything about her said *I dare you*, and he was a man who had never turned his back on a challenge.

"Poetry isn't what I want," he said in a low voice. "What I want is to fuck you."

She didn't so much as blink.

"Get yourself a copy of last month's *New York Fashion*. Open it to page seventy-eight. The lipstick ad. I'm right there and you can go into your bathroom and je—"

He said something raw and savage. The shredded gown fell to the floor as he hauled her against him and lifted her off her feet.

"Don't," she said, but his arms were hard around her, his mouth was on hers and the bulge of his erection was pressing against her naked belly. "Don't," she said again, but she was lying, lying, lying. If he stopped kissing her, she would die.

She needed this, needed him, and she gripped his hips with her legs as he carried her to the dresser and swept it clean of whatever small objects it held.

No silk bonds this time. No lingering seduction. She reached between them. Unzipped him and he drove deep inside her. Fast. Furious. No lead-up, no questions, nothing but this.

His need.

Her desire.

The sound of her cries as he moved.

The feel of her, hot and wet around him.

The power of him, primitive and male.

No mercy offered. None wanted.

A cry of incoherent joy burst from her throat. A groan of primitive satisfaction growled in his.

"Luca," she wept, "Luca…"

"That's right. Me. Only me. Never anyone else. Just me."

He felt the start of her orgasm, the delicate contractions of muscle around him. His vision blurred; his heart felt as if it might explode.

Not yet, he thought. Not until he heard the words.

"Tell me what you want, *bellissima*," he demanded. "Tell me!"

Her eyes, glazed and swimming with tears, met his.

"You. You. I want—"

He drove deep on last time. She cried out and fell forward in his encircling arms, and he whispered her name and tumbled into the starry abyss with her.

* * *

He held her that way for a long time.

She felt the heat of his breath against her throat, the thud of his heart against hers. His body was slick with sweat.

He smelled of sex and man.

She had always hated those smells. Getting rid of them was what hot showers were made for, but not tonight.

Tonight, she found herself burying her nose in the crook of his shoulder, inhaling him, making his scent a part of her.

It didn't make sense, but nothing she'd done tonight made sense. Nothing she'd done the entire day made sense.

Her world had turned upside down.

It was a terrifying thought.

Move, she told herself. *His arms around you make a lie of everything you believe, everything you know.* Instead, she found herself shutting her eyes, burrowing even closer and all but purring when he stroked his hand slowly down her spine.

He kissed her temple.

"You okay?"

She nodded. She was lots of things, but 'okay' would have to suffice. For the moment, that was about all she could manage.

Sex was an easy topic of conversation in her world.

How bad it was. How good it was.

Girls talked about it over coffee, over endless waits backstage at runway shows.

She'd never been part of those conversations—that was another mark against her, she suspected, that she didn't 'share'—but she'd heard enough to know that her comments, had she chosen to make them, wouldn't have fallen into either category.

Sex was sex. That was all it was.

Not tonight.

This was—it was—

"Cheyenne? Are you all right?"

She nodded. Talking would have taken too much energy.

"Because I was kind of fast."

That needed an answer, never mind her almost non-existent energy. "No," was the best she could manage.

She felt his lips form a smile as he pressed them to her temple again.

"Good. That's good." He gave a soft laugh. "Only one problem. I don't know if I can move."

At least, it wasn't just her. She couldn't have moved if a fire alarm had gone off.

Slowly, he drew back and framed her face with his hands.

"But we have to. Move, that is." He flashed a grin that was 100% pure male pride. "Otherwise, we'll scare the hell out of my housekeeper when she comes in Monday morning."

The image made her want to smile, but you didn't smile during sex. Well, this was after-sex, but it came to the same thing. Sex was sex. A bodily function.

"I can hear the news flash now," he said solemnly. "*Couple Found Hungry but Happy in Manhattan Penthouse. Details at eleven.*"

It was impossible not smile. Truth was, it was impossible not to laugh. When she did, he put his hand under her chin and titled her face up to his.

"Am I right?"

"About what?"

"About how I just described us."

Us. Why did such a simple word made her feel breathless? The safest move was to joke right along with him.

"Absolutely. I'm hungry enough to give up a tofu-and-egg-white scramble for a steak."

"I won't even comment on the tofu." His smile dipped; his thumb followed the arch of her cheek. "And what I meant was, are you happy?"

She stared into his eyes. Considered all the possible responses.

In the end, though, she took a deep breath.

And said, "Yes."

* * *

He asked her if she wanted to eat or shower first.

"I make a mean frittata," he said, flashing that million-dollar grin. "And I'm sure I can find a couple of steaks in the freezer."

The mention of food made her stomach growl. He heard it and laughed. She laughed along with him. Truth was, she was starved, but eating only meant delaying her departure by another half hour, and the trick now was to get out of here as quickly as possible.

Too much was happening too fast. She felt as if she'd stepped on a merry-go-round that was starting to spin out of control.

"They're both great offers," she said with a lazy assurance that she didn't feel, "but I want to shower first."

They were sitting on his bed facing each other, he cross-legged, wearing his zipped trousers, muscled arms folded over his bare chest, she with her feet tucked up under her and trying not to let him see the death grip she had on the edges of her gown.

"Fine." He got to his feet and held out his hand. "Shower it is."

"Oh, not together," she said quickly.

His dark eyebrows rose.

"I mean—you know, I need space in the shower."

"Not to sound immodest," he said, sounding exactly that, "but my shower's bigger than some bathrooms."

Yes. She'd noticed when he'd tended to her foot, and again a few minutes ago when she'd gone into the bathroom to pee. She'd seen his shower and it was, indeed, bigger than not just some but most bathrooms.

Trouble was, she didn't do that kind of thing.

Sharing a shower was too intimate, and yeah, she knew how

weird that would sound, considering that they'd had sex twice already. Well, three times. Four times, if you counted what had happened in the hotel…

The bottom line was that she didn't 'do' showers with a guy anymore than she 'did' spending the entire night with one, and it was troubling that she was already close to breaking that rule, considering a clock somewhere in his apartment had just struck three.

So she lied, told him she meant virtual space so she could wash her hair, condition it, do what she blithely described as a whole bunch of girl things that he didn't need to observe, and he listened, nodded, appeared to accept what was, basically, a load of BS.

"Then it's all yours," he said.

She smiled, stood up—and he reached for her, drew her into the curve of his arm and kissed her.

She wanted to melt into him. To wind her arms around him. To tell him she had never felt like this in her life, as if she could relax, trust him, be with him fully in all the ways she'd never been with another man…

What's the matter with you, Cheyenne?

She knew what men were, the reality of them. She knew the truth, and the only thing that separated this man from the rest was that he was exceptionally good in bed.

So she pulled away from his kiss, shot him her best model-in-the-eye-of-the-camera smile, and strolled into the bathroom.

She shut the door.

Eased out a breath and leaned back against it.

That was it.

He was very good in bed. Very, very good.

A lie.

There was more to it than that.

He seemed to be able to see through her. Into her. He knew when to demand. When to ask. When to take. When to give…

"Stop it," she whispered, and she slid free of the remnants of her gown, turned on the spray in the big glass box of a shower and stepped inside.

The cascade of water felt wonderful.

She let it beat down on her, turned the water hotter, watched tendrils of steam curve up the glass like the stalks of exotic flowers. Shelves held shampoo, conditioner and soap. She picked up the bottle of shampoo, sniffed it. It smelled like him. Like Luca. Fresh and clean, a scent that spoke softly of mountain meadows and golden sunlight.

She slicked the shampoo through her hair. Tilted her head back and let the suds drain away…

And gasped at the feel of hard, slightly calloused hands closing on her hips from behind.

She knew the right thing to do. To say. Smile at him over her shoulder, ask him please to respect her request for privacy.

He kissed her neck.

"Cheyenne," he whispered.

He turned her to him. And perhaps if he had done something sexual, touched her in a way that said this was about sex, she'd have made that request.

But he didn't.

He put his arms around her. Bent his head and took her mouth with such tenderness it brought tears to her eyes.

"I missed you," he said, and she knew she was lost.

* * *

He took her to bed.

Not for sex.

Instead, he drew back the duvet, gathered her against him and whispered, "Go to sleep, *dolcezza*."

She wanted to ask him that meant, *dolcezza*, wanted to tell him that it was long past time she went home, but all she could manage before closing her eyes was a jaw-creaking yawn.

He smiled, kissed her eyelids, and that was the last thing she remembered until she woke to the morning sun.

She sat up in the bed.

"Luca?"

He was gone. Her heartbeat stuttered.

Payback?

Then she heard a man singing. Was it Luca? It couldn't be the radio or the TV or an MP3 Player. The singer was obviously not a professional, just someone who loved… *Don Giovanni*? *Rigoletto*? She wasn't very good at identifying operas, but someone was definitely singing an Italian aria just a little off-key, and who could that possibly be but Luca?

Amazing, to awaken in a man's bed for the first time in her life and do it to the sound of a classic opera.

Cheyenne laughed.

How lovely. How unexpected. How…

How wrong.

What was she doing? Better still, what had she done? Staying the night. Sleeping with him. Really sleeping with him, not just using the word as a euphemism for sex. Letting him control the situation.

Control her.

She tossed back the duvet and only then remembered that she had nothing on. Was that little pile of clothing at the foot of the bed meant for her?

It had to be.

Gym shorts. A T-shirt. Leftovers from some mistress? Not unless the mistress had been as big as he was.

The clothes were his.

She pulled on the shorts. They hung almost to her ankles and, of course, they were enormous, but he'd thought of that—he'd left a canvas belt beside them.

Efficient of him, she thought coolly.

She used the belt as a tie, wrapped around her waist. Not that she wanted to think about ties just now and, Jesus, how had she ever permitted him to do that to her?

You let him do it because it had been exciting. Freeing—and wasn't that ridiculous? Being a man's captive was surely not freeing.

She needed coffee. Buckets of it, hot, black and strong. And, she thought, as she pulled the T-shirt over her head, that would be her very first stop. She'd grab a taxi, tell the cabbie her address, but tell him to stop at the nearest Starbucks before he took her home.

The T-shirt was a million sizes too big, but it covered her and that was what mattered.

All it all, it was one hell of an outfit, especially when she added her stilettos—Luca must have located them. Her evening purse was there, too, right beside the shoes.

What remained of her blue silk evening gown was draped over a chair.

She felt her face heat.

Quickly, she snatched up the gown, balled it up, went into the bathroom and stuffed it in a glass and silver trashcan.

What a pitiful sight. A humiliating sight! But there was nothing to do but leave it behind. It was only a length of fabric. What mattered was getting out of here before Luca appeared.

Back into the bedroom. Take a look around. Did she have everything? Shoes? Purse? God, what a sight she was, she thought as she caught a glimpse of her reflection in the mirrored wall opposite the bed.

It wasn't the first time she'd seen her reflection there. Last night, after they'd had sex the first time, Luca had brought her to that wall, stood behind her, cupped her breasts in his hands and told her to look at herself, to see how beautiful she was.

How much she was his creation, he'd meant, but he was wrong.

Starting the day in Texas, ending it in New York, the change in time zones and then the shock of coming face-to-face with the last man on earth she'd wanted to see…

Was it any wonder her behavior had been so bizarre?

But the world had righted itself, she thought as she combed her hair with her fingers. And she supposed she owed him some sort of thanks for having taught her that there was more to sex than she'd known.

And it was sex, not what he'd insisted on referring to as making love.

Not that she'd ever want to do that again.

The tied wrists. The gown torn from her body. The sense of being overpowered. Dominated.

A slow, hot burn flooded her skin.

Taken.

Taken for pleasure. With pleasure. Taken so that all you had to do was let yourself feel, feel what was happening without guilt or remorse…

"Hey."

Cheyenne swung toward the door.

Luca leaned against the jamb, hands tucked into the rear pockets of faded jeans, bare feet crossed at the ankles, white T-shirt outlining his shoulders and chest. His dark hair was mussed; there was stubble on his jaw.

He was mouth-wateringly beautiful and when he smiled, as he was doing now, he upped the ante another hundred percent because she had to admit, he had one amazing smile—sexy, innocent, charming and wicked all at once.

His gaze swept over her, head to toe. His smile tilted.

"You're a sight to warm a man's heart," he said softly.

He was a sight to warm a woman's, but she wasn't about to tell him that.

"It's the outfit," she said, batting her lashes. "Straight from Paris."

He grinned. "Who ever knew my old workout clothes could look so good?"

"That's the thing about fashion," she said brightly, plucking the purse from the bed. "It's full of surprises."

She started toward him. He didn't move. Her heart banged into her throat. She didn't want any kind of confrontation. What if he refused to let her leave?

"Going somewhere?"

"Home," she said in the same bright voice. "I have appointments."

"It's Saturday."

"Right. And I have appointments."

He waited until she reached him. Then, casually, he stretched one arm across the frame and wrapped his hand around the edge of the door.

"I made breakfast."

"I never eat breakfast."

"You haven't eaten since… When? We never got around to dinner at the *Horse Sense* party." His eyes darkened. "We never got around to it here, either."

"Really, I'm not hungry."

"Eggs. Pancakes. Bacon. Coffee."

"Sounds great, but I'm still not hungry."

"I am," he said, his gaze dropping to her lips.

Her heart thudded into her throat again.

"Well," she said briskly, "then it's good that you made breakfast. Please, could you step aside? It's getting late and—"

"Why are you running?"

"Running? I'm not running. I told you, I have—"

"We haven't even said good morning."

"Luca. Last night was—it was—"

"Yes." His voice was husky. "It was."

"But it's morning now, and I have to leave."

"When will I see you again?"

"I don't know. I have a busy—"

"*Si*. As do I."

There it was, the faint accent, the formal way of speaking that was a reminder he was from a different culture.

"Then you understand that planning ahead can be difficult."

"But planning is necessary." He touched his hand to her cheek, threaded his fingers in her hair, and brushed it away from her face. "For instance, you have appointments today."

"Yes. Exactly."

"And I have to be in Milan on Monday."

"Milan," she said gaily, "what a wonderful city! I did a couple of shows there two years ago."

"You should go back."

"I will, someday." She ducked her head a little, to escape the touch of his hand. The feel of it against her hair was—it was disconcerting. But he seemed oblivious to what was happening. He just kept shifting closer.

"Come with me."

"What?"

She looked startled. Well, hell, he'd startled himself, but now that he considered the suggestion, it was a damned good one.

"I said, come with me."

"Where?"

He laughed. "To Milan. My business won't take more than an afternoon. You can shop, do whatever you wish until I'm free."

"Thank you. That's a—it's an interesting offer, but—"

Luca lowered his head and kissed her.

That was all.

He didn't touch her with his hands, just his mouth.

And his mouth was warm and firm and he tasted of coffee—and the memories of the night washed over her. The feel of his body against hers. The caress of his hands on her breasts. Those lovely, ecstatic moments when she'd been naked beneath him, his to do with as he wanted, and the way those moments had ended, with him untying her hands when she was so hot, so filled with fever for him that winding her arms around him had seemed the only way she could keep from flying off the planet.

She whimpered against his mouth.

He groaned and his lips parted over hers.

For a heartbeat, just a heartbeat, Cheyenne let herself respond. She couldn't help it. Returning his kiss was everything and she leaned into him, let him taste her, let herself taste him and when she did, he gathered her to him, the length of her body against his, his arms around her, the sensation of being his enough to make her heart beat faster.

What if she said yes, she'd go with him? What if she stepped into this new world for just a handful of days?

Maybe he sensed her hesitation, because he drew her even closer.

"Come with me, *dolcezza*," he whispered. "I will make you happy. I will make you forget everything but me."

Reality flooded in on that soft, oh so masculine promise.

She jerked back, slapped her hands against his chest and tore her mouth from his.

"Is that what you think I want?" she asked. "To become

your sex toy?"

He raised his head. The passion in his eyes became bewilderment.

"What?"

She moved quickly, before he could reach for her again.

"Goodbye," she said. "And thanks for an interesting night."

Anger replaced bewilderment. An interesting night? Was that what she thought they'd spent together?

She swept past him, her head high.

His swung around and watched her, his jaw knotted.

He could go after her.

Catching her would be easy. Forcing her to take back those words would be even easier. She'd made the night sound like nothing, but that last kiss had made a lie of her words.

She'd been on the verge of surrendering again.

Another kiss. Another caress. She'd be in his bed…and this time, binding her wrists would not be enough.

She needed to be taught who was in charge.

She needed punishment. The sweetest torment. With his mouth, his hands, his body…

"*Cristo.*"

Luca sank down on the edge of the bed, lowered his head and plowed his fingers through his hair. What was happening to him? He was turning into a man he didn't know, and it was her fault, all her fault, all her doing.

He snarled something ugly in the language of his youth. Then he shot to his feet, took his iPhone from his pocket and punched up his contact list. It took seconds to choose a name and number. He barely remembered the face that went with it—

she was a banker he'd met a couple of weeks ago at a meeting; they'd talked and flirted and when she'd offered to enter her number on his phone—*in case you want to discuss finance*, she'd said, with a sultry smile—he'd said he was certain that he would.

Minutes later, he had a date for the evening.

By tomorrow morning, Cheyenne McKenna would be little more than a bad memory.

CHAPTER NINE

HIS DATE DIDN'T go as well as he'd hoped.

In fact, it was pretty much a disaster.

Aldo took him to the lady's brownstone in Brooklyn. And, of course, he had to double park. There was no parking in Brooklyn. There was no parking anywhere in the city, for that matter. No surprise there, but Aldo—Luca, too—knew Manhattan's ins and outs.

Why hadn't he taken a taxi?

Because you aren't thinking straight, he thought grimly, *that's why.*

His date was pretty, he thought as they killed time in a traffic snarl on the approach to the Brooklyn Bridge. Actually, she was beautiful, but she didn't have hair the color of midnight and eyes the color of a summer sea. She was smart, too, and probably charming, but how could he know that if he didn't pay attention to what she was saying?

Concentrate, he told himself.

He tried, but he lost half of what she said because instead of listening to her, he was listening to that last exchange with Cheyenne. He had offered to take her to Milan. She had told him she wasn't going to be his sex toy.

His what?

Was that what she thought the night they'd spent together was about? Him, wanting a sex toy? What about how she'd responded to him? Her moans? Her sighs? Her cries of pleasure?

Dio, what about it? A one-night stand. Okay. A one-day stand. He'd had those before, and he sure as hell hadn't tormented himself with memories or regrets when they ended.

"…never can be sure how things will turn out," his date said, and laughed.

No, Luca thought, you never could.

His date raised her eyebrows. She was waiting for a reaction. He had no idea what she'd been talking about, but laughing seemed appropriate so he laughed and she got a strange look on her face, meaning either laughing had not been appropriate or his laugh had sounded as phony to her as it had to him.

They reached the restaurant where he'd made reservations. It was quite a coup because the place had only recently received four stars from the *Times* and you had to call months in advance to secure a table, but Luca and the chef-owner had grown up together in Sicily, so he'd had no difficulty getting the reservation. Giovanni came out from the kitchen to greet them and Luca supposed the food was amazing, but he might as well have been eating at a neighborhood grill for all the attention he paid it.

How could he, when Cheyenne's voice was ringing in his

head?

He'd made breakfast. And she'd said, *I never eat breakfast.*

Really? Not even after hours of passion? Not even when her lover made it for her? Not that he was her lover, but the idea was the same. He'd prepared a meal for her and she'd reacted as if he'd offered her a bowl of gruel. Did she know that he had never cooked for a woman in his life? Never. Not once. Nor had he wanted to…

"Luca?"

He blinked. His date was staring at him. Evidently, they'd gotten through most of their meal because their plates were being cleared. Hers was, anyway; the busboy was looking at him expectantly.

"Are you finished eating, sir?"

Luca looked at his plate. He seemed to have moved the food around, but most of it was still there.

"Yes," he said briskly. "I am."

"Was everything all right, sir? If you'd prefer something else…"

"No," Luca said quickly. "Everything was fine. I'm just—" *Think. Think, before Giovanni comes out.* "I'm afraid I have a slight headache."

His date looked baffled.

Who could blame her?

A slight headache. Was that the best he could do? But he needed a way to explain why he hadn't been able to concentrate on her or make simple conversation unless you counted *Sorry, what did you say?* as scintillating banter.

Not that she bought the story.

She was quiet during the endless drive to Brooklyn—as they crossed the bridge, it occurred to him that this was his first time in the borough.

"I've never been in Brooklyn before," he said in a desperate attempt to fill the silence.

Bad move.

"And probably your last,' she said icily.

"No. Not at all. I mean—"

Aldo pulled to the curb in front of her brownstone. Luca started to get out of the car, but she beat him to it.

"No need to see me up," she said.

And she was gone.

Luca sat back and let out a long sigh of relief.

Aldo looked at him in the mirror.

"Are you all right, sir?"

He had to look pretty bad for Aldo to ask him such a personal question. Their relationship was polite though distant.

"Fine, *grazie*. Just a—a headache."

Aldo nodded. "Where to, sir?"

"Home," Luca said. "Straight home, *prego*."

When they reached his condo, he dismissed his driver for the night, went to his bedroom, put on all the lights and stared at himself in the mirror.

Cristo.

He looked like hell.

Eyes burning. Mouth thinned. Forehead furrowed. Shoulders tensed. He looked like a man who'd scare little kids—and it was Cheyenne's fault.

She'd walked out on him. Again.

Insulted him. Again.

Now he really did have a headache. It felt as if someone were playing a kettledrum behind his left temple.

Calm down. Take a deep breath. Hold it. Now exhale.

Alessandra had gone through a phase in her teens when she'd driven them all crazy, lauding the benefits of meditation. He and Matteo had teased her unmercifully, but years later they'd admitted—to each other, not to her—that they'd finally both tried it and maybe it had its uses.

Inhale. Hold. Exhale.

Every now and then, he still did the breathing thing. It came in handy when he was stressed by a tough business negotiation or after an exceptionally long flight. He'd never done it because of a woman, but what was that old saying?

There was a first time for everything.

Two firsts in one night, he thought, as he undressed. Brooklyn. And now, this.

He tossed his suit coat on a chair, did the same with his shirt. Maybe a shower would help.

His jaw knotted.

He thought back to the shower he'd taken with Cheyenne.

She hadn't wanted to shower with him, so he'd permitted her to think she'd won the argument. He'd waited until he heard the water pulsing down. Then he'd stepped into the stall and taken her in his arms.

He'd half-expected protests, but she gone into his embrace willing, gladly, burrowing against him as if she belonged there.

He hadn't made love to her then. Sex was usually what happened when he showered with a woman, but holding her had seemed enough.

Enough? It had seemed perfect.

Yeah, well, maybe all the sex the last couple of days had taken its toll. Matteo had ribbed him about old age at his thirty-second birthday party. For all he knew, there was truth to the jibe. It might even have been the reason he'd paid such scant attention to his date tonight.

Luca toed off his shoes, stripped off the rest of his clothes and looked at his reflection in the mirror.

The last time he'd stood here, Cheyenne had been in his encircling arms.

Seeing herself in the mirror had been another thing she hadn't wanted to do, but he hadn't even pretended he'd permit her to win that argument. Instead, he'd clasped her hand and drawn her to the wall of glass.

"Look at how beautiful you are," he'd said. cupping her breasts.

He'd seen the color rise in her face as she watched him play with her nipples.

Her breathing had quickened. His cock had sprung to swift, powerful life and she'd gasped when she felt it probing at her from behind.

"That's what you do to me," he'd whispered. "And this is what I do to you."

He'd slid his hand between her thighs.

Her head had fallen back against his shoulder; he'd cupped her, stroked her, kept stroking her until he'd driven her toward a climax that had shattered them both, and then he'd taken her back to the bed…

Merda!

His erection was swift and enormous.

So much for being too worn out for more sex.

Just the memory of what had happened in this room hours ago had given him a hard-on any man would be proud of.

Except, pride was not what he felt.

How had he permitted her to do this to him? Make him—what was the American word? Make him a patsy. And there it was again.

That word.

Permitted.

There were only certain things he should have permitted her to do. Wresting control from him was not one of them.

If he had it to do over, he would change the way he'd dealt with her.

He would permit her to be obedient in his bed. To touch him when he told her to do so. To submit to him when he ordered it.

To feel pleasure when he commanded.

His head told him those thoughts were insane.

His body told him they were what he needed to survive.

What *she* needed, to become his.

Not that he wanted her to be his. A stranger. A woman he hardly knew. Besides, thinking of a woman as his woman was foreign to him.

Why would he want such a drain on his emotions?

The answer was simple.

So he could have her whenever he wanted her.

He saw her in the mirror, the length of her pressed against

his chest and legs. Her head thrown back against his shoulder, watching as he teased her nipples, then sought the heat between her thighs.

His penis throbbed.

He should never have allowed her to walk away. She didn't want to be his toy? Too bad. She'd agreed to a game of his devising, but she had not played by the rules.

The game would end when he said so, not she.

And, *Dio*, if he didn't get some relief, he was going to explode.

Luca swung away from the mirror, strode into the bathroom, switched on all the lights and stepped into the glass shower stall. He adjusted the sprays so they would all hit him hard, turned the water to cold, and gasped at the shock of it against his fevered skin.

Useless.

He was still as hard as a thirteen-year-old boy with a purloined copy of a skin magazine in his hands.

He gritted his teeth. Grimly, in search of release, not pleasure, he called up an image of Cheyenne, hair spilled over his pillow, eyes blurred with passion, hands tied above her head.

Luca, she whispered, *Luca…*

He came instantly, shuddering as his climax tore through him. As the last drops of semen left his body, he bowed his head, flattened his hands against the glass wall, let his heartbeat return to normal as the icy water continued to pelt him.

Then he stepped out of the shower, returned to his bedroom and dressed.

Jeans. A pale blue shirt with the sleeves rolled up. Moccasins.

No underwear, because he damn well wouldn't need any. He stuffed his wallet in his pocket and then he was gone.

* * *

It was eleven o'clock. Still early by New York standards, and taxis were plentiful. The night doorman whistled one up in seconds.

"Soho," Luca told the driver. He still had her address in his phone and he read it to the guy.

Traffic was light. Fifteen minutes and he was standing outside her building.

It was only a few stories high, a big, well-kept Victorian, the kind of architectural gem that had escaped the wrecker's ball. Another evening, he'd probably have spent some time admiring it. Now, his only thought was how to get inside.

Was there a doorman?

There wasn't.

Instead, there was an unlocked glass front door that led into a handsome vestibule that—dammit—ended in another glass door.

That one was locked.

Luca looked around.

Built-in mailboxes adorned one wall. Call buttons were lined up on another. He checked the names. James Andrews. Alfred Bernstein. Lucy and Thomas Chang. Another few names and then he saw hers.

C. McKenna.

That ridiculous first initial thing again. Did she really believe that could protect her from predatory men?

From him?

The only problem now was how to get past that second door without pressing her buzzer and letting her know that he was coming, except it really wasn't a problem at all.

He had not always been rich. Going to Columbia University on a skimpy scholarship right here, in Manhattan, he'd spent a couple of semesters delivering pizza.

One of the first things he'd learned was how often somebody called in an order and gave you an apartment number without bothering to add that the downstairs door would be locked and if it were, which of half a dozen generally unlabeled buzzers was the correct one to press.

The solution? You chose one at random and pushed.

Luca checked the nametags again. James Andrews, apartment 3C.

C. McKenna, apartment 2C.

He hoped James Andrews wasn't in the middle of something important.

Bzzzz.

"Yeah?"

"Pizza," Luca said pleasantly.

"I didn't order pizza."

"Your name Andrews? James Andrews?"

"That's right."

"Well, that's what it says right here on the box. One large pizza, that's a deluxe pizza, for James Andrews."

The buzzer sounded. Luca grabbed the doorknob and

stepped into a narrow entryway. James Andrews would be annoyed and disappointed this evening, but he'd smile tomorrow when the local pizzeria delivered a large deluxe pizza as well as a bottle of their best Chianti.

Luca took the stairs two at a time.

There were three apartments on each floor. Apartment 2C was at the end of a short hall.

He hadn't considered what he'd say when she opened the door. How could he, when he was still hot with rage? Everything would depend on her because she'd be angry to see him…

Hell.

His eyes narrowed.

Nothing, not one goddamn thing would depend on her. There wasn't a way in hell he'd let her anger stop him tonight, not when he was angry enough for the both of them.

He lifted his hand. Reached for the buzzer and, instead, found himself hitting the door with his fist.

"Cheyenne!"

Nothing. Maybe she was out. Maybe she was with another man.

Maybe he'd lost his mind.

If he had, it was her fault.

Her fault. All her fault.

His anger went up a notch.

"Cheyenne!" Another bang of his fist against the door. "Open the goddamn door!"

He heard the faint creak of a door opening at the other end of the hall and he swung toward it.

"This is a private matter," he growled. "Mind your own

business."

Anywhere else, the threat would bring the cops, but this was New York. The door closed, and he turned back to Cheyenne's apartment.

"You're a coward, McKenna," he said. "Each time things get tough, you run."

He heard the slide of a deadbolt. The door opened only as far the chain would permit.

"Are you insane?" she hissed.

"Open the door!"

"I'll call the police."

"You do that and I'm sure Alene Beresford will enjoy hearing how we spent the last twenty four hours."

What felt like an eternity crept by. Then the door closed. He heard the rattle of the chain and the door swung open.

Cheyenne stood centered in the doorway.

She wore a white tunic, a kimono, whatever in hell women called those things that hid their bodies while hinting at the lush curves of breast and hip. Her hair was an untamed river of wet midnight silk cascading over her shoulders. She smelled of soap and water and he knew she must have just stepped out of the shower.

His throat constricted.

She was the epitome of everything wild and beautiful, and if he didn't have her soon, he was surely going to die.

"Did I tell you that you could leave me?" he said. "Did I give you permission to walk away?"

He heard his voice, heard his words and he thought, maybe he really was crazy. He had never spoken to a woman this way in his life, but he'd never let a woman turn his world upside down before, either.

"Answer me, dammit! Did I give you permission to leave me?"

"You truly are out of your mind! I don't need your permission for anything."

She was trembling. Her face was flushed. She was afraid of him and that was fine. It was what he wanted, what he'd come for.

"Yes. You do. You have to beg me when you want me to make love to you and beg me when you want me to stop, and you are never, ever to walk out on me unless I tell you to do so. Do you understand?"

"What I understand is that I never want to see you again."

She began closing the door. He jammed his foot in the opening and shouldered the door open. When she stumbled back, he caught her by the shoulders and kicked the door shut behind him.

He was out of control and he knew it, but only the explosion of the sun could have stopped him now.

"You're right," he said. "I *am* out of my mind, and it's your doing."

"Get out of here, Luca. Right now. Before—"

"Before what?" His fingers bit into her flesh. "Before what?" he demanded.

"Before I call the police!"

He laughed. Laughed! At her. At her threat. At the entire world she'd so painstakingly created.

"That's it," she said. "I'm calling the cops and to hell with both you *and* Alene Beresford! You really think you can come here and force your way into my apartment and—"

He caught her hand. Brought it to his lips. Pressed a kiss to her palm while his eyes bored into hers. All his anger had suddenly drained away.

"I want you," he said. "I need you. If I don't have you, I'm going to die."

She made a choked sound.

"Damn you, Luca!" Her voice shook. "Damn you, damn you, damn—"

Then she was in his arms.

CHAPTER TEN

HE'D IMAGINED THIS.

It was what had kept him going through the taxi ride.

Cheyenne, defiant. Refusing to surrender until he demanded it and then the feel of her in his arms, the taste of her mouth, the softness of her body against the hardness of his.

Imagining had been exciting, but reality was electrifying.

He was a man on fire; she was the sizzle of lightning that had lit the flame. He was burning with the need to take her and from the way she was returning his kisses, her submission, her desire for him was complete.

He lifted her off her feet.

She wrapped her arms around his neck, her legs around his hips.

"Where?" he said against her lips.

"Down the hall. To the right."

Her four-poster bed stood near a window. It was high but

not very wide, covered in what looked like a waterfall of white linen.

The long gown she was wearing had bunched up and she was pressed against him. He slid one hand the length of her spine and realized there was nothing under her gown. No bra. No panties. Nothing.

He groaned. He could feel himself throbbing against her.

"Cheyenne," he whispered, "*dolcezza…*"

"Yes," she said. "Now. Please, Luca. Do it. Take me. Take me…"

He fell back against the wall. Reached between them. Unzipped his fly. His erection sprang free, swollen and hot, and he drove into her.

She cried out and convulsed around him at the first stroke of his possession and he felt the tightening in his scrotum that meant he could have come right then, but he wasn't done with her.

Not yet.

Claiming her. Her surrender was what this was all about.

Luca gritted his teeth, fought back the urge to come and drove into her again. And again. She was sobbing; her breath was hot on his throat and when he drove into her a final time, she screamed, sank her teeth into his shoulder and he shuddered and let go, let his own climax drain him of anger, of need, of everything but the feel of the woman in his arms.

They stood locked together, him still inside her, both of them gasping for air. His muscles were trembling; he could feel his heart pounding as adrenaline coursed through him.

Finally, his breathing slowed. The world righted itself.

Slowly, he let Cheyenne slide down the length of his body until she was standing.

Her arms were still around his neck.

She stirred and he thought she might try to pull away. No way would he have let that happen, but she didn't make the attempt. Instead, she leaned into him and as he stroked his hand over her hair, he knew that whatever was happening between them could change his life, forever.

* * *

He smoothed down her kimono. Adjusted his jeans. Then he pressed a kiss to her hair.

She lifted her face to his and he kissed her mouth. She curved her hand around his jaw, loving the sexy roughness of his end-of-day stubble.

How long had they known each other? Two days? Two years?

A lifetime.

She smiled.

"What?" he said softly.

She shook her head, slid her hand to the nape of his neck, rose on her toes and kissed him.

"What a lovely way to end an evening," she murmured.

He smiled. It was a wicked smile, filled with promises, and it made her pulse quicken.

"It's not the end of anything," he said, taking her hand and drawing her to the bed.

She sat on the edge of the mattress and held her hand out to him. He laced his fingers through hers, but didn't sit down beside her.

She looked up at him. The moonlight was reflected in her eyes. How could she be lovelier each time he looked at her?

A smile curved her lips.

"What are you thinking, *cara*"

Her smile widened. Then, to his amusement, she giggled.

"You're laughing?" he said, trying to sound stern. "Just what a man wants after he makes love to a woman."

"It isn't that. Well, not exactly. I'm thinking of Mrs. DeCenzo."

"Who?"

"My neighbor."

"Even better. We make love and you think of Mrs. DeCenzo." Luca grinned as he sat next to her and curved his arm around her shoulders. "Would you mind explaining that?"

"She's elderly. And she's a widow."

"And?"

"And, what happened is a woman's fantasy. A man wanting her so much that he'll storm castle walls, slay dragons, do anything to have her." She blushed and buried her face against his shoulder. "Don't look at me like that."

Luca cupped her chin and raised her face to his.

"I am looking at you exactly as such a man would look at such a woman," he said in a low voice, "because I am that man, *cara*, and you are that woman."

He bent his head and kissed her mouth.

"Do you know how delicious you taste?" He kissed her

again. "Coffee. With cream and sugar."

"My dinner," she said softly.

"Only that?"

"I didn't have much of an appetite."

He sighed and drew her against his side.

"Neither did I," he said, remembering the plate of exceedingly expensive something-or-other he'd hardly touched. "Why no appetite?"

She gave him a smile that went straight to his groin.

"I kept thinking about you. About last night."

"Yes." His tone roughened. "As did I. It was an amazing night, *dolcezza*. I should have forced you to admit that instead of letting you leave me."

"How would you have done that?" she asked, very softly, and he could feel the atmosphere in the room change.

A muscle knotted in his jaw.

"I could have tied you up again. Not just by your wrists, but by your ankles, too."

"I'd have fought you."

"I am bigger than you, *cara*. Which of us do you think would win such a struggle?"

"But—but you wouldn't force me to do something I didn't want."

"No." He tilted her chin up. "We are learning. Both of us. For instance, I would not have thought this thing you are wearing is sexy."

Cheyenne slicked the tip of her tongue across her bottom lip.

"But?"

"But it is. It covers so much of you…" She caught her breath as he traced his index finger along the fabric that covered her nipples. "And yet, beneath it, you are naked. That makes it very sexy indeed."

His touch was light. Still, she could feel her breasts lifting, her nipples budding. Her breathing quickened and she closed her eyes and let herself glide with the sensation.

"Look at me," Luca said.

Cheyenne's eyes flew open.

"That's it, *bellissima*. Look at me as I pleasure you."

A little sound whispered from her throat. He bent to her, caught the sound with his mouth.

"You were naked beneath your gown at the ball the other night."

Both his hands were on her breasts now, his thumbs teasing the nipples. Hot wetness bloomed between her thighs. They'd just made love. How could she want him again?

"It—it suited the—it suited the…" She swallowed dryly. "Luca. I can't think when—"

"And naked again, tonight."

"Because I'd just come out of the—Oh God. Luca. Please…"

"What do you call this thing you are wearing, *bellissima*? A caftan?"

"Yes. I bought it in Morocco last year. We were doing a shoot and I went—I went shopping at a *souk*…" He bent forward and touched the tip of his tongue to first one nipple and then the other through the silk of the caftan. Cheyenne began to tremble. "What are you doing?"

"Nothing," he said calmly. "I am simply imagining you in

that *souk*, trying on caftans."

He sat back and traced a line from the valley between her breasts to her navel. Where would his hand stop? Where the caftan stopped? Where its long skirt was rucked up above her knees?

"Did you?" he said.

Her gaze flew to his. He wasn't as calm as he sounded. There were crimson stripes along his high cheekbones and his eyes were almost black.

"Did I what?" she whispered.

"Did you try on this caftan before you bought it?"

There was an edge to his voice. A warning. Soft, but real.

"I—I'm sorry. I don't—"

"It is a simple question *bellissima*. Did you try on the caftan?"

Her heart was pounding. His hand was at the hem of the caftan. What would he do next? Where would he touch her?

"No. I didn't."

"Because?"

"Because…" She bit back a moan. His hand was under the hem, stroking her thigh.

"*Cara?* You were explaining why you didn't try on this caftan."

"Because—because a *souk* isn't that kind of place. There are rules…"

"Rules?" he whispered, as the back of his hand brushed lightly over the soft curls at the apex of her thighs. "What rules?"

"Not rules, exactly. Traditions. About modesty."

His fingers stroked over her. Her lashes fluttered to her

cheeks as heat flooded her veins. She gave a little moan of frustration when he withdrew his hand and leaned back, but he wasn't done with her yet.

"Stand up."

His voice was hoarse and hard. A tiny shiver of fear went through her.

"Cheyenne. Stand up."

Slowly, she rose to her feet.

"Look at me. I told you that before. I want you watching me, do you understand?"

She nodded. She was weightless. Boneless. She was a cluster of nerve endings, a creature made of fire and need.

And what she needed was him.

"You're wet," he said in a smoky whisper. "Only from me touching you."

"Yes."

He put his hand over his fly. She could see the bulge of his erection under the straining denim.

"And I am hard, only from touching you."

Sweet Jesus. Surely, her knees were going to buckle.

"Do you want to see how hard I am, *dolcezza*?"

She whispered his name. It was all she could manage.

"Take off the caftan, Cheyenne, and I will show you."

She stared at him. If she took off the caftan, he would still be fully dressed and she would be naked. Years of modeling had taught her to see the human body as little more than a structure on which to hang clothing, but there was something about the thought of being bared to his eyes while he was not bared to hers…

“I told you to undress.”

Slowly, she pulled up the skirt of the caftan. Crossed her arms. Drew it over her head—and held it in front of her.

“I want to see you,” he whispered.

Her mouth was dry. Her skin was hot. And she wasn’t wet, she was soaked.

“Let go of the caftan.”

How could she possibly obey him? And yet, how could she disobey him? The gown fell from her hands. His eyes swept over her and she began to tremble.

He cupped her hips with his hands and drew her forward.

“Tell me what you want, *cara*.”

He knew exactly what she wanted. It was cruel to make her tell him that she wanted his mouth on her nipples. Her belly. Her thighs. That she wanted him to take her in his arms and kiss her, lay her back against the pillows and slowly, slowly take her on that ride that ended in paradise.

Why make her say it?

There would be such weakness in her asking. In her needing. In admitting that what had happened to her years ago had nothing to do with what was happening to her now, what had been happening since the minute she’d first laid eyes on him at El Sueño.

“Shall I help you, *bellissima*?”

He lifted his hands. Cupped her breasts. Took her nipples between his index fingers and his thumbs and teased them.

She moaned.

Had her breasts always been this sensitive? She’d never really let herself find out.

"Do you like it when I touch you?"

She nodded.

"I can't hear you."

"Yes. Yes. I like when you…"

"Watch," he said.

She looked down as he ran his hands down her body, over her hips, her belly, then parted her labia with his hands. Gently. So gently. He lifted his head and sought her eyes with his.

"I want your taste on me," he said. "On my hands. My body. My tongue."

Then he closed his mouth over her, and she would have collapsed if he hadn't caught her, gathered her in his arms and drawn her onto his lap.

"Cheyenne," he whispered, and he groaned, shifted his weight, his jeans, and suddenly he was deep inside her. "Cheyenne," he said, *mia bellissima* Cheyenne."

She sobbed his name.

Clasped his shoulders.

And rode him, rode with him, into the blazing inferno of a million billion stars.

* * *

They slept tangled in each other's arms, Luca as naked as Cheyenne, skin against skin, soul against soul.

She woke first.

He was still asleep, his face turned toward hers on the pillows.

It was an amazing face. Hard. Masculine. And beautiful. It was an amazing face for an amazing man.

Why had she run from him last night? She'd given herself lots of reasons, but not the true one.

She'd run because she was afraid.

Not of Luca.

Of herself.

She come awake in his arms yesterday, exactly like this, and realized that she was no longer in full control of her life. She had given some of that control to him.

It had seemed impossible.

So she'd run. Such a cowardly thing to do, but the fear of what was happening had been overwhelming. She'd gone over and over it for the rest of the day and no matter how she tried, she'd still been unable to make sense of it.

She had let Luca seize command.

She'd spent years creating the woman she was. Had she given up that woman for a few hours of sex?

She'd told herself she hated herself for letting it happen, hated him for making it happen, and whenever a memory intruded—Luca kissing her, Luca gathering her in his arms, Luca possessing her, oh, the sensation of him possessing her, she'd shuddered and told herself she wasn't shuddering with passion, but with humiliation.

And yet—and yet, early in the evening, when she'd heard a man's footsteps climbing the stairs outside her apartment, her first thought had been *Luca*. Her heartbeat had skittered. She'd waited beside the door, listening, listening…but the footsteps had plodded to the Stein's apartment and she'd realized it had only been their nephew, come to visit.

"Grow up," she'd told herself, and she'd stomped into her bedroom, showered, washed her hair and tweezed her eyebrows. She'd been contemplating giving herself a manicure when she'd heard other footsteps.

She'd known instantly that they were Luca's.

Good.

He'd come after her.

Now, she could tell him what she thought of him. That he was overbearing and self-centered and she despised him. And by the way, she'd only pretended to enjoy the sex.

Except, when she opened the door and saw him, felt the waves of fury and desire coming off him, the truth had almost sent her to her knees.

She loved what had happened between them. His domination, her acquiescence.

They were dancers, moving to a melody only they could hear.

He led. She followed—except they both knew that under it all, she led, too.

She'd convinced herself that showing need was weakness, but he'd shown her that it could be empowering.

Just thinking of his hands on her made her come alive—but it was she who made him come alive.

She, of all people. She, who'd always believed that sex was about men taking what they wanted and if it degraded a woman in the process, so be it.

But Luca took only what she wanted to give, and he gave back more than she'd ever dreamed she could want or have. He'd freed her of a past she thought she'd conquered, but which had, instead, almost conquered her.

She thought about telling him that, but why would she?

They were making love, not falling in love, and what man would want to hear a lover's dark secrets, especially when those secrets were ugly?

"A penny."

She blinked. "You're awake."

"Uh huh." He slid his fingers into her hair and brought her to him for a kiss. "Good morning, *cara*. And I'm still offering that penny."

"For what?"

"For the thoughts that made you look so serious."

"Ah. Those." She forced a smile. "They're so important that I don't know if I can share them with you."

He smiled, too. "Try me."

"Well…I was supposed to water my cactus garden yesterday."

"Your cactus garden," he said solemnly.

"It isn't a garden, of course, it's just a bowl. And the plants are really succulents. I water them once a—"

She caught her breath as Luca drew down the sheet and comforter and ran the tip of his tongue around one nipple.

"Such a lovely word," he murmured. "Succulent." His hand replaced his mouth. "Go on. Tell me more about these succulents."

"I—I started keeping them because—because when I traveled a lot, they didn't require much… Luca, are you trying to distract me?"

"Would I do such a thing, *cara*?"

She almost laughed. His attempt at sounding innocent was worse than hers at sounding exasperated.

"You would. You are. You—you—"

He was moving over her, kissing her mouth, trailing his hand over her hip and thigh. Her heart went into overdrive as teasing gave way to hunger, and she raised her arms and put them around his neck.

"Luca," she whispered.

"Cheyenne." His lips curved against hers. "It is time for a proper good morning."

He slid into her as if he belonged there. Her body welcomed him; her muscles tightened around his erection as she arched toward him.

The sensation was exquisite, beyond any she'd ever known.

"Succulent," he whispered. "So succulent…"

The world fell away.

* * *

He knew Soho, but not as well as she.

They strolled the cobblestone streets hand in hand.

The architect and builder in him was entranced by the handsome cast-iron buildings that dated back to the 19th century.

She loved the feeling of history. In a city known for replacing the old with the new, Soho was a treasure trove of handsome old architecture.

"Have you lived here long?" he asked.

"Since I came to New York," she said. She looked at him and laughed. "Well, maybe that's a bit of an exaggeration. I couldn't afford much of anything when I first arrived. I ended up taking a share in a loft."

"Sounds very bohemian."

"Not really. The realtor said the loft was in Soho, but it was on the edge of it, and I do mean 'edge.' The bathtub was in the kitchen, the stove was a two-burner hotplate, and the first time I came home after dark, I saw what I thought was a dog running up the stairs. A chihuahua, or maybe a fox terrier. Well, I love dogs so I called to it and when it didn't stop, I went after it."

Luca raised her hand to his lips and kissed it.

"Why do I suspect this will not end well?"

"It was a rat. I'd seen rats before. Where I grew up… But I'd never seen a rat that size. Luckily, I realized what it was just before I cornered it." She shook her head. "I was very, very careful after that."

"How old were you when you came to the city?"

"Seventeen."

"So young? And you were already on your own?"

It was the wrong thing to say. He could almost see the walls going up.

"Models usually start their careers at an early age."

"And your parents had no objections?"

Another bad question. The walls were not only going up, they were starting to sprout crenellations and towers.

"Forgive me," he said, kissing her hand again. "I ask too many questions."

"No," she said quickly. "I just—I don't like talking about

myself, that's all." She smiled, and he could see the wariness beneath it. "It's a boring topic."

"Nothing about you is boring," Luca said, and he stopped in the middle of the crowded sidewalk and kissed her. This was New York; nobody objected. The crowd simply parted and swept around them as if they were boulders in a stream.

When he raised his head, what he saw in her eyes filled him with joy. "Are you happy, *bellissima*?" he asked softly.

He'd half-expected her to hesitate before answering, but that didn't happen

She laughed and touched his cheek. "Very happy."

A dozen thoughts skittered through his head. Most of them were dangerous because they made no sense. He reminded himself that they hardly knew each other and besides, the relationship wouldn't last.

He never wanted relationships to last.

He was not a man seeking permanency. He had places to go, things to do. Aside from all that, he had seen far too many fools believe in something as useless and meaningless as love.

Not that what he felt for Cheyenne was love, or anything even close to it. He liked her; he found her desirable.

Incredibly desirable.

No surprise there.

She was a beautiful, bright, sophisticated woman, fun to be with, interesting to talk to, and as eager to explore the pleasures of their sexual relationship as he was.

And yet—and yet, there was more to it than that.

There was a vulnerability to her that was at odds with the tough exterior she presented to the world. A softness. A sweetness. He had the feeling he'd found a part of her she kept hidden and that there was still more to her than she'd permitted him to see, and if he let himself think about that too long, if he let himself think that there was more to this than terrific sex…

"A penny," she said.

She was laughing up at him, repeating what he'd said to her last night.

He wanted to offer a clever answer, but his thoughts were spinning and all he could manage was to kiss her again.

Then he cleared his throat, laced his fingers through hers, and led her into *Balthazar* for brunch.

The café was, as always, crowded, noisy and wonderful.

She ordered strawberries and coffee.

He looked at her as if she was a creature from an alien planet.

"I have to watch my weight," she said. "In my profession…"

"I'll watch your weight," he said, stroking an imaginary handlebar mustache.

She laughed. It was an old, foolish joke, but she loved that he'd made it. Besides, why worry about her weight? She really didn't have much of a profession anymore. The calls her agent sent her on were more and more scarce.

"Okay," she said. "I'll have a poached egg. Dry toast. And coffee."

"The lady," Luca said, "will have Eggs Benedict."

"Luca. All those calories!"

He took the menu from her hands, added it to his and handed them to the smiling waiter. "I'll have an omelet. Mushrooms, cheese, whatever. And don't forget those strawberries."

"Yes, sir."

"We'd like a bottle of champagne to start."

"Will Dom Perignon Brut be all right, sir?"

"The 2003? Yes. That will be fine."

The waiter left. Luca reached over the table for Cheyenne's hands.

"You're spoiling me."

He grinned. "Am I succeeding?"

She smiled. "I take it you've been here before."

"A few times."

"With women you date who live in Soho?" she said, and instantly hated herself for asking the question. "Luca. I'm sorry. That is so unlike me—"

"With my brother," he said gently, "and, once or twice, with my sisters." He leaned forward. "Are you jealous, *cara*?" His eyes darkened. "I hope that you are."

"No. I'm not jealous. I…"

She ran the tip of her tongue over her bottom lip. He considered leaning in a couple of inches more and replacing the tip of her tongue with his.

"I don't—I don't usually… You've found a version of me that I don't know. Does that make sense? I don't know how else to phrase it."

"It is the same for me." His voice was low; his fingers tightened on hers. "It is as if we are on a journey of discovery."

"Yes. That's the way I feel, too."

"So stay with me, *bellissima*. We will travel this road together, *si*?"

She nodded, but he saw the uncertainty in her eyes and he silently cursed himself for being a fool.

"Nothing will harm you, Cheyenne. I swear it."

Something would. Life would. Reality would, because this was not reality and she knew it. This was all a risk, but she would take it, gladly. She would take any risk for him.

The champagne arrived and as the bottle was opened and poured, they both sat back and returned to the easy give and take of two people just beginning to get acquainted.

Over the eggs, she asked about the brother and sisters he'd mentioned.

He told her about Matteo, who, it turned out, had his law offices nearby. About Bianca, who was studying for her Master's degree in psych at New York University. About Alessandra, who had studied design at the Fashion Institute and was seeking a job in the industry.

"Does she have a portfolio?"

Luca grinned and said whatever that was, he was sure that she did.

"Well, I know lots of people. Maybe I can…" Cheyenne paused and blushed. "Sorry."

"About what?"

"I got ahead of things. I mean, there's no reason you'd want your sister to meet me. I mean, we met, of course, at El Sueño, but getting together for coffee or lunch…"

She was right.

Why on earth would he want one of his sisters to meet the woman he was sleeping with? The designation made him wince. To meet his lover. That was better.

Besides, for some reason, the thought made him smile.

"She would like you," he said softly.

"I'm sure I'd like her, too. I only meant—" She sipped some champagne. "So," she said brightly, "you were all educated in the States?"

"We all took our degrees here, yes."

"No comparable schools in Italy?"

Luca's jaw knotted. "Our father was American."

"Ah. So you came here to live with him."

"No."

The 'no' was abrupt. Cheyenne flinched.

"Forgive me," she said. "I didn't mean to pry."

"You didn't. It's just that…" Hell, he thought, why hide it from her? "Our father was—he was a fraud, and not at all what he pretended to be." He drew a deep breath. "Our mother will never know because she is gone—and we, my brother, my sisters and I—are only just learning how to deal with it."

This time, it was she who reached for his hand.

"I'm so sorry."

His fingers meshed with hers. "Sometimes," he said, trying to lighten things, "families are not all they're supposed to be."

She tried for a laugh and hoped she'd managed to make it sound real.

"Isn't that the truth."

"Here is another truth, *cara*. I must leave you tomorrow to fly to Milan."

She understood. It was goodbye time. A couple of days and now it was over.

She hadn't expected more than that. The truth was she hadn't expected as much as they'd had. There was no reason to feel such a sudden weight in her heart.

"Come with me."

She looked up. The expression on his face was so intense it almost took her breath away.

"Come to Milan, with me, *bellissima*. I'm asking again. Say that you've changed your mind and that you will let me take you with me."

"It's impossible. I mean, you want me to put everything aside and go away with you at the last minute? We only just met. We don't know anything about each other. I'd have to be crazy to go with you—and you have to be just as crazy to ask."

He smiled. "Is that a yes, McKenna?"

Cheyenne smiled, and all that he had ever dreamed of was in that smile.

"That's what it is, Bellini," she said, and he leaned over the table and kissed her.

CHAPTER ELEVEN

HE HAD A private plane.

Why didn't that surprise her?

Everything about him spoke of success and power.

He explained he and Matteo used it primarily for business, that their accountants had determined it was logical to make the purchase, and then he laughed and said the problem was that he was still unaccustomed to having money and there were times he found himself apologizing for it.

"I know how that feels," Cheyenne said. "When I was a kid, having a dollar in my pocket was like having a fortune. Then I began modeling and I got lucky, and sometimes I'd look at the numbers in my checkbook and wonder if it all belonged to me."

They were sitting in a pair of leather chairs, side by side, in the center of the spacious cabin. Luca had introduced her to the pilot, the co-pilot and to Ted, the flight attendant, who'd served them lunch.

"This is sooo decadent," Cheyenne said happily, over cannoli and tiny cups of espresso. “You’re going to spoil me.”

“I hope so.”

“I’ll never be able to fit into sample sizes.”

He raised his eyebrows. “Sample what?”

“Sizes. The clothes designers create for their collections. You have to stay skinny, if you want to work.”

“I like you just the way you are. I especially like that drop of chocolate on the tip of your nose.”

She started to wipe the chocolate away with her napkin, but he got there first, leaning in to kiss the offending drop away.

“Definitely decadent,” she said softly.

“No sacrifice too great,” he said solemnly, and when she laughed, he kissed her again. Then he pushed aside the table on which their coffee and desert had been served and took her hand. “Is it interesting?”

“Is what interesting?”

“Modeling. I imagine it must be very glamorous… What?”

“It isn’t glamorous at all, certainly not when you’re starting out. I remember how my feet would ache at the end of the day after I’d gone from one casting call to another. At least when you reach the go-see level—”

“What is that?”

“A go-see is when a client specifically asks you to interview. There are open calls, where anyone can show up, and casting calls, where you’ve been invited to stop by, and then there are the go-sees, meaning someone has specifically requested you.”

Luca gave a dramatic shudder.

“And I thought trying to join a fraternity was bad.”

She smiled. “Did you join one?”

"No. I had no time for such things." He rolled his eyes at how stuffy that sounded. "I had a scholarship, but it was for tuition only. I had to work, but I know enough about the process to think that what you've described is a lot like hoping to be asked to join a fraternity."

"It's not fun, that's for sure. You and a million other girls are vying for the same couple of slots. They talk to you, maybe take a couple of photos. If you're what they're looking for, they call you back."

"You are surely always what they are looking for, *bellissima*."

"No. I wasn't. I did toothpaste ads. Detergent ads. I posed for catalogs. It wasn't until I was modeling for almost a year that I got lucky."

"Lucky, how?"

"Well, I was with a small agency. The good thing was that they worked with a limited number of models. The bad thing, which I hadn't thought of at all, was that they didn't have enough top contacts. So, anyway, I was leaving an open call one morning and I was feeling really discouraged—it was a year all the best models were blonde Nordic types—and a woman came up to me in the street, said she was from a modeling agency and that she'd seen a couple of things I'd done. She gave me her card. She said she thought I had...don't laugh...a new face."

He laughed anyway.

"A new face?"

"You know. I didn't look as if I came from Sweden or Germany."

"What she meant was that you were absolutely beautiful, *cara*. And she was right."

Cheyenne smiled. “Whatever she meant, it was the turning point for me. No more casting calls, no more go-sees. The new agency sent me for a styling… A new hairdo and new makeup,” she explained. “Which, in my case, meant no more using a curling iron, no more tweezing my eyebrows into thin lines, no more trying to de-emphasize the fullness of my bottom lip.”

“What a tragedy it would be to do anything to that delicious bottom lip,” he murmured, running the tip of his finger across it.

“Six months later, I made the cover of *Beauty Today*. And my career was off and running.”

“Then did it become glamorous?”

“It certainly improved,” she said with a little laugh. “And, sure, I guess it was kind of glamorous. Lots of travel. Lots of gorgeous clothes. Lots of interesting people. But there were negatives. Go to bed early, get up early, watch every mouthful you eat, avoid the sun, say the right things, be cooperative, you know, be easy to get along with… It was glamorous, but it was hard work, too, in some ways more than waitressing, which I’d done, or even cleaning houses.”

“Cleaning houses?”

“For a little while, when I was in middle school.”

“How old were you?”

“Twelve.”

“Aren’t there laws against child labor in America?”

“Laws don’t apply if nobody knows what you’re doing.”

He looked shocked. Appalled. She thought of how much more shocked he’d be if he knew the other things she’d done as a child, and then she realized she’d told him too much. Stupid.

And amazing, when she had never before mentioned her past to another soul.

"Yes, but a child, cleaning houses…"

"It's a perfectly legitimate job," she said stiffly. "And it paid for my school supplies and clothes."

The chip that materialized on her shoulder was the size of a boulder. Luca, who had experienced his father's disdain when he'd learned his son was supplementing his college scholarship by delivering pizza, was sure he understood it.

"Of course it is," he said. "I just hate to think of you working so hard."

He could see some of the tension go out of her.

"Sorry," she said, "but when my mother found out what I was doing, she told me I was an embarrassment."

He wanted to ask why her mother hadn't provided her with school supplies and clothing, but he knew it might be best not to. At the moment, it was enough to wonder if a man could despise a woman he'd never met.

"On the contrary," he said, trying to sound calm. "It is something to be proud of. That you worked hard to be able to buy things you needed." He hesitated. "And what did your mother do?"

She drank. She gambled. Mostly, she sold herself to the highest bidder, and when that wasn't enough…

"*Cara*? What is it?"

"Nothing," Cheyenne said quickly. "Just—my mother is dead. She died five years ago."

Luca's hand tightened on hers.

"I'm sorry."

"Don't be. I mean, we weren't very close…"

She paused. He could see her trying to regroup. She was in pain, and it hurt his heart to see her that way.

"*Dolcezza*. What's wrong? Talk to me. Let me help you."

"Nothing's wrong," she said briskly. "It's just, you know, this trip down memory lane reminds me of something I once read, how it takes forever to climb to the top and no time at all to plummet to the bottom."

Luca knew she was deliberately changing the topic. If she needed to do that, he would let her.

"Surely that doesn't apply to you," he said, smiling.

"It might. I haven't been working much lately."

He looked as bewildered as she felt. Why did that ease the hurt?

"But why?"

"They say I've become difficult to work with."

"Difficult in what way?"

His voice was suddenly that of a knight preparing to ride off and battle dragons for his lady's honor.

That he wanted to protect her made her want to throw her arms around him.

That she had once again told him something so personal troubled her.

"Who is the 'they' saying this of you?"

"My agent," she said. "And some of the people I work with. They say that I'm too—too controlling."

She watched his face. No raised eyebrows. No signs of anything so far.

"That I, uh, that I want to do things my way."

Was that a tiny twitch at the corner of his mouth?

"You know," she said. "That I always want to be in charge. In control."

Until now, she hadn't spoken the words out loud. Kept inside, they'd seemed unfair. Said aloud, did they possibly contain a whisper of truth?

And, yes. That was a definite twitch.

"Look, I just want things to be done properly, that's all. Is there something wrong with that?"

"Certainly not."

"Then why are you laughing?"

"I'm not laughing."

Of course he was. Did he think she was blind?

"I, of all people, would never think of you as wishing to be in control. We both know that's an idiotic perception. Why, that day at Sweetwater, you were the very soul of conciliation and reason."

"I am entitled to my own ideas." Jesus. She sounded like a fool. "What I mean is, if a person knows what is correct, why shouldn't that person say so?"

"Indeed."

"Other people should appreciate the input."

"Without question."

"Dammit, Luca, stop agreeing with me."

"Consider it stopped."

She hit his shoulder in frustration. Then, to his delight, she began to laugh.

That was good. It was excellent. For a few minutes, he had seen an awful darkness in her. It had made him feel helpless, and he was not a man who enjoyed feeling helpless.

"You're a woman who knows her own mind, *cara*. That's a fine trait—but every now and then, easing back, you know, combining control with cooperation, can be a good thing."

She thought about arguing, but a little voice inside her told her that he was right. She sighed and slumped against him.

"I know. But sometimes, it's hard to do."

He stroked the hair back from her temple and tilted her face to his.

"You do it with me," he said softly.

He could almost see her thinking that over. Then she nodded.

"And that's a new thing for you, *si*?"

Another nod. And then, a smile that made him want to kiss her—so he did.

It was a tender kiss, but as it went on, the tenderness mixed with awareness and that awareness became desire.

Luca rested his forehead against hers.

"Would you like to try this new thing again, *bellissima*? Being cooperative? Just so we can be certain we know how to do it correctly?"

She smiled. "Now?"

"Right now. All you have to do is ask."

She laced her arms around his neck.

"Make love to me."

"Say it properly."

"Please," she said, her mouth a breath from his. "Make love to me, Luca."

He lifted her in his arms.

"What a good girl you are, *cara*. And because you are so very, very good, you're going to get a reward."

He kissed her and carried her through the plane to a handsome bedroom in the rear of the cabin. Then he shut the door, locked it, undressed her, undressed himself, and taught them both what command, control and cooperation were all about.

* * *

Milan had always been one of Cheyenne's favorite cities.

One of her first big breaks had occurred there, during September Fashion Week almost a decade ago.

Four top designers had asked her to show their clothes. She became a fashion "name" virtually overnight. How could she have anything but a special affection for Milan? Venice had its Grand Canal, Florence had its David, and Rome had its Coliseum, but Milan had the *Via Monte Napoleone* as well as her heart.

And if you gave the city a chance, it was happy to show you its hidden parks and cathedrals and ancient works of art.

"I only wish we were here in season," Luca said as they stood on the wide balcony of their suite while the last rays of the sun touched the Duomo with pink and gold. "I would take you to La Scala."

She put her head back against his shoulder and smiled.

"I heard you that morning."

"What morning?"

"That first morning we were together. You were singing an aria."

He chuckled. "Howling it, you mean. When we were kids, Matteo used to threaten to smother me if I didn't stop what you so graciously refer to as 'singing.'"

"I think you sounded wonderful."

"I used to think so, too, until he recorded me and played it back. When he did, I decided it was truly a miracle that he hadn't carried through with the threat."

Cheyenne smiled as he put his arms around her waist and drew her back against him.

"It must be nice, growing up with a brother."

"Don't forget the two sisters." Luca rolled his eyes. "Brothers can be annoying, but sisters…"

"What?"

"Well, you have to worry about them all the time. Who are they dating? Where are they going? What are they doing? Are they taking foolish risks? Are they blind to the possibility of trouble?"

"Are you much older than they are?"

"Four years older than Bianca, five years older than Alessandra."

"Mmm. I can see that must have been hard. Big brothers worrying about teen-aged girls, I mean."

"I wasn't talking about them as teenaged girls." He chuckled, bent his head, nuzzled her hair aside and kissed her neck. "I'm talking about now."

Cheyenne laughed. "You're lucky they let you."

"That's the point. They don't. And they get—"

"Huffy."

"*Si*. They get huffy if they find out, or if I ask too many questions."

She turned in his arms. "But they love you for it."

"Bianca has used other terms. So has Alessandra." He smiled. "But, yes, they love Matteo and me, and we adore them. What about you?"

"What about me?"

"Do you have sisters?"

Amazing. A simple question, and he could see those walls going up again.

"No."

"No family? What about your father?"

"I have no father."

He almost said that was impossible. Everyone had a father, even if it was a father they preferred not to acknowledge.

Then he realized that her choice of words had been deliberate.

"I'm sorry, *cara*."

"There's nothing to be sorry for. He was never part of my life. All I know about him is that my mother named me for him. He was Cheyenne."

"A Plains Indian tribe, right?"

She nodded.

"And he taught you the language?" Luca grinned. "I'll never forget the look on that punk's face when you cursed him out."

She grinned back at him. "That was a nice moment, wasn't it?" Her grin faded. "Actually, my father took off l before I was born, but I knew a kid in school whose family was Cheyenne and he taught me a couple of words."

"Well, your mother named you wisely. A beautiful, proud name for a beautiful, proud woman." He caught a strand of her hair between his fingers and played with it. "My mother named me, too, but her choice was far less dramatic. She named me for her great-grandfather. At least, that's what she told me. The truth, I think, is that she picked the first name she could come up with, because my father was not there to offer any suggestions."

"Was he away on business?"

Luca smiled grimly.

"He was away, spying for his country. Or playing at being the great general who would save the world. Your choice."

"I don't understand."

"No. Neither did we." He paused. "Do you remember asking me if the Bellinis were related to the Wildes? Well, you were right. We are."

"Cousins?"

"Siblings," he said flatly. "Half-siblings. Our father married our mother in Sicily even though he was already married to a woman in America."

Cheyenne stared at him.

"You mean—"

"I mean that he was a bigamist. And," he added, with a tight laugh, "I cannot believe I am telling you about it. It is such a dishonor. Such a disgrace. Such a—"

"The dishonor is your father's, Luca. He should be proud to have a son like you."

He took her hand and brought it to his lips.

"This is the first I've told anyone."

"You don't have to worry. I'd never—"

"Yes. I know. What I was going to say is I didn't expect that sharing the truth would make me feel as if I've been freed from a darkness. Does that make sense?"

A therapist had long ago told her almost the same thing. *Face who you are,* he'd said, *and realize that there is no disgrace in what someone else imposed on you,* but it wasn't so.

How could it be, for a truth like hers?

To her dismay, sudden tears filled her eyes.

"Cheyenne, *dolcezza*, are you weeping?" Luca drew her closer, rested his chin on the top of her head. "Don't weep for me, sweetheart. Never weep, I beg you."

"I'm not weeping," she said, as her tears flowed onto his shirt.

He dug a pristine white handkerchief from his pocket.

"Let me see your face." When she did, he dried her eyes, then held the hankie to her nose. "Blow. Good. And again."

She made a honking noise the second time. Luca smiled and gathered her to him again.

"I'm sorry for being so silly."

"You're not silly. You're wonderful." He clasped her shoulders and looked into her eyes. "And I'm going to reward you." He laughed at the rush of pink that swept into her face. "By taking you to La Scala," he said. "It isn't the season for opera, but there's a concert tonight. How does that sound?"

"Wonderful." She smiled and linked her hands behind his neck.

"And," he said, "I promise you another reward tonight, after we return here." He brushed his lips lightly over hers. "Does that please you, *cara*?"

Everything about him pleased her. His voice. His smile. His touch. Just being with him pleased her.

The enormity of the realization stole her breath away. She wanted to say something light, to offer the kind of sophisticated response she'd given other men in the past, but this was Luca, not any other man, and what she felt for him was—it was—

"Tell me that I please you," he said gruffly.

She raised her eyes to his. There were truths so ugly she would never share them, especially with him, but this was one truth she wanted him to know.

"You please me more than I ever dreamed possible," she said softly. "You make me—you make me happy."

Her sweet admission, the way she was looking at him, put a lump in his throat. He wanted—he wanted—

He wanted her.

Physically, yes, but he wanted something more, and it scared the hell out of him. It was safer to kiss her, then kiss her again until he felt the fire leap between them.

"Turn around," he said gruffly. "Hold onto the balcony rail."

"Here? On the balcony? But someone might—"

"Turn," he commanded.

Her body's response, the hot rush of desire that swept through her, was instantaneous.

She turned her back to him, clasped the rail, heard the snick of his zipper, felt his hands under her skirt taking down her thong, and then he was inside her and she was one with him, lost to the place, to the hour, to everything but Luca.

* * *

The concert was wonderful, but being together was the best part.

After, they stopped for a light supper at an elegant little *ristorante* near their hotel. Luca ordered a bottle of Barone Ricasoli Chianti Classico, bruschetta and antipasto.

Once their wine was poured, he said that he would be busy the next morning.

"Will you be in meetings?"

"Dull stuff, most of it. I've arranged for a car and driver to show you the city."

"I'd much rather walk around on my own," she said. "Besides, I know Milan very well, remember?"

"Ah. Yes, of course. You worked here."

"More than that. My career really took off here. Four different designers wanted me to do their shows." She sighed at the memory. "It was a heady experience for a kid."

"Of course they wanted you." He smiled. "They weren't fools. I'm sure you could make a dishrag look sexy and desirable."

"That's the idea," she said, smiling back at him.

"To make dishrags look good?"

She laughed. "To make whatever you put on look good, even if it's—"

"Cheyenne! *Mia bella* Cheyenne*! Come stai*?"

A tall, good-looking man had appeared beside their table, beaming at Cheyenne. He took her hand and kissed it.

Cheyenne smiled.

Luca frowned.

"Franco! How wonderful to see you. I'm fine, thanks. And you?"

"Also fine, but I have been desolate these last months, not seeing you, you exquisite creature! Where have you been hiding?"

"I haven't been doing much travelling lately."

"But now you are here, in Milano, and you did not tell me that you were coming? For shame, my love. For shame!"

Luca cleared his throat as he got to his feet and held out his hand.

"Luca Bellini," he said gruffly. "And you are…?"

"Oh, I'm so sorry," Cheyenne said. "Luca, this is a dear old friend, Franco Savo. Franco, this is Luca Bellini."

Savo turned his smile on Luca. The men shook hands.

"How nice to meet a friend of Cheyenne's."

"I am her very good friend," Luca said in a tone that left no doubt as to what he meant.

Cheyenne looked from one man to the other. Luca was jealous. Normally, that would have angered her. She had no use for men who had such proprietorial attitudes about women, but what she felt now wasn't anger at all.

This was her lover, and what she felt was pure delight.

Savo dipped his head. "You are a fortunate man."

"*Si*, I most certainly am."

"And you are Italian?"

"I am Sicilian."

Cheyenne almost laughed. Her lover—her beautiful, exciting lover—wasn't just staking his claim; he was drawing a line in the sand.

"Ah. *Un Siciliano*. And Ms. McKenna has come to Milan to meet with you? Are you in the fashion business?"

Either Franco hadn't gotten Luca's none-too-subtle message, or he was having fun at Luca's expense. Either way, Cheyenne was enjoying the show.

"I am not. And Ms. McKenna did not come to Milan to *mee*t me, she came to Milan *with* me. We are together, Cheyenne and I."

Cheyenne sighed. It was time to put an end to the game.

"Franco is a designer. I modeled for him several times." She paused. "He and his wife," she said, emphasizing that word, "are world-famous."

"*Si*. My Maria is in the powder room. I am sure she will be delighted to… Wait! There she is now. Maria, *dolcezza*, come and see who is here!"

A stunning blonde hurried toward them. The color that had striped Luca's cheekbones vanished in a flurry of introductions, handshakes and air kisses. Luca invited the Savos to join them; Franco explained that they were just leaving. More handshakes and air kisses.

Then Maria said, "Wait! Cheyenne, will you still be in Milano tomorrow? Because if you will…" She looked at her husband, who nodded. "If you will, we have a huge favor to ask."

"A favor?"

"*Vogue* is coming to do a spread on us."

"That's great!"

"*Si*. It is, indeed. We will be offering glimpses of our next collection—you know the kind of thing it will be. We have three girls coming in for the shoot." Maria named them. Cheyenne said yes, perfect, wonderful…and then Maria took a deep breath. "But we built the set, the entire concept of the shoot, around Jane Houston."

"A fantastic choice." Cheyenne glanced at Luca. He looked like a man hearing a language that was not his own for the very first time. "Jane is absolutely stunning," she told him. "She's one of those girls who makes everything she wears look like a million dollars."

"Like you, *cara*," he said softly.

The Savos smiled.

"We think so, too," Franco said. "That is why Maria's idea is so perfect."

"What idea?" Cheyenne asked, looking bewildered.

"We just had a text message from Jane's agent. Jane is ill. She won't be able to make it tomorrow."

"Oh, that's awful. I'm so sorry she's—"

"As illnesses go, this is a good one." Maria smiled. "Jane is pregnant. She's begun suffering from morning sickness—and we are scheduled for seven o'clock!"

"You and Jane have similar coloring," Franco said. "In fact, though we adore Jane, if we'd known you were available… Cheyenne, dearest one, we know it is a great deal to ask. You are on holiday, you and Luca probably have plans, but if you could possibly step in—"

"She can't," Luca said, at the same instant Cheyenne said, "I can."

They looked at each other. The silence became palpable. Franco Savo gave a discreet cough.

"Um, Maria and I will be at the bar, having a nightcap. Let

us know your decision, Cheyenne, yes?"

"Yes," Cheyenne said, but she never took her eyes from Luca.

"*Bellissima*," he said softly, as soon as the Salvos had walked away, "this is a holiday. Why should you work?"

"You'll be working, too. "

"Yes, but that's different."

"How is it different?"

"Well—well, I run a business."

"And I have a career."

Hell. He'd said the wrong thing. It wasn't that he didn't appreciate her career, but—but he'd envisioned himself at work, with her waiting for him to return to her at home. Well, not at home. At the hotel.

"I like working, Luca. It's what I do. Who I am."

"And if I were to say no?"

She sat back. There was a sudden coolness in her eyes.

"I would tell you I make my own decisions."

Yes. He knew that. And as much as he admired her for it, he wanted her to be… What? A little more dependent?

A little more needful of him, not just in bed but out of it?

Dio! Even having such thoughts was crazy. The last thing he would ever want of a woman was that she'd organize her life around him—and what was with that image of her waiting for him at home? This relationship, if you could call something that was only a few days old a 'relationship,' was about passion and fun, not about domesticity.

He took a drink of his chianti.

"Of course you do," he said pleasantly. "I only meant that I hoped you working tomorrow would not interfere with the plans I've made."

"What plans?"

What plans, indeed?

"Well, my meeting will take most of the morning. I thought we'd drive south afterward. To Tuscany. Where I keep my horses."

That did it. Her face lit.

"Oh, I'd love that! And the timing should be fine. I know how these shoots go. I'll be done by early afternoon."

"Good. *Va bene*. That's it, then."

"Luca." She sat forward and reached for his hand. "This could be the chance I've been waiting for. If I can show the people who count that I'm easy to work with…" She laughed at the way his eyebrows rose. "Okay. If I can show them that I'm not impossible to work with, I'll be back in the game."

"And that's important to you."

"Yes. It's terribly important."

He nodded, smiled, brought her hand to his lips. "Good," he said except, what he really wanted to say was, *What about me? Am I not important to you, too? Am I not, perhaps, even more important?*

But only a fool would say such a thing. Only a fool would want such a thing. Only a fool would build his life on emotion.

And if there was one thing Luca Bellini was never going to be, it was a fool.

CHAPTER TWELVE

BY TWO THE following afternoon, they were on the road, heading for the village in the Tuscan hills where Luca bred and raised Arabians.

"How did your meeting go?" Cheyenne asked.

"It went well." He flashed her a quick smile. "Actually, it went very well. I'm going to design and build a new skyscraper in Manhattan. Fifty stories, all glass. I'm excited to start work. And you? How did things go with the *Vogue* shoot?"

"Oh, it was fine! I'd worked with the photographer before, which made things easier, and I managed not to tell him what angle to shoot from." She made a face. "I didn't even tell the makeup guy that I look better with red lip color than peach."

Luca chuckled. "Of course you told him."

"Well, maybe I hinted…"

He laughed, and she joined in.

"I'm impressed," he said.

"Me, too. Seriously, the agency rep was there and he said

he'd give me a call."

"But not too soon." Luca reached for her hand. "We're not going to do anything but enjoy ourselves for the next few days."

Cheyenne smiled at him. "I'm already doing that."

He'd rented a car, a bright red Ferrari. He had the same model at his ranch, he said, and he loved driving it. The car flew like the wind, eating up the miles, hugging the tight corners of the impossibly narrow, twisting roads that led south.

He'd scoffed at the idea of taking the *Autostrada del Sol.*

"The *autostrada* is fine for speed, but it's an insult to a car like this one to put it on a straight road and give it nothing more important to do than get its driver and passengers from Point A to Point B. Besides," he said, with that sexy grin Cheyenne adored, "there's nothing to keep us from testing the car's speed on the *autostrada* another day."

The further they drove into Tuscany, the more beautiful the rolling hills, meadows and small, ancient towns became.

Cheyenne was entranced by the scenery and by the car, too. She said it reminded her of an ad she'd done for Ferrari, posing beside a vintage Testa Rossa.

"Do you know what year it was?" Luca asked.

"Yes. A '58. Perfectly restored, of course."

"Ah. The most beautiful car ever made."

"When they told me what it was worth, I was afraid to touch it."

Luca grinned. "Matteo would be proud of you."

"Does he own a Testa Rossa?"

"Only God and Matteo's accountants know what he owns," he said, laughing. "My brother loves fast cars. Ferraris.

Lamborghinis. He's even American enough to own a vintage Corvette."

"Did your family spend a lot of time in America when you were growing up?"

"We never went to the States at all." He double clutched and downshifted as they approached a tight curve. "We used to ask our father to bring us there on vacations, but he always had an excuse. Now, of course, we know the reason. We were a secret more easily maintained in Sicily."

"But all of you chose American universities. Was it hard? Coming to a new country, I mean."

"Not really. We spoke English, of course, because of our father." His jaw tightened. "That was one good thing he did for us."

Cheyenne put her hand over his on the wheel.

"Is he still alive? Your father? I mean, maybe he can explain why he did what he did."

"He's very much alive, and he spent the July fourth holiday trying to explain it." A muscle flickered in Luca's jaw. "It was an explanation that left much to be desired."

"But at least he tried to explain. My mother—some parents never do."

Luca caught her hand in his.

"You were not close with her," he said softly.

She wanted to laugh, or maybe to cry, but either might give too much away. Instead, she gave the safest answer.

"No."

There was a brief silence. Then Luca said, "Did she mistreat you, *bellissima*?"

"Why would you ask me that?" She pulled her hand from his.

"I only meant—"

"I know. And I'm sorry I jumped on you. I just…I don't like to talk about her."

"Then we'll talk about something else. For instance, do you see that road leading into the hills?"

"The one lined with those beautiful tall trees?"

"*Si*. Italian Cypress." He shot her a quick smile. "They're like you. Tall, slender and elegant."

She laughed, and he reached for her hand again.

"They sigh when the wind goes through them. I always thought that was a wonderful sound, but the sound of your laughter is what is truly perfect."

She laughed again, but the laughter caught in her throat. Luca looked at her with alarm.

"What is it? Have I said something to upset you?"

"No. Oh, no. It's just that—that—" She took a deep breath. "I'm glad you asked me to come to Milan with you," she said softly, "and I'm very, very glad I said yes."

He wanted to stop the car, take her in his arms and tell her that it was the same for him, that he'd asked her to come with him because he'd thought it would be fun, that it would be an interlude they'd both enjoy, but that it was becoming more than that, that she was somehow changing him…

But it was more than he'd ever imagined saying to any woman.

And far more than his mind was willing to process.

* * *

She fell in love with his ranch.

Rolling green hills. Stately cypresses. Towering oaks. There was even a grove of olive trees, some gnarled and ancient, yet still bearing fruit.

Cheyenne had always loved animals; one of the things that pleased her about her place in upstate New York was that the woods and meadows were home to deer and foxes. There were deer and foxes here, too, and one evening, at dusk, a badger ran across the trail ahead of them.

And then, of course, there were Luca's horses.

She fell in love with them at first sight, especially with a white stallion.

"He's an old man," Luca said as the horse came across the paddock to them, tossed his head, then accepted a carrot from Cheyenne's outstretched hand. "And he was the very first Arabian I bought. I didn't know much about them back then." He smiled as the horse pushed his nose into the curve of Cheyenne's shoulder. "He likes you."

"Such a sweet boy," she crooned. "What's his name?"

No answer. She looked at Luca.

"Luca? What's his name?"

Her lover was blushing! It was a charming sight and it made her smile.

"His name is Baby. Don't look at me that way, *cara*. I didn't name him. It was the name he came with and since he knew it and responded to it, I didn't want to… What?"

"I had—I knew a horse named Baby a long time ago. Well,

that wasn't really his name. He didn't have a name at all, so I took to calling him Baby." She looped her arm around the stallion's neck, but she seemed to staring into the past. "He was old, too. Very old."

Why did he have the feeling this was another story that wasn't going to have a happy ending?

"The people who owned him lived down the road. They kept him tethered behind an outbuilding. His mane, his tail were all matted. Sometimes, they forgot to feed him and to refill the big old copper bucket that was supposed to hold his drinking water."

"There are some evil people in this world," Luca said cautiously.

"I began to visit him every day. I combed him. I brought him water. And I fed him—they had lots of feed and hay in their barn for their other horses, but they—they forgot about Baby."

"Cheyenne. *Cara*. If this upsets you—"

"My mother didn't like me doing things for Baby. She said—she said it made me mess up my clothes, and that I always smelled of horses, and that none of her—her friends would like me that way."

Dio! Could a man go from despising a woman he'd never met to abhorring her?

"But you took care of Baby anyway," he said softly.

"Yes. And then, one day..."

Her voice cracked. Luca cursed. He reached for her, but she stepped back. The stallion snorted, lowered his head and nibbled the grass.

"One day, he when I got to him, he was down. Not lying

down—I knew horses did that. This was different. He was down, and breathing hard."

"Sweetheart. Don't."

"I couldn't get him up. I tried and tried, but I just couldn't."

Luca waited. He felt sorrow for the horse and greater sorrow for a skinny child, because surely she had been skinny, struggling to bring the dying animal to its feet.

"I called the police. At first, they wouldn't listen. They said it was a private matter. We had a local TV station. KLUS. They ran a program they called *Us Helping You*. They advertised it all the time. 'Phone us when the authorities won't help you,' they'd say."

The stallion whinnied and stepped away from her, lowered his head and nibbled at the grass. Cheyenne watched him, her posture rigid, her eyes dark.

"And you were how old, *cara*?"

"Thirteen."

"Thirteen," he said, wishing he could have been beside her then to protect her from whatever was coming.

"A reporter showed up. The people who owned Baby sent for my mother. She tried to make me go with her, but I wouldn't. And then the police came. And when they saw what things were like…" A sob burst from her throat, and she buried her face in her hands. "If only I'd done something sooner," she whispered. "If I'd reported his owners right away—"

"Sweetheart, no, you did all that you could." Gently, Luca took her hands from her face. "Think of the months of kindness you'd shown him." Were horses aware of such things? He had to believe they were, and he told her that. "He must have loved you for all you'd done for him."

"What I know for sure," she said softly, "is that I loved him with all my heart."

"So," he said, trying desperately for a positive ending if not a happy one, "the owners were fined, yes?"

She nodded. "That's what the police said would happen."

"And your mother understood you had done the right thing..."

Cheyenne looked at him and he knew that for the rest of his life, he would remember what he saw in her eyes.

"My mother took me home," she said in a toneless voice, "and beat the crap out of me."

"Jesus Christ," he said, because the softness of the various Italian words for God no longer seemed to be enough.

"It wasn't the first time. The difference was... That day, I hit her back."

Luca could feel the rage swelling inside him. The savagery. He wanted to kick in a fence post. To punch his fist through a wall. Most of all, he wanted to take Cheyenne in his arms and tell her he would never let anything or anyone hurt her again, but he knew how fragile this moment was.

Everything in him warned that he and his beautiful lover were standing at the edge of a precipice.

She stared at him. Then she laughed. It was the laugh of a brave, tough, heartbroken thirteen-year-old kid.

"I gave her a black eye."

"Good girl." He cleared his throat. "And what happened next? Did you have anyone you could go to for help?"

She hesitated. He could almost see her withdrawing.

"Things worked out."

It was an answer that raised more questions than it answered. "How?"

She shrugged. "They just did."

"Yes, but surely—"

"I don't want to talk about it anymore. Okay?"

He nodded. And wondered what in hell to do or say next.

She had opened herself to him. He knew enough about her now to realize that it was not something she did easily. The question was what to do about it.

He wanted to soothe her. To gather her close and hold her. He wanted to tell her that if her goddamned mother were still alive, he'd—he'd—

"Hell," he said, and he gave up logic and reached for her.

She came to him stiffly, arms at her sides, and he suspected she was already regretting that she'd told him all she had. He knew that a wiser man might know the right things to say to ease her pain, but he wasn't a wise man.

He was a man whose life was spiraling out of control.

Terrifyingly, magnificently out of control.

So he held her and rocked her and, after a while, she sighed, looped her arms around his neck and leaned into his embrace.

He shut his eyes and rested his chin on the top of her head.

"And," he said softly, "Baby is the reason you wanted to buy Sweetwater Ranch. To donate it to *Horse Sense* so that abused horses could be assured of… What?"

"*Horse Sense* is for kids," she said, looking up at him smiling. "It runs something called equine therapy. Kids—abused kids, disabled kids, kids with problems—are taught to ride and care for horses. There's something about bonding with a gentle animal that can change a child's life."

He felt foolish and told her so.

"No," she said, "don't feel foolish! It's a new field—why would you know about it? Besides, I love that you were willing to donate money to an organization you believed had to do with animal welfare. You're a truly good person, Luca Bellini."

He shook his head.

"You are what is good, *bellissima*," he said.

She looked deep into his eyes. Then she framed his face between her hands and brought his mouth down to hers.

He kissed her, and then there were no more words.

There were only the things that lovers had always told each other with their hands, their hearts, their very souls.

* * *

Luca phoned his P.A. and told her to cancel his appointments for the rest of the week.

"All of them, sir?"

"All of them," he said.

When he ended the call, smiling at how politely shocked Jessica had sounded, he began planning the first real vacation of his life.

He wanted to show Cheyenne Tuscany, but what parts? Should they drive through Siena and stop at the small, family-owned vineyards that dotted the hills? Head for Florence, the Uffizi Museum and some of the most beautiful paintings and sculptures in the world? Visit La Torre di Pisa and snap one of those silly photos that made you look as if you were holding up the leaning tower?

That night, as she slept, he left the bed and sat mapping things out by the light of a small lamp at a desk in his bedroom. He was quiet and the light was on low, but she woke anyway and asked, sleepily, what he was doing.

"I am trying to figure out what I should take you to see and when."

He was frustrated. She could tell by the strength of his accent. She sat up against the pillows, the light blanket over her breasts, ready to pull on the silk robe—his silk robe—that lay on a chair beside the bed and see if she could help him when an amazing thought occurred to her.

"Luca?"

He was sitting with his back to her. She could see his dark hair standing up in little tufts and she knew that meant he'd been running his hands through it.

"Luca."

He sighed and swung toward her. "*Si, dolcezza.* Is the light keeping you awake? I am almost done here and then—"

"I have an idea," she said softly. "Why don't we just get into the car and drive?"

He frowned. "No plan?"

"No plan." She smiled. "Should be interesting, don't you think? A pair of control freaks like us, just going wherever the mood takes us."

For a long moment, he said nothing. Then, a smile she'd come to know and adore curved his lips.

He'd been working on an iPad. She watched as he shut it off

and placed it on the desk.

"Wherever the mood takes us," he said.

She nodded. "Why not?"

He rose to his feet. The way he was looking at her, combined with the heat of his smile, sent her heart racing.

"A good idea, *bellissima*. An excellent idea." He walked towards her, his steps slow and deliberate. He'd pulled on a pair of sweatpants when he left the bed, only the pants and nothing more. She looked at the beautiful lines of his body, the muscled shoulders and chest, the tight abs, and the race of her heart quickened.

"Luca?" she whispered. "What are you thinking?"

"I'm thinking that going wherever the mood takes us is an interesting idea." Without taking his eyes from her, he opened the door to his closet, reached inside and plucked something from it. A scarf. A blue scarf. Silk. Or maybe cashmere, the sort of thing he might tuck into a coat collar on a cool day. "For instance," he said, his voice gone thick and low, "I am in the mood to have you feel, but not see. To feel, but not touch."

They had gone out to dinner; his jacket, shirt and tie lay on a chair and he paused only long enough to pick up the tie. A blue silk tie.

Her mouth had gone dry, but not the rest of her. She could feel the dampness starting between her thighs.

He stopped beside the bed. Undid the cord of his sweats. Stepped free of them.

His erection was huge and powerful, but when she reached for him, he shook his head.

"Let go of the blanket, *cara*."

The blanket fell to her waist.

He looked at her breasts. It was enough to make her nipples bud. A little moan rose in her throat.

"You have such beautiful breasts," he said softly. "Such perfect nipples." His eyes met hers. She felt as if she could fall into the darkness of those eyes and stay there forever. "Do you like it when I look at your breasts, *bellissima*?"

She nodded.

"Tell me."

"I like you to look at my breasts," she whispered.

"And when I touch them? Taste them? How do you feel when that happens?"

"I feel—I feel as if my bones are turning to liquid." She gasped as he bent to her and sucked the tip of one breast into the heat of his mouth. Her hands rose; she dug her fingers into his hair, but as soon as she did, he lifted his head.

"I am the one who will touch, *cara*. Not you. Do you understand?"

She nodded. Her heart was beating hard and fast. He was going to make love to her in the way that had become their own.

He would dominate her and in submitting to that domination, she would become powerful. He would be as much hers as she would be his, and nothing, absolutely nothing in the universe could equal the feeling of it.

"Tell me that you understand."

"I understand."

"Are you sure?"

"Yes. I understand, Luca. You are the one who will touch.

Not me."

"Good girl. Now, put your hands behind your back."

Her hands shook, but she did as he'd instructed. He sat down next to her and pressed his lips to the place where her neck and shoulder joined as he wound the silk tie around her wrists. She could hear the little sounds she was making, soft whispers and softer moans. She was desperate for him to be inside her. Instead, he reached for the scarf.

"I'm going to blindfold you, *cara*. You won't be able to see what I do to you. You will only be able to feel. Do you understand?"

"Yes."

"Say it. Say, 'Luca, I understand.'"

"Luca," she whispered, "I understand."

He leaned in, took her mouth in a deep, drugging kiss. Then he drew back, looped the scarf around her eyes and tied it behind her head.

Now she was in total darkness. And her hands were bound.

She was his. Completely his.

Her body throbbed. Melted. She could hear the rasp of her own breath. She waited, waited…

Oh God!

The lightest brush over her nipples. His fingers? His hand?

She moaned with pleasure.

And again. No. Not his fingers. His lips. The whisper of his breath against her sensitized flesh. She arched toward him, wanting more. The heat of his mouth. The caress of his tongue.

The bed sighed.

He was stretching out beside her.

He was watching her. She could feel his eyes on her. But she needed more. His touch. His kiss.

A cry broke from her throat.

His hand was tracing the outline of her body. Throat. Breast. Hip. Her skin felt singed.

It wasn't enough.

"Please," she whispered.

He caught the plea with his mouth. His tongue swept over hers. She gave a little sob; her head fell back as he cupped her breast and feathered his fingers over the dusty rose tip.

"Is this what you want, *dolcezza*? Me, touching you? Kissing you?"

"Yes," she said, "yes yes yes yes…"

At last, he drew her nipple into his mouth. The sensation was indescribable. She could feel herself coming apart and when he slid his hand between her thighs, found her with his fingers, she cried out in ecstasy.

She wanted to hold him. To see him. She begged him to free her hands, uncover her eyes, but he wouldn't, he wouldn't, and she sobbed with pleasure, with frustration as he kissed his way down her body, over her belly, to her thighs, as he nuzzled them apart and put his mouth to her, God, his mouth…

The wave broke over her, more powerful than any before. She felt herself rise with it, felt it reach its apex before it drew her down and down, taking her under, and she was breathless, she was dying, and then the wave lifted her, brought her out of the darkness.

"Cheyenne," Luca groaned as he entered her, and she screamed his name as he took her with him into the hot, bright light of the sun.

* * *

Seconds passed. Minutes. She had lost all concept of time.

Luca lay over her, his heart hammering against hers.

He had reached back and untied her wrists; now, her arms were wrapped tight around him. The scarf had loosened and was draped around her throat. Her mouth was pressed against his shoulder. The taste of his skin—salt, heat, man—was on her lips.

What was happening to her?

She was losing herself.

Everything that she'd believed herself to be was changing. She was a leaf drifting from shore, drifting on the slow current of a stream.

She didn't understand it.

What had become of her need to control? To command? To be in charge of herself, her life, of everyone and everything around her?

And yet, she still was in charge.

Her decisions were her own—including the decision to let the man in whose arms she lay show her a side of herself she'd never known existed.

He stirred. Shifted his weight. Started to lift himself off her.

She held him more closely.

"I am too heavy for you, *cara*," he said.

He was right. He was much too heavy for her, but she wanted

his weight on her, wanted the feel of his body against hers.

"Stay," she whispered, and she felt his lips curve against her throat as he smiled.

"I would not dream of going anywhere."

She sighed as he rolled to his side with her in his arms, heart to heart, belly to belly. His face was a breath from hers. She looked into his eyes and what she saw there was what she knew he must see in hers.

It was a time for complete honesty, and she knew it.

"I don't," she said, "I don't understand what's happening."

He didn't try to pretend her words confused him.

"No," he said. "Neither do I."

"I'm going to tell you something..." She swallowed dryly. "Don't laugh."

He raised his head a little, just enough so he could kiss her.

"I would never laugh at you, sweetheart."

She nodded. "You need to know that I—I never liked sex very much. It was just something, you know, something people do." The truth went well beyond that. Perhaps some day she could tell him so. For now, this admission was enough. It was more than she'd ever made before.

"And now?"

"And now—and now, I know that you were right. What we do isn't sex. It's—"

"It is making love."

"Yes. And it's...it's..."

"Amazing."

"Yes."

"Incredible."

"Uh huh."

"Magnificent."

She laughed. Who'd ever have believed you could lie in a man's arms and laugh?

"Don't get carried away, Bellini."

He grinned. "Male ego, *cara*. My apologies." He propped himself up on his elbow, kissed her mouth, her throat, her breasts, and a bolt of that very ego he'd just apologized for shot through him when she stirred under his kisses. "But I wonder..."

"What do you wonder?" she said, catching her breath as he drew her nipple into his mouth.

"Well, I wonder about plain vanilla."

His hand was on her belly. On the soft curls below it. Impossible, that she should want him again. Need him again.

She smoothed her fingers through his hair.

"Plain vanilla what?" she murmured, even though she knew.

"Lovemaking. No games. No toys. Just you and me." His fingers moved lower. Over her. Into her. "Could we have sex that way and still find it amazing?" The world began to tilt. "And incredible?"

He moved over her, slid inside her. She clutched his shoulders.

"And magnificent," she said, because no matter how they made love, it was all of that.

And more.

* * *

They spent the next day driving the countryside, stopping for lunch at a charming café in the village of Montepulciano and for espresso at a *piazza* in Montalcino.

Hand in hand, they headed back to the Ferrari. When Cheyenne said she wanted to drive, Luca clapped his hand to his heart.

"You know how to drive a stick shift?"

She blew a strand of hair off her forehead. "Have you forgotten the day we met?"

His grin was sexy, wicked and wonderful. "How could I possibly forget that day, *cara*?"

She dug an elbow into his ribs. "I meant the truck. I was driving one, remember?"

He gave a deep sigh to hide his delight. The truth was, he'd been waiting for her to ask.

"Go ahead," he said, handing her his keys. "But drive slowly, *si*?"

"Slowly, of course," she replied.

She did drive slowly… for the first couple of minutes. Then she put her foot down hard and the Ferrari's engine roared.

It was exactly what he had expected, and he laughed. She did, too. He fought hard against the desire to do what he'd done that first time—grab the wheel, force the car to the side of the road, take her in his arms and kiss her.

Instead, he wondered how it was that he could be so happy when he'd been so full of anger and despair only a week ago.

He knew the answer. It was she. Cheyenne. She had changed everything.

* * *

They had dinner at home, on a brick patio lit by candlelight and what were surely a billion stars.

His cook had outdone herself. The meal was perfect, from the from the Insalata Caprese that began it to the ricotta cheesecake that ended it. Luca opened a bottle of Brunello they'd bought at a centuries old vineyard in Montalcino. They drank the wine, talked, laughed, looked at the pictures they'd taken with his cellphone the day before, including the silly selfies from Pisa that made it look as if they were holding up the famous leaning tower. Then they danced to music carried to the patio from speakers tucked into the branches of the two towering oaks.

When the moon had ridden high into the night sky, Luca kept Cheyenne in his arms even as the strains of the last melody faded away.

"We have to leave tomorrow," he said softly. "I have business in New York and I cannot put it off any longer."

She leaned into him so that her head rested under his chin. She'd known the magic had to end, but hearing him say the words was hard.

"I wish we could stay here forever," she murmured.

He tilted her face up to his.

"We can do the next best thing, *bellissima*. When we return to New York, move in with me."

CHAPTER THIRTEEN

HE'D TAKEN HER by surprise.

He saw it in her face. She was shocked by what he'd said. Well, he understood that, because he'd shocked himself, too.

Waking in the morning with her in his arms, falling asleep that same way, even just seeing her sitting across from him at breakfast, he'd found himself thinking how nice it was to have her there.

That had been the first surprise.

He'd always liked his privacy. Growing up under the ever-watchful eye of a Sicilian mother, he'd had a bellyful of answering questions about where he was going and what he was doing. His years at school hadn't helped: first the harsh confines of boarding school in Palermo where your every act was subject to the dictates of an unsmiling priest, and then the regimented routines of the prep school his father had insisted he and Matteo attend on the English moors.

His first taste of freedom had come when he'd left Europe to go to college in America, despite his father's insistence that he attend an Italian university.

Answering to nobody but himself had been a remarkable experience and he'd never seen a reason to change the practice.

Until Cheyenne.

A couple of days ago, when he'd realized he could no longer put off returning to business, he'd thought how good it was that he was mostly going to be working out of his New York office. It would be easy to see her as often as he wanted.

Not really.

She lived in Soho. He lived on the East Side. On a map, the distance between the two locations wouldn't look like much. Factor in Manhattan traffic, the pressure of differing schedules, and they might as easily have lived in different cities.

That morning, watching her dress, it had occurred to him that one of them could move.

She, of course. Not he.

He could find her something handsome and spacious on Park. Or Madison. Or—why not?—right near him on Fifth.

And then he'd thought, why do that when she could simply move in and live with him?

For a second or two, he couldn't believe he was considering the idea. He had never, ever asked a woman to live with him. And then he'd thought, what did that matter? There was a first time for everything.

Not that he'd actually ask her.

It was just an idle thought, something to toss around, maybe eventually to discuss with Matteo. Matteo was logical. Matteo was a lawyer. Matteo would help him see the good and bad without emotion getting in the way.

Not that his own emotion was getting in the way.

He was having an affair with an interesting woman. He enjoyed being with her. Why not make being with her simpler? And then he'd thought, *What the hell am I doing?* and he'd emptied his head of all those nonsensical ideas.

Except, evidently, he hadn't.

He was holding her in his arms, facing the reality of life returning to normal, and he wanted her with him.

Now, all he had to do was convince her. From the way her mouth had dropped open, it wasn't going to be easy.

"There's plenty of room in my condo," he said.

Brilliant, Bellini. That is certainly a reason she would want to live with you.

He tried again.

"My place is more centrally located than yours."

Another outstanding reason.

"There's so much to see and do in my neighborhood. Shopping. Proximity to the Park..."

Cristo! He sounded like a real estate agent. He swallowed hard.

"We are good together, *cara*," he said softly. "Why should we lose that?"

At least she was not looking at him as if he were crazy.

"We don't have to lose it," she said, just as softly. "We can see each other as often was we like, once we're back in the city." She touched her hand to his cheek. "I'm honored that you asked me."

"Honored," he said, with a little laugh. He clasped her hand, brought it to his lips, kissed the palm.

"Honored," she said. "And—and deeply touched."

He didn't want her to feel honored or deeply touched, he wanted her to be as eager to hold onto what they had as he was. Still, part of him was breathing a sigh of relief because, when you came down to it, what was it that they had? Friendship? Passion? Something else?

Really? Something else, Bellini? Surely, you should have an idea of what that 'something else' is before you step off the edge of a cliff?

The rational answer was 'yes,' and by the next morning, he was once again a rational man.

Last night's idea had been the result of a week of Tuscan sun and the best sex he'd ever experienced.

And she was absolutely correct. They could see each other all they wished, once they were back in Manhattan.

* * *

That was what they did.

Saw each other all they wished—and that turned out to be every day.

It was inconvenient for one or the other of them to have to go home late at night just to get a change of clothing for the next day, so they compensated.

She left a few things to wear at his place. Jeans. T-shirts. A couple of silk blouses, shoes, panties, bras… His closet was big enough so that she had a rack and a wall of shelves to herself.

Her toothbrush hung next to his in the bathroom and when he opened a drawer in the vanity one morning, he found a lip gloss, a brush, a comb, a compact and a little tube of something called *EyeLights*. He opened it, sniffed it, wondered why on earth a woman as beautiful as Cheyenne would think she needed cream to put under her eyes or around them or whatever it was women did with such stuff.

In the past, if a woman left a lipstick or a comb behind, he'd seen it as an intrusion in his personal space, but seeing her things mixed in with his was different.

It made him feel good.

He began leaving things at her place, too. Toothbrush. Razor. A couple of T-shirts and jeans. A suit, then two suits. Dress shirts. Ties. Socks and boxers. Mocs as well as black shoes. She cleared out a dresser drawer for him and she didn't have a closet the size of his, so his suits ended up hanging among her dresses, but he was fine with that.

She was, too.

There was something—what was the word? Comforting. That was it. There was something comforting in just knowing his things were there.

His doorman and concierge greeted her by name. Her neighbor, Mrs. DeCenzo, did the same with him after he rang her doorbell, introduced himself, kissed her wrinkled hand and presented her with a dozen long-stemmed roses.

July gave way to August. Then, one balmy Sunday morning Matteo showed up, unannounced, to find out if Luca wanted to join a game of soccer some friends were putting together.

Well, not entirely unannounced.

It was routine for the concierge to announce visitors, but Matteo was accustomed to going straight to the elevator. He had his own key. The brothers had always exchanged keys to their homes.

This time, the concierge was wise enough to call Luca on the house phone.

"Mr. Bellini," he said, "I thought you might want to know that your brother is on his way up."

By the time Matteo stepped from the elevator, Cheyenne and Luca were having coffee on the terrace.

They looked innocent…unless you noticed that her face was flushed and Luca's sweatshirt was inside out.

"Matteo," Luca said, clapping his brother on the back. "What a nice surprise."

Matteo looked from Luca to Cheyenne. "Indeed," he said politely

"You remember Ms. McKenna?"

Matteo said that he did.

"She stopped by to discuss, ah, to discuss plans for her ranch. "

If this was the way people looked when they discussed plans for ranches, Matteo thought with delight, the world would surely discuss ranches more often.

"Such dedicated people," Matteo said. "Working even on a Sunday."

"Business always comes first," Luca said stiffly.

Matteo smiled, shook hands with Cheyenne and declined his brother's offer to join them. "As you said, business comes first, and I am sure you would prefer to get back to it."

Luca glared at Matteo as he walked him to the door.

"That remark about business was inappropriate," he growled.

"I have no idea what you mean…unless… Is something going on between you two?"

"Certainly not. But just to avoid confusion, I would appreciate it if you would not mention any of this to our sisters."

"Why would I do that?" Matteo asked, looking aggrieved at being told such a thing. And was it his fault the news slipped out the next day, when he called his sisters?

They wanted all the details and though there weren't many, the three Bellinis agreed.

Something was going on.

The trick would be in discovering what—and in getting a good look at Cheyenne McKenna. If their brother was seeing her, there had to be more to her than the bitchiness they'd all observed July fourth weekend.

Luca, no fool, suspected Matteo would pass the news along.

He waited for it to trouble him—and realized that it didn't. In fact, he began to think it would be nice to introduce Cheyenne to his family under better circumstances than when they'd all first met.

He realized another thing, too.

He was more than happy. He was content.

By day, he was deeply involved in work on the residential glass tower he was designing. By night, he was deeply involved with Cheyenne.

He loved ending the day with her, going out to dinner or ordering in pizza, even if she preferred hers with broccoli instead of pepperoni. He loved the way they shared what the day had been like. She was thrilled because she was working again. Just as she'd hoped, the job in Milan had changed things. Top-notch offers were rolling in, and she'd already been booked with several designers for New York's famous Fall Fashion Week.

She told him that she'd learned to keep her advice for photographers and makeup artists and everybody else to herself.

"Most of the time," she added.

Luca grinned and kissed her.

She sighed as she nestled in his arms.

She *had* learned to curb the need to exert control. She also knew it was Luca's doing.

In bed and out, she could trust him. Give herself to him.

Be her real self with him.

For years, she'd hidden the true Cheyenne McKenna from the world. Maybe it was one of the reasons she'd had so much success as a model. She had the right looks—the slender but curvy body, the coltish legs, the fine-boned face, the sexy stride, all of that—but so did a lot of girls.

Her strength was in becoming the precise girl a designer or advertiser needed.

A girl straight out of the Old West? She was it. An exotic beauty from the Arabian Nights? Of course. A seductress who could convince men that the perfume she wore would magically turn their wives and girlfriends into duplicates of her? Consider it done.

She could still do those things, lose herself in an assumed

persona while the cameras clicked, but now, away from the cameras, she could also be Cheyenne McKenna.

She could laugh with Luca. Be silly with Luca. Go for long walks with him, share the *Times* with him on a rainy Sunday, stop at a hotdog stand just because the hotdogs you got from a corner cart in Manhattan were the best in the world. Spend a long weekend together at her little country place, introduce him to her horses and watch with delight as the still-shy pair of animals took to her lover as if he'd always been part of their world.

She'd let Luca see who she really was.

He knew about her mother. About Baby. He knew *her*, the good her and the bad her…

Except, he didn't.

He didn't know the ugliest, darkest part of who she was.

She told herself there was no reason for him to know. Nobody had to know everything about another person.

Unless—unless you were building a life together. Honesty counted then, didn't it? But they weren't building a life together. They weren't even living together…

And then, one evening, she faced the truth.

In all the ways that mattered, they *were* living together.

And he had begun talking about the future.

He spoke of the future in little ways—making idle plans for Thanksgiving, for Christmas—but she knew it marked a change in their relationship.

She wanted that change more than she'd ever wanted anything, but how could she think of the future when the past was always ready to reach out and grab her by the throat?

A shrink, the only one who'd ever done her any good, had assured her that the things that had been done to her had been exactly that. Things that had been done to her. Forced upon her. She had not brought them on, she had not wanted them. In all the ways that mattered, she had not participated in them.

"You were a child," the shrink had said gently. "Twelve years, then thirteen years old. You were a little girl, helpless, terrified, alone. You were not responsible for what happened to you. And you were brave. You went from being a victim to taking charge of your life. That's a wonderful accomplishment."

She told that to herself. She tried to believe it. But it didn't work.

Why had it taken what had happened to Baby to make her stand up for herself?

The shrink said that Baby had been the catalyst that forced her to face what was being done to her. Until then, she said, Cheyenne had protected herself from the ugly reality of her life by shutting down.

"When your mother got drunk or stoned and handed you off to a man," the shrink said, "you took refuge within yourself by pretending nothing was happening—but you couldn't do that when it came to the horse. You'd stopped permitting yourself to feel anything, but Baby was different. You felt his pain, and you loved him enough to fight back."

It was, the shrink said, why she treated sex the way she did. Being in total control with men kept her from feeling anything. It gave her a sense of power that drove away childhood memories.

"Will it ever be different?" Cheyenne had asked during one

of their last sessions.

The shrink had done an un-shrinklike thing. She'd reached over and squeezed Cheyenne's hand.

"It will be," she'd said, "if you keep working through these things. If you let yourself begin to feel. You'll finally acknowledge that you were a brave child who grew into a courageous woman and when you do, you'll find a wonderful man who will love you for who you are and not just for who you permit the world to see."

One night, she was sitting in a corner of Luca's long white couch, reading a magazine. He was reading, too, lying stretched out with his head in her lap. And without any warning, she looked down at her lover's face and faced the truth.

She was in love with him.

She loved everything about him, from their wildest, most passionate lovemaking to—she smiled to herself—to the plain vanilla kind.

She loved lying in his arms without having sex at all.

The other night, as always, he'd drawn her to him in bed and started to caress her.

She'd stopped him.

"I just got my period," she'd said softly.

"I want you anyway," he'd murmured. "Don't you know that, *cara*?"

She'd blushed.

Silly, but she had. And she'd told him that she loved what he'd said, but the thing was that when she had her period, she got crampy and headachy, and for the first day, anyway, she mostly felt rotten.

"Oh, sweetheart," he'd said. "I'm so sorry."

Did she want some tea? Aspirin? A heating pad? Did she want him to rub her back? Was there nothing he could do? He'd treated her as if she were made of glass and he'd held her close through the night, no sex, nothing but care and concern and—and—

Love.

Wasn't that what he'd shown her? That he loved her…

A cellphone rang. His. He sat up, dropped a light kiss on her hair and reached for the phone.

"Who?" she heard him say. He frowned, got to his feet and began pacing as he spoke. "Well, I don't know. I mean, it is kind of you to—No. I agree. There is no real reason not to—Still, the situation is…" He paused. She could see him take a deep breath. "You're right. It is time. I shall be there." He looked at Cheyenne. "*We* shall be there. *Si*. Yes. Cheyenne McKenna. Yes. Cheyenne. She and I are—we are—we are together. *Va bene.* We'll see you then."

The call ended. Cheyenne stared at Luca. She waited. And waited. Finally, he cleared his throat.

"That was Jacob. Jacob Wilde."

She nodded.

"There is going to be a party at El Sueño. A Labor Day celebration."

She nodded again. This was serious. There was that telltale sudden appearance of his accent.

"He says it is a Wilde tradition. A family tradition. And he says that since the Bellinis are family, you know, since we are Wildes, too…"

"I'm glad you're going," she said, meaning every word. "But I heard what you said about taking me with you. Thank you for that, but I don't belong there. I mean, this is a family thing."

He crossed the room in half a dozen long strides, gently clasped her shoulders and lifted her to her feet.

"I could tell you that I want us to go because it's a chance for me to take another look at Sweetwater Ranch and get started on planning renovations."

"Oh, that's lovely! I didn't think that you'd—"

"I could tell you that it would be fun to get away together for a few days." His kiss was as tender as it was hard and deep. "Or I could simply tell you the truth. You belong wherever I am. I love you, Cheyenne. I love you with all my heart."

"Luca." She felt her eyes fill with tears. "Luca—"

"And you love me."

She gave a watery laugh at that bit of arrogance, that Luca Bellini arrogance that she'd come to adore.

"Tell me," he demanded, as he had so many times before. "Say the words I need to hear."

What he needed to hear was the ugly truth of her past, but right then, the only truth that mattered was the one blazing in her heart.

"I love you," she said. "I love you, love you, love you..."

He gathered her into his arms and took her to his bed, to their bed, and they made love with such passion and tenderness that, at the end, she wept.

CHAPTER FOURTEEN

"...AND THEN," ALESSANDRA gasped, amidst peals of laughter from everyone gathered around the fire-pit in the back yard at El Sueño, "and then, Bianca and I looked at each other and we pointed at Luca and Matteo and we said, 'They did it!' And our mother grabbed each of them by an ear, marched them into the house and sent them to bed without any supper."

"Which was fine with us," Luca said, grinning, "because supper that night was *maccheroni al formaggio* and even when you say it in Italian, macaroni and cheese is still macaroni and cheese."

"And we hated macaroni and cheese," Matteo said. "I still do."

More laughter.

Lissa wiped her eyes. "How come we never thought of laying the blame on our brothers?"

Jaimie and Emily exchanged mischievous smiles.

"Speak for yourself," Jaimie said. All the Wildes and Bellinis looked at her. "One time, you guys had been home from school, winter break or something, and I had just gotten my driver's license and I wasn't supposed to take a car out without permission, but Em and I were supposed to meet a couple of guys at Angie's Café and so we, uh, we 'borrowed' that black pickup we used to have, remember? Things would have been fine except we forgot to refill the gas tank, and—"

"And," Emily said, "Father flew in the next day and he took the pickup out to check on a couple of oil wells—"

"And he ran out of gas." Jaimie giggled. "He had to walk back to the house and he was furious. ' Who drove that truck and didn't top off the tank?' he said, and we both knew he'd ground us if we told him the truth, so—"

"So," Emily said blithely, "we said one of you guys must have done it."

"Never could trust 'em for a minute," Travis said, looking at Luca and Matteo and grinning.

"How come I wasn't going to Angie's with you?" Lissa said.

Emily rolled her eyes. "That was the winter you were too busy drooling over Donny Hayes, remember?"

"His name was Donny Hayden," Lissa said with mock indignation. "And I did not drool." She batted her lashes. "Well, okay. Maybe a little."

Lissa's husband wrapped his arm around her shoulders and hugged her to his side. "Aha," he said. "A secret past."

She smiled at him, and all the love in the world was in that smile.

"Jealous?" she asked sweetly.

Nick kissed her. "No," he said, and kissed her again, "because you're not Donny Hayden's, you're mine."

Everybody sighed.

"What a scene," Caleb said. "Probably straight out of Nick's next movie."

"Well," Nick said, "now that you mention it…"

They all laughed.

Cheyenne sat in the curve of Luca's arm, warmed by the fire, by the wonder of seeing people who had been enemies coming together as a family, but warmed most by the joy of being with the man she loved.

They'd flown in yesterday and rented a car for the drive to the ranch.

She'd been on edge. On edge? Terrified, was more like it. She was about to meet her lover's brother and sisters, his half-brothers and half-sisters, their spouses, their kids…

She was about to meet all the people who mattered to him and yes, she'd met them before, but that only made it worse because that first meeting, right here at El Sueño, had certainly not gone well.

"Nervous?" Luca had asked, when they pulled up at the house.

"No," she'd replied, but her teeth had chattered.

He hadn't laughed, hadn't teased her. He'd simply leaned across the console and kissed her.

"I love you," he'd said. "And so will everyone else."

The first few minutes had been a little sticky. They'd been the last to arrive. Same as the last time, the Wildes and Bellinis had all been gathered at the big table in the dining room; they'd been eating lunch and talking non-stop, but they fell silent when she and Luca entered the room.

All those upturned faces. The polite smiles. The questioning eyes. Given the chance, Cheyenne would probably have turned and run, but Luca hadn't let that happen.

He'd put his arm around her shoulders and drawn her close.

"Everybody," he'd said, "this is Cheyenne." A pause. "Just in case you don't remember meeting her before."

He'd said it lightly. A few people smiled.

"She owns Sweetwater Ranch." She stiffened, and he drew her even closer. "Which is about to become a place where kids with problems learn to trust the world, thanks to Cheyenne and an organization called *Horse Sense*."

That drew more smiles, looks of interest and a couple of knowing nods.

"But the most important thing you should know about her," he'd said, "is that I love her." A gasp. Stares. "And she loves me," he'd added, and that had done it.

Everybody had started talking at once, Matteo had high-fived Luca, Lissa had told them all to shove over, Emily had taken plates and silverware and napkins from the sideboard and just that easily, Cheyenne had been made a part of the group.

And, she thought now, as she watched the flames of the fire shooting into the night sky, it was one heck of a group.

An actor. A chef. A psychologist. A CFO. A VP. A couple of lawyers. A university professor. A financial guru. A guy who ran a half a million acre ranch as well as one of his own. Another guy who owned a high-level security company. Two men who designed and built structures known around the world.

It would have been easy to be impressed, maybe even intimidated, but they were all really nice people. They'd made her feel as if she belonged here, asking her about the places she'd been, the ads she'd done, the world in which she moved.

Amazing.

Only a couple of months ago, questions about her life had seemed intrusive. Luca's love had changed that. He'd shown her that the world could be a welcoming place instead of a judgmental one.

As for his big family… She liked them all, but she felt especially comfortable with his sisters, maybe because they so obviously adored him.

"Whoops," Lissa said. "We're out of cookies."

Bianca said that she would go into the house and get more. Alessandra offered to go with her.

"Me, too," Cheyenne said, and rose to her feet.

"Come back here, woman," Luca said with a fake growl.

She leaned down and kissed him.

"Two minutes," she said. "I promise."

"Two minutes," he said, smiling at her. "And then I'm going to come after you."

She laughed. His sisters did, too, looping their arms through hers as the three of them walked across the grass, through the back door and into the kitchen.

"You've moved the mountain," Bianca said, as the door closed behind them.

"You have, indeed. You've given us back the Luca we used to know."

Cheyenne smiled as she transferred chocolate chip cookies

from a big platter to a wicker basket.

"He's a wonderful man."

"He is. He always was." Alessandra licked a drop of chocolate from her finger. "But to see him so happy…"

"We all took the news about our father hard. You know about that, *si*?"

"Yes. Luca told me."

"Well," Bianca said, "we all suspected our father had a dark secret. Even as children, we knew something was not right. And when we learned the truth…"

"We were all hurt and angry," Alessandra said, "but Luca was filled with rage." She smiled. "Now, that rage is gone. He is different. What I mean is, it is a long time since we saw our brother so—so—"

"Relaxed," Bianca said.

Alessandra nodded. "And so trusting."

Cheyenne felt her smile tilt.

"Really? The Luca I know has always been trusting."

"Well, that's the point. The Luca you know is the Luca who loves you. You have changed him."

"He's changed me," Cheyenne said, a little too quickly. "I mean—I mean I had some trust issues myself. Everyone does."

"Not like our Luca," Alessandra said softly. "I think he may have been the one our father hurt the most. Bianca and I grew weary of his endless promises to spend holidays with us early on. So did Matteo. But Luca…there is a part of Luca that tried very, very hard to believe that though our father was not perfect he was, at heart, a good man."

"We can remember being very young," Bianca said, "five and

six, perhaps, and already suspecting that there was no point in thinking that our father would come home for Christmas, as he always promised, or for our birthdays. Matteo and Luca were older. Ten. Maybe eleven. And Matteo knew, as we did, that our father was given to making promises he wouldn't keep. Luca would say he knew it, too, but—"

"But," said Alessandra, "he was the one who sat up until midnight Christmas Eve, waiting for the sound of our father's car, the one who would not open his birthday presents because he was sure our father was going to come through the door at any minute. Luca clung to the hope that our father would not disappoint him longer than the rest of us did."

Bianca nodded. "And he paid the price. You know, growing up with a father we couldn't trust and with parents whose marriage must have been an endless series of deceits affected us all. As most children do, we learned to sublimate our feelings."

Alessandra groaned. "*Dio*, must you speak psychobabble?"

"It isn't psychobabble, it's the truth." Bianca looked at Cheyenne. "Alessandra and I learned how important it is for women to be strong and independent. Matteo convinced himself he would never marry. Well, the lesson my sister and I learned is actually a good one. As for Matteo—Matteo may yet meet a woman who will change his mind."

"And the moon may turn out to be made of green cheese," Alessandra muttered.

Bianca made a face. "The point is," she said, reaching for Cheyenne's hand, "it was Luca who concerned us the most. We feared he would have a sad life, that he would never learn to trust anyone, to believe in someone enough to permit himself to love her."

"And then you came along," Alessandra said softly, "and now our brother is whole."

* * *

Cheyenne couldn't go back outside to that happy, laughing bunch of people and pretend to be part of them.

Not yet.

"You two go on," she told Luca's sisters. "I'm going to make myself a cup of tea."

She didn't drink tea unless she was sick, but nobody knew that.

"We'll stay with you," Bianca said, but Cheyenne said, no, they couldn't do that.

"Everyone's waiting for those cookies. If they don't get them soon, they're liable to storm the kitchen."

They laughed. Bianca hugged her; Alessandra kissed her cheek. Finally, the door shut after them.

And Cheyenne let the phony smile drop from her face.

Now what?

Get herself under control, that was what. Grab that much-vaunted control that had carried her through life, and hang onto it.

Pin a smile on her face. Go back to the fire-pit. Laugh and joke, and sit with Luca's arm around her.

Luca, who loved her and trusted her.

"Oh, God," she whispered.

She wrapped her arms around herself, paced out of the kitchen, through the big dining room, then down the hall.

He trusted her.

And she had repaid that trust by lying to him, by withholding the truth that would surely have driven him away, because she was not a woman that a good, decent, kind man like Luca Bellini would want in his life.

What man would ever want a woman like her?

The story she'd told him about what the day Baby died... It had only been part of the truth. Yes, Mama had beaten her black and blue, and she had finally hit her back, and the next day, the school had called the authorities.

But there was more, much more to it than that.

The day Baby died was the day she had finally refused to let Mama 'give' her to a man.

The nightmare had started months earlier, with touching. Mama had boyfriends who'd liked having fun. That was what Mama called it. Having fun.

"They just want to have a little fun, sweetie," she'd say. "Come on. Let Tommy touch those little titties. He won't hurt you."

Tommy. Or Jerry. Or Billy. What did it matter?

And when she'd sobbed and begged and said *No, no, please Mama, I don't like this,* Mama would turn cold and mean. Children were supposed to obey their mamas, she'd say, and to help with chores. 'Having fun' was Cheyenne's chore, and it was time she got used to it.

On her thirteenth birthday, 'having fun' escalated into something even worse.

Far worse.

"Happy birthday, sweetie," Mama said, her eyes big, black holes from whatever she'd been shooting or snorting. "Today you're gonna be a big girl. A real big girl."

Mama had led her into the back room of their trailer. A fat man who stank of whiskey and sweat had been waiting, sitting on the edge of the rumpled bed with his pants around his ankles.

"Be nice," Mama had said to her.

She'd shut the door, the man had grinned…

Bile rose in Cheyenne's throat. To this day, she couldn't think of what had happened without being sick.

That had been the first time, but not the last.

It had happened three times after that, and when she'd refused to do it, Mama had grabbed her and shoved her into that back room. Cheyenne had thought about ending the horror like a girl she'd read about in the paper, cutting her wrists, just letting go of everything…

And then, she'd discovered Baby. Sweet, sad, neglected, abused Baby.

Loving him had saved her.

Losing him had given her the courage to take hold of her life, because what she'd told Luca about that day wasn't exactly true.

Mama had beaten her, all right, but not because Cheyenne had reported the horse's brutal death to the police.

She'd beaten her because when they got back to their trailer, Mama had folded her arms over her skinny bosom and said there was only one way Cheyenne could make up for the trouble she'd caused.

There was a man waiting for her in the bedroom.

Cheyenne had thought of her beloved Baby and how he had died because she hadn't been strong enough to save him.

And she'd thought, *I will never be weak again.*

"You hear me, girl?" Mama had said. "Move your skinny ass, right now!

Cheyenne had taken a deep, deep breath. Breathed it out. And said that she would never do what Mama wanted her to do again.

Mama had grabbed her by the arm. "You go on back there and make that man happy or so help me Christ, I'll beat you black and blue."

Cheyenne had spat in her mother's face, just as she had done to the hoodlum the night Luca had found her walking home. Luca had saved her then, but there'd been nobody to save her from Mama that day so long ago, and Mama had done just what she'd threatened. She'd beaten her harder than ever before. A man had come barreling out of the bedroom and thundered past them, and Cheyenne had taken the blows and taken them, and then she'd screamed with pain and rage, balled up her fist and punched her mother in the face.

That night, she'd slept on a bench hidden in a tangle of bushes in the trailer park. The next morning, she went to school and straight to the principal's office, walked right into that office without knocking and when the woman looked at her and said "Ohmygod, what happened to you, child?" Cheyenne told her.

All of it.

Everything, starting with 'having fun' and ending with what had gone down the previous day.

The principal had called Child Services. Cheyenne had gone into foster care, and foster care had been what had saved her.

She knew there were endless stories about how awful foster care was and, no, it hadn't been wonderful, but she'd been lucky. She'd been sent to a small group home for girls, she'd been helped by good people, she'd gone to New York and made something of her life, she'd put the rest behind her…

Tell all that to Luca?

No.

Never.

He would stop loving her even though he might pretend that he still did, at least for a little while, because he was a good man. He was the best man in the world, and she was—she was—

The back door slammed.

"Cheyenne?"

She froze. It was Luca.

"*Bellissima*, where are you? My sisters said you were making tea."

Her heart began to pound. She couldn't let him see her like this. The truth was, she couldn't let him see her at all. She had to get away, get back to New York, write him a letter, tell him that—that she'd changed her mind, that she was too busy to think of love.

"Cheyenne!" There was an urgent ring to his voice now; she could hear his footsteps in the kitchen.

Think! Think!

There was a big pottery bowl on a table near the door in the front hall. She'd laughed at how people had dropped their keys in it.

"How do you ever find the right ones?" she'd said, and Luca had grinned and said sometimes it was the luck of the draw.

"Cheyenne," Luca shouted, "*cara*, where are you?"

She dug into the bowl. Luck was with her tonight. Luca had put the keys to the rental car on a keychain hung with a silver L, and it was that silver L around which her fingers closed.

"Cheyenne," Luca said, from almost right behind her, and she flung open the front door and raced to the car.

Sobbing, she got inside, stabbed the key into the ignition lock and stepped on the gas.

The last thing she saw in the side mirror was her Luca, running down the driveway after her.

CHAPTER FIFTEEN

LUCA STOOD HALF a mile down the long driveway, panting, bent over with his hands on his knees.

He'd run as fast and hard as he could, but no way could he catch up to a car, especially one doing at least seventy miles an hour.

Now, even its taillights had vanished into the darkness.

What the hell had happened?

One minute, Cheyenne had been snuggled up to him, smiling and laughing. Then she'd gone into the house and—

And now, she was gone.

He heard a vehicle pull up behind him. He swung around, held his hand up against the glare of headlights.

"Luca!"

The lights dimmed, doors opened, and Matteo and Travis stepped down from the cab of a pickup truck.

"What's going on?" Matteo asked.

"Cheyenne," Luca gasped. "She's gone."

Travis ran his hand through his hair. "Gone where?"

Luca shook his head.

"Jesus. What happened?"

"I don't know. She took off." He dragged in another lungful of air. "Something must have gone wrong in the house. With Bianca and Alessandra."

Matteo shook his head. "I don't think so. When they came back, they were both smiling. In fact, Alessandra told me what a wonderful woman Cheyenne was, and Bianca said the same— What are you doing?"

"I'm going after her," Luca said as he slid behind the wheel of the truck.

"We'll get everybody out looking," Travis called, but Luca had already floored the gas pedal and the pickup was racing down the driveway.

* * *

He had only been to El Sueño once before, but he knew the roads well enough to know that a left at the end of the mile long driveway would take you further down a narrow country road. A right would eventually take you to the main road.

Which way would Cheyenne go?

Luca thought fast and took the right.

The pickup was responsive, its engine surprisingly powerful, but she'd had a head start. Not even a winking taillight was visible in the darkness ahead.

A few more minutes and he'd have to make another decision.

Assuming he'd chosen correctly and she'd headed for the main road and the highway, which way had she gone from there? Dallas lay in one direction. Nothing much of any size lay in the other…

Nothing except Sweetwater Ranch.

The main road was just ahead.

Where would she have gone? Luca took a breath, damn near stood on the brakes, and made the turn that would take him to Sweetwater.

All he could do was hope he had made the right decision.

The pickup ate up the miles.

He was driving faster than was reasonable, but nothing was reasonable tonight.

Why had she run away? She'd been happy. They'd been happy. What had changed?

His headlights cut a swathe through the night. Something ran across the road. He swerved and missed it. The turnoff for Sweetwater had to be coming up soon and he tried to remember something, anything that might serve to let him know that he was coming up on it—

There! A tall tree, long-ago split by lightning. The brakes juddered and protested as Luca skidded into the turn and onto a narrow gravel road.

Long minutes later, Sweetwater Ranch rose on the horizon.

No lights.

Nothing.

Just the dilapidated house rearing up in his headlights and, beyond it, the one functional building.

The barn.

And outside it, the rental car, the driver's door hanging open.

He drove over the grass towards it, hit the brakes, stopped the engine. The headlights blasted a path through the darkness, but he'd need light inside the barn. He leaned over, yanked open the glove compartment. Back home, at his ranch in Tuscany, he insisted on a flashlight in the glove compartment of every vehicle on the place. He could only hope that Jake kept the same standard at El Sueño

And…yes! Luca's fingers closed around the flashlight. He turned it on, shut off the truck's lights, and stepped out into the night.

Silence, except for the tick, tick, tick of the cooling engine, surrounded him.

"Cheyenne?"

Nothing.

He called her name again. This time, a lone katydid answered.

Luca started through the high grass, playing the beam of the flashlight over the dark barn. The door was closed.

"Cheyenne," he said again, as he pushed it open.

More darkness… What was that?

Something moved in the far corner. An animal? An owl?

"Cheyenne," he said, "*dolcezza, per favore,* you have to be here. You have to be…"

Something moved again…

No. Not 'something.' It was she. Cheyenne. She was crying. Sobbing. His heart thudded. Was she ill? Hurt?

He cast the flashlight's beam on her and rushed forward.

"*Cara*. Sweetheart—"

She shook her head, spun away from him. "Go away!"

The anguish in her voice stopped him. Years before, when he was a boy hiking the cliffs in Sicily, he'd found an injured osprey. He'd wanted to save the bird, but his desperate attempts had only driven it closer and closer to the edge. In the end, the osprey had fallen. Luca had never forgotten the terrible sight, nor had he forgiven himself for making a bad situation worse.

He stopped a couple of feet away.

"Are you injured?" he said softly.

She shook her head.

"Are you ill?"

Another shake of her head.

"Will you turn around so we can see each other?"

"There's nothing to see."

"There is you, *cara*," he said. "You are always what I wish to see."

"Luca. Did you mean what you said? About—about caring for me?"

"About caring for you?" He gave a sad little laugh. "I love you, Cheyenne. With all my heart."

"If you do… If you really do, then—then please, go back to El Sueño."

"And leave you here, alone?" His voice roughened. "Do you take me for a crazy man?"

"I know you mean well, but—"

"What?"

"But everything became clear tonight. I—I don't want what you want out of life."

"And what is it you think I want?"

"The things your brothers and sisters have. Some of them, anyway. Marriage. Children." Her voice broke. "A house in the country, a dog, a cat—"

"And?"

"And—and I realized that I—I don't."

He wanted to go to her. Grab her. Demand to know what in hell she was talking about. Instead, he did the hardest thing imaginable. He stood still and said, "What do you want, then?"

She drew a ragged breath. This was going to be the tough part. Convincing him that she was telling the truth, but she was good at convincing people of things, that the soap she was selling was the reason her skin was soft, that the shampoo she hawked was why her hair was so lustrous. That was her talent, convincing people that she was someone she wasn't.

Surely, she could convince Luca, too.

"I want my career."

"And I have stopped you from having it?"

"A model at the top can't afford to have any baggage. I have to be able to travel at a second's notice, to spend time on keeping myself fit and—and—"

"Bullshit!"

Luca covered the couple of feet that separated them, clamped his hands on her shoulders and spun her towards him as the flashlight fell to the oak floor, spilling just enough light so he could see the truth, the real truth, in her eyes.

"I love you," he said fiercely, "and you love me, and you're going to tell me what this is all about if I have to shake it out of you." His eyes darkened. "Or kiss it out of you," he whispered, and he drew her into his arms, claimed her mouth with his…

She was lost.

How could she not rise on her toes, wind her arms around his neck, sob his name, return his kisses with frantic kisses of her own?

"Tell me you love me," he said, not as a demand, but as a plea that went from his heart to hers. "Tell me, *bellissima*, or I am nothing."

"I love you," she said. "I love you. I'll always love you."

Luca cupped her face in his hands. "Then why did you run away from me? If you love me—"

"Your sisters—"

"*Merda*! What did they tell you that upset you so?"

"They told me something I already knew." Cheyenne smiled, despite her tears. "They told me that you were a fine, wonderful man—and that you had been a sweet, trusting boy."

"Sweet?" Despite everything, he laughed. "My sisters said that of me?"

"What they said was that when you were all growing up, you were the one who kept believing in your father."

His mouth twisted. "That was not a sweet thing, *cara*. It was stupid."

"It was sweet. You trusted him. You believed in him."

"I suppose that I did, for a very long time. And it was foolish, but I—I loved him. When you love someone, you put your trust in them to be what you believe them to be."

"I know." She bit her bottom lip. "And—and that's what you've done with me. You believed me to be one kind of woman But—but I'm not."

"Sweetheart. Whatever it is you're trying to tell me—"

"I'm trying to tell you," she said, "that what I said about the horse I loved, about that day, about my life, were only bits and pieces of the truth. And once you hear the truth, everything will change."

"Nothing will change," he said. "How could it? *Cara*…"

"I lost my virginity the day I turned thirteen. Mama said it was—it was my birthday present, although that was hardly the first time a man had touched me."

She saw the shock in his eyes. Felt the pressure of his arms around her ease. This was the end, she knew, but she loved him too much to hide the truth anymore.

"I was barely twelve," she said softly, "the first time it happened…"

* * *

She told him everything, and spared herself nothing.

She described her childhood. The trailer. Her mother. She did it dispassionately, and told him all of it because she was determined to hold nothing back.

She stumbled, but only briefly, when she described 'having fun.' She thought she saw his mouth tighten, but the light was bad and she couldn't be sure. Not that it would have surprised her.

What she was describing, after all, was not only 'having fun,' but her pathetic attempts at fighting back.

"I know I didn't try hard enough," she said.

"Because?"

"Because, if I had," she said, in a tone of absolute reason, "the men would have stopped doing those things to me."

Luca was very, very still. In fact, he seemed to hardly breathe. If only the light were better. If only she could see his eyes.

"And how would you have done that? Tried harder, I mean."

"I don't know. Grabbed something, maybe. Hit the man. I just should have done better."

He nodded. Why was he so motionless?

When she got to the part about her thirteenth birthday 'celebration,' she was even more ruthless.

"I know, absolutely, that I could have stopped it."

Luca responded with another one word question.

"How?"

"The same way. By hitting him with something."

Another nod. And more of that awful stillness. "A lamp? A skillet?"

"Something," she said, surprised at the irritation in her voice. "I just should have done more than I did."

"Which was?"

"I kicked him. Between the legs. But not hard enough or he'd have—"

"Stopped."

"Yes."

"Did you try to kick him again?"

"Yes."

"And?"

She shrugged. Looked over his shoulder.

"He was big," she said, and cleared her throat. "You know.

Fat. He lay on top of me and—"

There was a long, terrible silence. "And then," Luca said, moving closer to her, "you found something to love. A horse you named Baby."

"This isn't about—"

"But it is," he said. "You gave your love to Baby. And he gave his love to you. And then—and then, he died."

A moan rose in her throat. She clapped her hands to her mouth to silence it, but Luca took her hands and held them tightly in his.

"And on the very day you lost him, your mother took you home to—to be with a man."

His voice cracked. She knew the reason. Now he understood just how disgusting a creature she was.

She nodded. "Yes."

"But you refused" He lifted her hands to his chest. "You spat on her. And she beat you."

"Why are you repeating all this? I already told you—"

"So you hit her back."

Cheyenne's chin rose.

"You hit her hard enough to hurt her, and the next day you went to school and told the principal what was happening."

"What do you want me to tell you?" she said, her voice strengthening. Her eyes met his. "Do you want me to apologize? Because I'm not going to do that, despite the way you're looking at—"

Luca hauled her into his arms and kissed her.

He kissed her and kissed her. She tasted tears, and they were not only hers, they were also his.

"Cheyenne," he whispered, "my beautiful, brave, amazing Cheyenne. How could you have thought that the story of all you overcame to become the incredible woman you are would keep me from loving you?"

She stared at him. "But what I let happen to me…"

"You were a little girl, *cara*. An innocent child. The men who abused you were—they were…" His mouth thinned. "And your mother. *Cristo*, your mother…" He swallowed hard. "Cheyenne. I love you with all my heart."

Luca could have sworn he saw stars suddenly glow in her eyes.

"If anyone had asked me, I would have said I couldn't love you more than I already did." He smiled. "I would have been wrong, sweetheart. I love you all the more for knowing the woman you truly are."

Cheyenne knotted her fingers in his shirt, rose to him and kissed him. "Do you remember when you said we were going to make love, not have sex?" Her voice broke. "You were the first man, the only man I've ever made love with."

He bent his head and brushed his lips over hers.

"*Tu sei mia, dolcezza, e io sono tuo,*" he said softly. "You are mine, sweetheart, and I am yours."

"Forever," Cheyenne whispered.

"Forever," Luca agreed.

Outside, a big ivory moon rose into the star-filled sky, and a chorus of crickets burst into song.

EPILOGUE

THEY WERE MARRIED at El Sueño on Christmas day.

The Wilde sisters and sisters-in-law came up with the plan. They suggested it to Bianca and Alessandra—all the women had become close. When they told Cheyenne what they'd been thinking, she said she loved the idea.

By the time she mentioned it to Luca, he could only sigh, roll his eyes and admit that he had come to be very fond of his half-brothers and half-sisters, and that the horseman in him had grown increasingly fond of the ranch itself.

Renovations at Sweetwater were moving ahead faster than anyone had expected. The house was beautiful and in such good shape by early December that they held Cheyenne's bridal shower there.

The day of the wedding dawned bright and cold. It had snowed the night before, not enough to spoil the festivities, but enough to look very much like the frosting on the gorgeous six-layer wedding cake Lissa had baked.

Everything was perfect, from the stunning bride in a long white gown of handmade lace to the handsome groom in a custom-made black tux to the Christmas garlands and white satin ribbons that hung from the fireplace mantels and stairways.

The ceremony was beautiful, the reception perfect, the dinner elegant.

After dinner, while Cheyenne changed into her going-away clothes, five men who had started as bitter enemies and had become pretty good friends—Jake, Caleb, Travis, Matteo and Luca—took a short break out on the porch. They toasted each other with glasses of excellent Scotch, and then they toasted the groom and his bride.

"You're a lucky man," Matteo told his brother.

Luca grinned. "And you, *mio fratello*, are next."

Matteo shuddered. "*Non me*," he said, "not me!"

All the brothers laughed—and then Jake said, "Look!"

He was pointing at an old path that followed a brook through the woods to the beginning of the long gravel road that led to the house.

"What?" the others asked.

Jake frowned. "I'm not sure. I thought I saw...something."

The others shook their heads.

"I don't see anything," Caleb said.

Travis grinned. "Maybe it was Santa."

They all laughed.

"Maybe," Jake said.

Except, what he'd thought he'd seen was their father. John

Hamilton Wilde. Four star general or four star spy, take your choice, looking alone and sad and, hell, old as he watched them from the cover of the trees.

"Time to go in," Matteo said. "We have to get my brother out of his monkey suit and into some real clothes."

The brothers high-fived each other, but Jake hung back when they headed for the door.

He took another look at the woods.

No. What would the old man have been doing, hanging around today? They had not invited him to the wedding. A couple of the girls had toyed with the idea, but not even they could ultimately bear the thought of sharing a day of such family happiness with him.

Yeah, but despite everything, John Hamilton Wilde was their father…

"Jake? Dude, you coming?"

Jake drew himself together, turned his back to the woods and walked briskly across the porch.

It was crazy to feel sorry for the SOB who had caused them all so much pain

"Crazy," he muttered, and closed the door behind him.

Dear Reader:

Did you fall in love with Luca? I hope so! If you did, if you enjoyed his story, let me know. Drop me an email, or you can review it online. Reviews are the best way to let an author know you like her writing.

Pride is the first book in my brand new series, In Wilde Country. There are three more books to come! Passion (Matteo's story), Power (Alessandra's story), and Privilege (Bianca's story). Be sure and look for them.

And have you read the first Wilde books? There are four. The Prince of Pleasure. Emily: Sex & Sensibility. Jaimie: Fire & Ice. and Lissa: Sugar & Spice. All were bestsellers! There's a novella, too. It's called On the Wilde Side. It's the story of General John Hamilton Wilde when he was young, and I think it will surprise you!

Please be sure and sign up for my newsletter at http://www.sandramarton.com so you can always know what I'm writing, what's new in my life—and so you can be eligible for some fun gifts and surprises!

Remember, you can always find me at my website, at Twitter, and at my Facebook Friends page or my Facebook Fan Page.

I'm looking forward to seeing you!

With love,

Sandra

Made in the USA
Middletown, DE
18 April 2015